continued ...

"In this modern Southern romance, charming bad boy Reese and sassy Gabby's chemistry sizzles. McLane gives readers characters they'll care about as she expertly weaves a tale of love and past regrets."

—*RT Book Reviews*

Moonlight Kiss

"Alluring love scenes begin with the simplicity of a kiss in this romantic Southern charmer."

—*Publishers Weekly*

"A sweet love story set in the quaint Southern town of Cricket Creek. Reid makes for a sexy hero who could melt any heart." —*RT Book Reviews*

"A very charming story, and I would be more than happy to read the entire series." —The Bookish Babe

"McLane nails the charm, quirks, nosiness, friendliness, and sense of community you'd experience in a small Southern town as you walk the streets of Cricket Creek … engaging and sweet characters whose chemistry you feel right from the start." —That's What I'm Talking About

Whisper's Edge

"This latest foray to McLane's rural enclave has all the flavor and charm of a small town where everyone knows everyone else and doesn't mind butting in when the need arises. With a secondary romance between members of the slightly older generation, *Whisper's Edge* offers a comforting read where love does 'trump' insecurities, grief, and best-laid plans." —*Library Journal*

"Visiting Cricket Creek, Kentucky, feels like coming home once again." —*RT Book Reviews*

"Cute, funny, and full of romance."

—Love to Read for Fun

"LuAnn McLane has a rich and unique voice that kept me laughing out loud as I read."　　—Romance Junkies

Pitch Perfect

"McLane packs secrets, sex, and sparks of gentle humor in an inviting picnic basket of Southern charm."
　　　　　　　　　　—*Ft. Myers & Southwest Florida*

"A delightful . . . charming tale."　　—*RT Book Reviews*

"Entertaining [and] lighthearted."
　　　　　　　　　　—Genre Go Round Reviews

"McLane writes a romantic, lighthearted feel-good story."
　　　　　　　　　　—Romance Reviews Today

Catch of a Lifetime

"I thoroughly enjoyed this amusing tale of baseball fanatics and a quiet little town that everyone falls in love with. The residents are all amusing and interesting . . . pure entertainment!"　　　　　　—Fresh Fiction

Playing for Keeps

"A fun tale."　　　　　　—*Midwest Book Review*

"Charming, romantic . . . this new series should be a real hit!"　　　　　　　　　　—Fresh Fiction

"McLane's trademark devilish dialogue is in fine form for this series."　　　　—*Publishers Weekly*

"No one does Southern love like LuAnn McLane!"
　　　　　　　　　　—The Romance Dish

ALSO BY LuANN McLANE

CONTEMPORARY ROMANCES

Walking on Sunshine: A Cricket Creek Novel
Sweet Harmony: A Cricket Creek Novel
Wildflower Wedding: A Cricket Creek Novel
"Mistletoe on Main Street" in *Christmas on Main Street*
anthology
Moonlight Kiss: A Cricket Creek Novel
Whisper's Edge: A Cricket Creek Novel
Pitch Perfect: A Cricket Creek Novel
Catch of a Lifetime: A Cricket Creek Novel
Playing for Keeps: A Cricket Creek Novel
He's No Prince Charming
Redneck Cinderella
A Little Less Talk and a Lot More Action
Trick My Truck but Don't Mess with My Heart
Dancing Shoes and Honky-Tonk Blues
Dark Roots and Cowboy Boots

EROTIC ROMANCES

"Hot Whisper" in *Wicked Wonderland* anthology
Driven by Desire
Love, Lust, and Pixie Dust
Hot Summer Nights
Wild Ride
Taking Care of Business

Written in the Stars

A CRICKET CREEK NOVEL

LuAnn McLane

A SIGNET ECLIPSE BOOK

SIGNET ECLIPSE
Published by New American Library,
an imprint of Penguin Random House LLC
375 Hudson Street, New York, New York 10014

This book is an original publication of New American Library.

First Printing, October 2015

For more information about Penguin Random House, visit penguin.com.

ISBN 978-0-451-47050-8

Printed in the United States of America
10 9 8 7 6 5 4 3 2 1

Penguin
Random
House

This book is for Tim and Maria. Your love story that began as teenagers and blossomed as adults is proof to me that some things are written in the stars.

Acknowledgments

I want to give a special thanks to my sons Ryan and Tim McLane for answering my questions about craft beer. Your delicious home-brewed ale was the inspiration for having a craft brewery in Cricket Creek, Kentucky. Thanks to craft breweries all over the world for the amazing ales with clever names. Oh and of course all of my beer tastings were done in the name of research.

Thanks again to the wonderful editorial staff at New American Library. I am so lucky to have lovely covers that capture the essence of the story. I want to thank Christina Brower for the attention to detail and for keeping me on track. With this team behind me, I couldn't ask for a better finished product. Thanks to Jessica Brock and Kayleigh Clark for promoting the Cricket Creek series and for teaching me how to navigate social media. I have learned so much from both of you. A very special thank-you goes to my editor, Danielle Perez. From brainstorming cover ideas to tackling revisions, you continue to challenge me and make me a better writer.

As always, thanks to my agent, Jenny Bent. When we first met, you told me to dream big, and you've made my dreams a reality.

And thank you so much to my readers! Connecting with you on social media and meeting you at signings and conferences brings me such joy. My goal will always be to give you a story that makes you laugh and believe in happily ever after.

1

The Eye of the Storm

"Siri, I have not arrived!" Grace Gordon tucked a lock of her windblown blond hair behind her ear and sighed. "This is getting super annoying." She held the phone close to her mouth and spoke slowly and clearly, "Walking on Sunshine Bistro at Mayfield Marina, Cricket Creek, Kentucky."

"The destination is on your left. You have arrived."

"No! A big red building is on my left! There isn't a bistro or marina in sight." With her free hand, Grace gripped the steering wheel of her rented convertible and teetered on tears of frustration. "You suck," she said to Siri, but then winced. "Sorry," she said quickly, and then remembered that she was talking to a computer-generated voice. But still, no need to be rude.

"No need to be sorry," Siri assured her.

"Okay, that was a little creepy," Grace mumbled, and tossed the phone over onto the passenger seat. Pressing her lips together, she gripped the steering wheel with both hands while wondering what to do next.

When her phone pinged, Grace reached for it, hoping it was her sister answering the million texts she'd sent her over the past hour. "I should have known," Grace said as she read a message from her mother asking if she'd arrived safely. "No! I'm completely lost," she said while she typed with her thumbs.

Of course, her mother immediately called. Becca Gordon always stepped in when her children were in distress, and she had an uncanny way of knowing even without a phone call. She could usually calm down Grace's mild-mannered sister, Sophia, but Grace was more like her half brother, Garret . . . a handful and then some. And, oh, how she missed Garret too!

"Gracie, love, you should have been there by now. Am I right?"

"Mum, what don't you understand about I'm *lost*?" Grace drew out the word *lost* for a few seconds. "As in I don't know where in the world I'm at except it's somewhere in Kentucky."

Her mother chucked softly. "Oh, Gracie . . ."

"It isn't funny!" Grace tipped her face up to the sky just as a bird flew by and pooped on her jeans leg. She let out a squeal of anger.

"Oh, come on, darling, it's not that bad."

"Really? A bird just . . . just had the nerve to *crap* on me!" She looked around for a napkin from her unhealthy fast-food lunch. Right, the napkin and wrapper had fluttered out of the convertible like butterfly wings, making her feel all kinds of guilt.

Her mother laughed harder.

"Mum! Seriously? What's so funny about my misery?"

"Well, for starters, you revert to an English accent when you get angry or upset. I'm sorry. I just find it rather amusing."

"Seriously? Have you forgotten that you're English and I've lived with you in London for the past two years? That I've traveled back and forth to England all of my not-so-normal life?"

"Your not-so-normal life made you into the amazing

and successful woman you are today. Would you have it any other way?"

"Well, when you put it that way . . ." Grace had to grin. "Of course not."

"I thought so. And, darling, to answer your question, I might be in my fifties, but I'm not forgetful yet. And I've not forgotten that you can get turned around in your own backyard."

"It makes going on a holiday an adventure, and I've discovered some really cool places taking the road less traveled," Grace said a bit defensively, but she had to grin again. "And you were often with me."

"Fair enough. You get your lack of sense of direction from me. Sorry about that."

Grace looked down at her soiled thigh and then cast a wary glance skyward.

"Aren't you using your GPS?"

"Siri is being rather difficult, I'm afraid. This was only supposed to be a two-hour drive from the Nashville airport to Cricket Creek. I'm well beyond that now."

"So I gather that you rented a convertible like you wanted to?"

"Yes, and it was nearly instant regret. I thought it would be fun rolling through the countryside in the late days of summer with the top down. But driving on the interstate was scary as hell! Everything was super loud. Trucks were terrifying, kicking up rocks and so on. And I littered by accident." She wasn't about to tell her mother it was a cheeseburger wrapper. Even though her mother's modeling days were over, Becca Gordon still consumed only healthy food. "Now I get the whole *Thelma and Louise* ending."

"Put the top up, silly girl."

Grace winced. "Um, I might have zoned out when that whole part was explained to me. Something about a switch and clamps." She looked around, nibbling on her lip. "I was distracted by the cute guy who rented me the car."

"Well, good."

"That I don't remember how to put the top up?"

"No, that you were distracted by a cute guy. You've been all work and no play for far too long, Gracie."

"Ha! I could say the same thing about you. When was the last time you went out on a date?"

Her mother sighed. "Like they say, all the good ones are either taken or gay."

Gracie couldn't really argue with that one.

"Sophia will know how to put the top up."

"Right, I know, she's the smart sister. I'm the creative one. La-de-da."

"Oh, that's rubbish. All three of you are smart and creative and gorgeous. Sophia had a convertible, remember?"

"Yes. Well, at this rate, by the time I find the bistro it will be dark and she might have already gone home."

"Have you called Sophia or Garret?"

"Are you kidding? I've blown up their phones. Sophia's goes straight to voice mail, so her phone must be dead. Garret isn't answering, so I'm guessing he might be in the recording studio or taking care of Mattie. I can't wait to see her baby bump."

"Yes, poor little thing was put on bed rest. Garret has been sick with worry. I will be so happy when the baby girl is finally here."

"Me too! I am going to be the best aunt ever. Hey, but speaking of dead phones, my phone is getting there too. I'm going to give Siri another go before my phone peters out."

"Don't you have a car charger?"

"I forgot it."

"Is there someplace you can stop and ask for directions like we did back in the good old days?"

"No, it's all country roads . . . trees . . . cows." She angled her head. "There is a building in front of me, and I think there might be lights on. Maybe I should check it out."

"Gracie . . . ," Becca said in her worried-mother voice. "I don't recommend going into a random building," she said, which really meant don't you dare go in there.

"Don't worry, Mum. I have to be close to the bistro at this point. There's water to the right of this building, so I have to be somewhat near the marina too. I'll be fine," she said, but the woods suddenly looked a bit sinister. She squinted, looking for beady little eyes. Sometimes having a vivid imagination wasn't fun.

"Okay. Well, text or call me as soon as you can. Promise?"

"I will. I promise. I love you."

"I love you too. Give everyone a big hug for me. I'll be there as soon as Garret and Mattie's baby girl is born next month. I've already cleared my schedule for most of the summer." Although her mother was still CEO of her own clothing company, as soon as she'd found out that she was going to become a grandmother, she'd put the wheels in motion to turn the reins of her company over to capable people.

"Sure thing. Bye, Mum."

"Do be careful. Bye now, Gracie."

After ending the call, Grace got a bit teary-eyed. Her mother and Garret were the only ones who still called her Gracie. Funny, but she often thought that her vintage name didn't fit her outgoing personality and that she and quiet little Sophia should switch names.

Grace closed her eyes and inhaled sharply. Oh, she wanted to see her sister! And Garret too. She'd gotten to know Mattie while Garret was in London filming the popular talent show *Sing for Me*. Grace was so happy that her former wild-child musician half brother had settled down with such a wonderful girl. And Garret was going to be a daddy soon. Unbelievable!

Grace dabbed at the corners of her eyes. She wasn't much of a crier, but the sheer frustration of being close and yet so far was getting to her. A glance into the rear-view mirror made her cringe. "Oh wow, that can't possibly be accurate." The gold clip had given up on keeping her long blond hair under control hours ago. She ran her tongue over her teeth and felt a little something.

Oh, please let it be a sesame seed.

Wide-eyed, she looked at her teeth in the mirror and saw a black speck. "Dear God, is that a bug on my tooth?" Grace rubbed at it with her finger and then checked it out. Okay, just a tiny gnat, but still . . . ew.

Grace desperately wanted to rinse her mouth with water. She groaned and then remembered that she had a couple of bottles in her carry-on bag in the trunk. The water would be warm, but at this point she didn't care. Besides, stretching her legs would feel amazing. And she needed to find a leaf or something to wipe the bird doo off her jeans.

Just as Grace opened the car door, she heard a rumble of thunder. "Don't even . . ." She tilted her face upward and peered at the sky, which had gone from cheerful blue to gunmetal gray. Maybe it was just getting dark, she hoped, but then a raindrop splashed on her forehead. Just one. "Please . . . God, no." She held her breath and waited. Nothing.

Sweet, false alarm.

"Okay, time to figure out how to put the top up," Grace said, thinking it couldn't be that difficult. And then, without even another clap of thunder for fair warning, the heavens opened and it started pouring. Wind whipped her hair across her face and she became instantly soaked to the skin. With a shriek of alarm and a glance of regret at the convertible, she ran for the empty building, hoping for an open door and no rats, spiders, or creepy things. Luckily, the door opened and she hurried inside, dripping wet and thoroughly pissed off at Mother Nature. "Is there no end to this crappy day?" she wailed.

"You've still got a few hours left," said a deep voice laced with the South. Startled, Grace looked around and saw metal tanks, lots of them, and it smelled . . . weird. Dear God, what had she walked into? Some kind of drug-making thing? "Got caught in the storm?" he asked, but failed to appear.

Grace spun around, but still didn't see anyone.

"Just a little pop-up thunderstorm. Trust me. It'll soon pass over."

"If you're God, you can stop with the practical jokes."

"Practical jokes?"

"You know, the bug on my tooth, the bird doo on my leg, and now the unexpected rain." She looked around but didn't see the man behind the voice amid the tall tanks and coils. Something hissed and sputtered. To her right was a large vat with something thick and frothy floating in it.

"I'm glad you found shelter. It's coming down hard out there."

"Yes, it is." But Grace didn't know whether to be glad or not. Perhaps she should have listened to her mother. Because Grace had grown up in big cities, she'd been taught to be wary, but her curiosity usually trumped the need for safety. If she were a character in a haunted-house horror movie, she would be the one going into the basement with a flashlight. Her mum would be the one ushering people to safety, and Sophia wouldn't have ventured into the house in the first place.

Grace looked around, thinking it was rather odd finding this whatever-it-was factory out here in the middle of nowhere. Although she was intrigued, her fight-or-flight instinct was starting to kick in, with flight winning. Swallowing hard, she took a step backward, thinking she might need to make a quick exit.

"Well, I'm sure not God, so I have to ask, who are you and where did you come from in the pouring rain?"

"I think that's my line." Grace always resorted to false bravado when she was scared or intimated. When something clanked, she edged another step toward the door.

"Well, this brewery is mine, so I think it really *is* my line, if you don't mind me sayin' so."

"Beer?" Grace looked around and felt a measure of

relief. "So this is a brewery." She looked around again. "Wow . . . and you're the beer guy."

"Brewmaster, thank you very much. And considered a god to some, so you weren't too far off base," he said with a hint of humor. "By the way, I'm up here."

Grace tilted her head back and saw the source of the voice up on a ladder doing something to a big tank that looked kind of like the world's largest teakettle. He'd poked his head around the side so she could finally see the man with the Southern Comfort voice. "So, there you are."

"Here I am. Not heaven, but close enough." He gazed down at her, and Grace simply couldn't look away. Longish dark hair framed a handsome face. But he was no pretty boy. Oh no, he had a strong jawline, Greek nose, and high cheekbones. His rugged good looks were heightened by a sexy five-o'clock shadow. Oh, but it was his mouth that captured her attention. Looking at those full lips made her feel warm and tingly, like she'd just taken a shot of potent whiskey. Realizing she was staring, Grace lowered her gaze and looked around. "A brewery, huh? I could use a pint about now."

"Welcome to my world."

"Thank you. It appears quite interesting." When Grace looked up again, he gave her the slightest of grins, almost as though he didn't smile too often, and then descended the ladder so quickly she wondered how he didn't fall. As he walked her way, Grace noticed how his wide shoulders tested the cotton of a standard black T-shirt tucked into faded jeans riding low on his hips.

She just bet he had an amazing butt.

"You look lost."

"Perhaps because I am . . ." At five foot nine, Grace was rather tall, but she had to tip her head back to look at his face. She could see that he had light blue eyes framed by dark lashes. *Wow . . .*

"Am what?"

"Lost. Sort of, anyway." Grace was about to ask him

the location of the bistro, but a loud crack of thunder had her jumping, sending droplets of water into the air. "Oh! My top is down!"

"Your top isn't down. Trust me—I would have noticed." There it was . . . that ghost of a grin again.

"No!" Although it made her realize that her wet pink shirt was clinging to her skin. She plucked at it. "I mean the top of my car . . . convertible. I hate to ask, but could you help me put it up?"

"Sure." With a quick nod he hurried out the door and ran right out into the wind and rain like it was nothing. Feeling a bit guilty, Grace watched from the doorway while the top slowly rose and then folded downward against the windshield. He swiftly latched it down and then hurried back to the building. "Here, I thought you might want your purse. It was under the dash but getting wet."

"Oh." Grace took the Coach purse and hugged it to her chest. "Thank you so much. I'm sorry you got drenched." But Grace wasn't sorry she got to see the black shirt clinging to him like a second skin. He was muscular, but not in a beefy iron-pumping way; it was more like his physique was a result of physical labor.

"No big deal." He shoved his fingers through his wet hair.

"The car's a rental, so I didn't know how to put the top up." Grace felt her cheeks grow a tad warm, but she lifted her chin. "I should have paid more attention during the demonstration."

"There must be instructions."

"Oh, I guess there's a manual in the glove box. I was about to figure that out when the rain started coming down." Grace shrugged and then winced. "I just hope the interior dries out."

"Well, it's definitely soaking wet, but it's going to be warm and sunny tomorrow, so you can put the top down later and it will dry out just fine." He extended his hand. "By the way, I'm Mason Mayfield."

"Grace Gordon. Oh wait, Mayfield? You must be Mattie's brother!" She shook his hand, relieved that she was finally on the right track. "I simply can't wait for the baby to be born."

"I am Mattie's brother. Nice to meet you, Grace. And I'm looking forward to being an uncle too. Although the thought of holding a tiny baby terrifies me. Welcome to Cricket Creek."

"Oh right, come to think of it, I did see pictures of you in the wedding album that Mattie showed me while she was in London when Garret taped *Sing for Me*." She thought that Mattie's brothers were both super hot in a tux. "I'm Garret's half sister. Sophia's sister."

"Wow." Mason tipped his head to the side. "I wouldn't have guessed that you were Sophia's sister."

"I know. We don't look alike at all." Grace gave him a sheepish grin. "Or act alike."

"Or sound alike."

"I spent way more time in London than Sophia, especially recently. The accent kind of comes and goes depending upon my mood—according to my mother, anyway."

"I did meet your mother at Mattie and Garret's wedding. Lovely lady. I'm surprised that you weren't there."

Grace shook her head and groaned. "I got snowed in at the Denver airport and missed my flight. Trust me—I tried to find a way to get there, like Steve Martin in *Planes, Trains and Automobiles*. I would have ridden in the back of a truck full of clucking chickens. But it was a total fail."

"That's too bad. The wedding was a good time. So, were you in Denver skiing?" The question was innocent enough, but the slight arch of his eyebrow got under her skin a little bit. Now that he knew who she was, Mason most likely thought she was a spoiled diva going on endless holidays and shopping sprees. She couldn't blame him, really. After all, she was the daughter of a former fashion model once married to one of the most famous hard rockers of all time. But although Grace loved to travel, her journeys were usually business related in some way, inspiration for whatever new project she happened to be working on, if nothing else.

"Business, actually," Grace answered, rather crisply, but then she felt as she as if she was being a bit rude. After all, he'd just run out into a raging storm on her behalf. "I'm a horrible skier. The fact that my name is Grace is kind of funny, actually. I'm prone to accidents, mostly because I'm looking somewhere other than where I'm going. And I don't always know where I'm going."

"Well, be careful in here. There are some things you don't want to fall into." He pointed to the big vat full of frothy stuff.

"I will." Grace hated that she and Sophia were usually thought to be rich, spoiled brats. Neither she nor Sophia rode on the coattails of anyone—including their biological father, who worried more about making money than spending time with his daughters. She was about to tell Mason what she did for a living when lightning flashed through the windows, followed by a deafening boom of thunder. Grace yelped and then shivered.

"Oh, hey, are you scared of storms?"

"Not so much, but this seems to be a quite a doozy. I am a bit cold, though. I have dry clothes in my suitcase if you wouldn't mind getting it for me, but I have to warn you that it weighs a ton."

"Hey, don't worry. I don't want to get your suitcase wet, and it's getting muddy out front. I've got a better idea. I'll be right back with something dry for you to put on."

"Thanks, but I don't want you to go to any trouble."

Mason shook his head. "I'm not about to watch you shiver." He flicked a glance toward the front window. "And the storm doesn't seem like it's going to let up anytime soon."

"Okay, then, something dry would be splendid."

"I'll be right back."

Grace watched Mason walk away, finally getting to

admire his jean-clad butt. *Yep, very nice.* She took a deep breath, able to calm down a little bit.

Grace looked around, intrigued by all of the machinery. While she did enjoy drinking good craft ale now and then, she'd never given much thought to the actual brewing process. From the looks of things in the huge room, brewing beer was much more complicated than she would have imagined.

Rain pounded on what she vaguely remembered was a tin roof, and in spite of feeling a damp chill, she thought the sound was somehow soothing after her rather stressful drive from the airport. Normally she loved to drive. Having lived most of her adult life in London, she commuted by the Tube, walked the streets, or traveled by taxi. So driving through the countryside had always been one of her favorite pastimes on a lazy Sunday afternoon. Grace grinned, thinking, yes, she often got lost, ending up in a random village where she explored shops and dined at local restaurants, sometimes with her mother, who would come along for a ride that was always bound to turn into an adventure. But Grace hadn't had a lazy or carefree day in a very long time. Of course, all of that had changed as of last week, and now she had more time on her hands than she knew what to do with . . . and it felt rather odd.

Grace noticed that the metal machinery gleamed and the smooth concrete floor appeared spotless. Curious by nature, she glanced around, thinking that she'd never look at a pint of ale the same way. Lost in thought, Grace turned when she heard his boots clunking across the concrete floor.

Mason walked toward her with long strides. He'd changed into a dry white T-shirt that had the Mayfield Marina logo scripted in green across the front. His jeans were replaced by gray sweatpants, and he carried a big plastic bag. He handed it to her. "We sell a few racks of clothes over at the marina. Should be everything you need in there."

"Thanks. Wait—you went all the way to the marina?"

"It's just a short jog down the road. I was already wet." The slight grin returned.

"Really? So where is Walking on Sunshine Bistro, then?"

"Across from the marina, up on the hill a little ways."

"Wow." Grace shook her head slowly. "So I've been this close the entire time?" She held her thumb and index finger an inch apart.

"Yeah, you weren't too terribly lost, if that makes you feel any better."

When Mason handed Grace the bag, she felt a little tingle at the touch of his fingers. "No! I feel worse. I've been right here all along. How silly is that?"

"You must have missed the right turn. Did you drive by some cabins by a lake?"

"Um, yeah." Grace nodded. "Like, three times. Don't tell me. Is that where Mattie and Garret live?"

"No, they live in a cabin overlooking the river. It's actually within walking distance from here too."

Grace groaned.

"Hey, don't feel so bad. GPS and cell phone reception can be sketchy out here, especially when the weather gets crazy."

"Crazy? I thought you said this was a pop-up thunderstorm."

"Late-summer weather around here is hard to predict sometimes." Mason shrugged his wide shoulders. "I was wrong," he said, and as if on cue, lightning flashed, followed by another deep boom of thunder. "A tornado watch was just issued a few minutes ago. Cold fronts moving through can cause havoc with the weather.

"What?" Grace swallowed hard, wondering if the tin roof would handle a tornado or peel back like the lid of a sardine can. "Should we go for cover or something?"

"I have an alert system on my phone. If we get an alarm or siren, we'll head into a closet or the bathroom. We don't have a basement."

"Oh boy. And to think this day started out so normal. Well, normal for me, anyway."

"It's only a tornado watch, not a warning. It'll be fine."

"It's been my experience that when people say *it will be fine* is when all hell breaks loose."

"Is that so?" Mason actually full-on smiled, softening his features. Grace wondered if he knew that his smile was a lethal weapon rendering the female population defenseless. "Well, if all hell breaks loose, I'll keep you safe." The smile faded and she could tell that he meant business.

"Good to know," Grace said in a breezy tone, but she believed him. Although Grace had been taught by her mother to be independent, something about having Mason protect her made her feel warm in spite of the damp clothing.

"I'll keep an eye on the weather."

"Keep *both* eyes on the weather."

Mason chuckled. "Okay, I will. I think you'll find everything you need in the bag. The bathroom is over there on the left." Mason pointed over his shoulder. "As a reward I'll get you a bottle of ale while we wait out the storm."

"A storm that could spawn a tornado. I guess if I'm going to go flying into the sky, I might as well have a beer in my hand."

"I'll drink to that. So what do you prefer? Something mild? A brown ale? An IPA blonde?"

Grace had to hide her grin. She could tell by his expression that he thought she was a wine or martini kind of girl, and he was right, but about a year ago she'd gone to a beer-tasting festival with some girlfriends and she'd been surprised at how many she'd enjoyed. "Actually, Mason, I'm a fan of something dark and more intense."

"You don't say." He shoved his hands in his pockets and rocked back on his boots. Since when did she find work boots sexy? *Since right now.*

"Do you like chocolate?"

"More than breathing."

"Well, then, I've got you covered. I'll bring you a light medium-body porter that delivers lots of chocolate flavor."

"Sounds amazing."

"It took me a few tries to come up with something I was satisfied with," Mason said, and then turned away. "The chocolate part was tricky," he said over his shoulder. "Hope you like it."

"I'm sure I will . . ." Grace's voice trailed off softly as she watched his progress. Something warm and delicious washed over her, and she was startled to realize that the foreign feeling was desire. Her mother had been right. She'd been working so hard for the past two years that romance hadn't entered her mind all that much, but it had just resurfaced with a vengeance. Grace was surprised her clothes didn't steam dry right there on her body.

Grace was intrigued by her instant reaction to Mason Mayfield. She usually took a while to warm up to a guy, starting with mild attraction that led to conversation and then maybe a date. As she walked toward the bathroom, she mulled over why she was so drawn to Mason. Perhaps she was used to city-living metrosexual men, who, by contrast, made country-boy Mason seem so virile.

Just hormones, Grace thought, trying to shrug it off.

Regardless, Mason was one sexy man. She opened the door and flipped on the light, but then made the mistake of looking at her reflection in the mirror. "Holy hell, I look like I've already been through a tornado," she said, thinking that the instant attraction most likely wasn't mutual.

"Oh, stop," Grace said, reminding herself that she was in Cricket Creek only to help Sophia out at Walking on Sunshine Bistro and to visit with Garret while they all waited with bated breath for his baby girl to arrive. According to her mother, Garret and Mattie hadn't settled on a name yet, even though her mother had tossed endless suggestions at them. After the birth of the baby, Grace would most likely move back to London, where she would start up another company now that she'd sold Girl Code Cosmetics, her wildly successful line of edgy urban makeup. Getting involved with anyone local, including sexy Mason, wouldn't work out in the end, and she needed to remember that important fact.

With a groan Grace peeled her wet clothing off and then dug inside the plastic bag to see what he'd brought for her to change into. She located white sweatpants with *Mayfield Marina* scripted in green lettering down one leg. A scoop-neck light green T-shirt and matching hoodie were in the bag as well. "Nice," she said with a smile.

After slipping into the dry clothing, Grace dug around in her purse for a comb and any cosmetics she could find. A few minutes later she'd pulled her hair back into submission and added some eyeliner and lipstick. Wrinkling her nose at her reflection, she said, "Well, that's as good as it's going to get."

And then the lights went out.

For a moment Grace simply stood as still as a statue, while thinking in a rather calm manner that she'd never experienced such pitch-black darkness. Surely her eyes would adjust and she'd be able to see enough to make her way out of the bathroom. She blinked and then squinted, but she couldn't see anything. She did the classic test, holding her hand in front of her face. Nope ... nothing.

Grace considered herself to be a pretty brave person, but she'd never been a fan of the dark. To this day she had a night-light in her bathroom. Grace swallowed hard and her heart thudded. Should she yell for Mason? No, surely he'd come looking for her in a few minutes. After all, he knew where she'd gone, Grace thought, and then snapped her fingers, remembering that she had the flashlight app on her phone. She fumbled around, bumped into the sink, hit the toilet seat, and came up against the wall before finally locating where she'd dropped her purse. "Yes!" she said when she found her phone, but her triumph was short-lived when she realized that her battery was dead.

With a growl of frustration, Grace decided she needed to exit the bathroom and give a shout out for Mason. She dropped her useless phone back into her purse and fumbled around for the doorknob, somehow thinking that when the door was open she'd have at least moonlight shining through the windows or something to guide her along.

Nope . . . just thick black darkness.

"Oh, well . . ." Grace hefted her purse over her shoulder and took a baby step forward, but then remembered the big vat of frothy stuff and decided to stay put and shout for Mason. She inhaled a deep breath, thinking she needed some volume, and then spotted a beam of light coming her way. "Oh, there you are! Thank goodness!"

"Sorry. I had to look for a flashlight," Mason said as he reached her side. "I hope you weren't too scared."

"Oh, of course not," Grace said, barely resisting the urge to grab his arm and cling. "It's still just a warning, right?" And then she heard the wail of sirens. "Oh no!" Grace pictured a funnel cloud twirling toward them like in *The Wizard of Oz*. "Is this the real deal?"

"Maybe."

Grace could hear the howl of the wind and then pinging against the windows. "What's that?"

"Hail," he answered gravely.

"Crazy." Grace didn't panic often, but when she did it was full-blown anxiety. "Mason, what should we do?" She wanted to fist her hands in his shirt and pull him close, but she stood there and tried to appear calm.

"Go into the bathroom for shelter."

Grace nodded and then heard something that sounded

like a freight train coming their way. She reached for Mason's arm this time. "What in the world is that horrible sound?"

"I'm not sure, but let's hope it's not a tornado."

"Oh my God!"

"We really need to head to the shelter of the bathroom. Let's go."

2

Bring on the Rain

MASON USHERED GRACE INSIDE THE BATHROOM AND shut the door. Although outwardly calm, he felt uneasy. If the electricity stayed off for very long, the backup generator would have to kick in. And what if a tornado hit the building? He groaned, not wanting to think about it.

"What was that noise for?"

Mason pointed the flashlight at her. "You mean outside? It's still hailing."

"No, I mean the groan that just came from you. Groans are never a good sign," she said, although Mason couldn't quite agree with that statement.

"Are we in for something horrible?" She sat down on the floor and looked up at him with a wide-eyed, wary expression.

"I'm sure we'll be fine and this will blow over," Mason said with more assurance than he felt. The weather station had predicted a cooldown, and he believed it.

"Okay . . . okay." She gave him a jerky nod. "You don't have that chocolate ale on you, by chance?" Grace asked with an edge of humor.

"No, I thought the flashlight was more important at the time. Now I'm having second thoughts." Mason tried to grin, but the loud boom of thunder made him wince. He sat down beside Grace, ready to shield her with his body if necessary. "I'm sure we'll be safe. This building used to house boats, and it's built like a fort. I just don't want any damage to the roof or windows. I've sunk my savings into this brewery, and I don't want to lose my ass from an act of nature."

"You have insurance, right?"

"Of course I do," Mason replied, wondering if Grace thought he was some sort of country bumpkin without a clue. His look must have telegraphed his thoughts, because Grace winced.

"Sorry. It's in my nature to immediately start thinking about that sort of thing. I didn't mean anything by it."

Mason gave her a small nudge with his elbow. "Yeah, just when I was going out into the danger zone for the chocolate porter."

"No! Stay right here!" When Grace put a restraining hand on his bent knee and squeezed, he thought it was kind of cute. "There might be a cow flying through the air or something."

Mason chuckled. "I'll just dash out and be back in a minute."

"No!" Grace repeated, but in truth Mason wanted to know what was going on out there. "Are you crazy?"

"All country boys have a little crazy in them. My brother, Danny, is worse, but I have my moments of *hey, watch this*."

"This isn't going to be one of them. I'll block the doorway."

"Yeah, like that will work," Mason said with a chuckle.

"You might be surprised. I'm tougher than you might imagine."

"So you're a rather-be-safe-than-sorry kind of girl?"

"Ha, not hardly. I'm always up for a new challenge. I'm all about the bigger the risk, the bigger the reward theory."

"Or the opposite can be true." Mason barely held back another groan. "I really think I want that beer now."

"We'll drink to our safety after the whatever-it-is going on out there passes over."

"I'll leave the flashlight for you."

"Are you kidding? What if you fall into that vat of foamy stuff? Or—"

"I'll use the flashlight on my cell phone. Plus, I know my way around this building even in the dark. I'll be right back." Odd, but Mason felt the urge to give Grace a quick kiss of reassurance—but of course he didn't. He pointed the flashlight at her face and thought that her eyes appeared a bit big with fear. Maybe he shouldn't leave her. "But don't you move."

"Don't worry about that! I don't want to get hit by a flying cow or land up in Oz."

"Okay, well then, stay put. I'll be right back." In spite of her squeal of protest, Mason hurried out into the taproom, where he located a couple of bottles of chocolate porter and hooked two of them through his fingers. Lightning flashed like strobe lights and the wind howled, but if a tornado had indeed touched down, it had thankfully missed his brewery, at least for now. But his phone still indicated that the storm warning was in effect for another hour, and although funnel clouds were spotted during these late-summer storms where fronts collided, having a tornado actually touch down was rare. Still, after having been caught in a nasty storm out on the lake when he'd been so hell-bent on winning a fishing tournament that he'd not taken heed of the weather warnings, Mason now took the sirens seriously.

Mason paused to text his mother to make sure everybody was okay. Her positive response made him feel much better. But when thunder boomed again, he felt a fresh flash of apprehension. He hoped to have enough stock to have a beer-tasting party for friends and family in a couple of weeks, and having a storm do damage would just suck big-time. "Come on, Mother Nature, give a guy a break."

Mason's family owned Mayfield Marina. But like his sister, Mattie, with the bistro, Mason had invested his own savings in the brewery. He'd been pretty much telling Grace the truth about sinking his last dime into converting the boathouse into a brewery. Mason's nest egg from his pro fishing days was nearly depleted. Plus, he wanted to protect his friend Shane McCray's sizable investment in the brewery. Losing his own money would suck, but even though Shane was a country music superstar, he didn't want him to lose his investment either.

"Mason? Are you okay out there?" Grace shouted. When Mason rounded the corner he could see the beam of her flashlight shining here and there, as if searching for him.

"I'm fine!" Mason hurried her way and met her just outside of the bathroom. "You're not very good about staying put."

"I was getting claustrophobic in there."

Mason had to chuckle. "Right. I think you're just what my mom would call a busybody."

"Who, me?" she asked, but when thunder rolled like angels playing bowling ball, she backed up toward the bathroom.

"Yeah, you."

"Okay, I confess that I always want to know what's going on. I was concerned for your safety too, if you must know."

"Were you going to come to my rescue?"

"I would have made a valiant attempt that would have most likely ended with an epic fail, but it's the thought that counts, right?"

Mason was about to give her a comeback, but he realized that she was being serious, and he believed her. "Good to know, I guess. We have about another hour before the warning is lifted. Hopefully the lights will come back on before then." After she sat down, he handed her a bottle of beer.

"Oh, I love the swing-top cap. So cute!"

"My beer isn't cute." Mason sat down beside her and bent his legs. "It's robust . . . manly."

"Please don't pound your chest."

"Just sayin'."

"We'll see about that." Grace opened the swing top and took a sip. "Oh, wow, this is so good."

"It should be served in a snifter beer glass so you can put your nose in it."

"I want to put my whole face in it." She licked her bottom lip.

"So, what do you taste?"

Grace took another sip. "Chocolate, of course . . . mmm . . . oh . . . cinnamon!" She took another lingering sip. "A hint of coffee, perhaps? Am I right?"

"All of the above." His tone was casual, but he really wanted to know. "So, are you serious? You really do like it?"

"Let's make sure." She took another sip. "No, I don't like it."

Mason let out a breath. "Okay . . . what don't you like? A little too much for you, huh?"

Grace put a hand on his forearm. "You didn't let me finish, O so lofty brewmaster."

"Sorry. Go on."

"I love it, Mason. Rich and dark . . . with a sweet aroma that comes through, even without a snifter glass."

"How does it feel in your mouth?" The question was common in beer-tasting lingo, but the suggestion took his thoughts in another direction. *God* . . .

"Mmm, velvety in my mouth . . . Does that make sense?"

"Absolutely. You have a sensitive palate."

"Dessert in a bottle!" She arched an eyebrow. "Now, you must admit this is kind of a girly beer." She shined the flashlight on his face.

"I don't admit any such thing." Mason reached over and took the flashlight from her and tilted it upward, shedding soft, shadowy light on the room. "Well, watch out, the ABV is seven point eight percent. It will knock you on your very girly-girl can."

"I'm not a girly-girl. And I can handle any . . . BAV you throw at me."

He grinned. "ABV, or alcohol by volume."

"I knew that. I was just seeing if you were paying attention," she said, but he could hear the laughter in her voice.

"Right." When he took a swig, his arm brushed against her shoulder, making Mason keenly aware of how close they were in the muted darkness. Her floral scent mingled with the chocolate porter, and both went straight to his head. "Girly . . . ," he muttered, trying to shift his brain in a different direction.

Grace lifted one shoulder. "Just sayin'. You could market this toward women, for sure. Lots of ladies still don't know about craft beer and how delicious and decadent it can be. I only found out that I was a fan when I went to a beer-tasting festival with friends. You should think about bringing women into the fold. Market toward them and capture a demographic that's being ignored."

"Nah, my taproom is going to be geared toward dudes," Mason said, but he was pleased that Grace seemed to really enjoy the porter. "The other side of the main brewery is where I'll have the taproom. My brother, Danny, is going to help me build a really sweet bar that will run the length of the room."

"Will it be a restaurant as well?"

"No, I won't be serving food, at least not at first, but Walking on Sunshine Bistro is just up over the hill. Mattie will cater some events and I'll do pig roasts and stuff like that for special occasions." He took a sip of his ale, thinking that he was damned good and chocolate porter wasn't an easy beer to brew. "Maybe tailgating for big ball games or bonfires in the fall. I'm going to have a few flat-screen TVs, darts, maybe some poker games, and of course corn hole."

"Um, what in the world is corn hole?" She tilted her head in question.

"A beanbag toss into slanted wooden targets, but the bags are actually made with dried corn kernels. So you've never even heard of it?"

"Nope. Is it something unique to Cricket Creek?"

"Supposedly corn hole started in the Cincinnati, Ohio, area, then trickled across the river into Kentucky and has made its way south and throughout the Midwest. The corn-kernel-filled bags is where the name of the game came from."

"Oh. Makes sense."

"But, yeah, popular around here too. We have tournaments at the marina now and then." Mason usually wasn't much for small talk unless it was about fishing or brewing beer, but he could hear the wind blowing, and rain pelted hard against the windows and roof. Grace seemed a little bit uneasy, so he wanted to take her mind off the storm.

"Are you good at it?"

"At what?"

"Corn hole."

"Of course. Maybe you would be too."

"As I mentioned, I'm not athletically inclined."

"All you have to do is toss the bags into the hole. It's pretty easy. I'm sure I could teach you."

"Ha, not likely. The fact that my name is Grace is a bit of a joke. I was a little-bitty thing until junior high school, when my legs seemed to grow overnight like my mum put me on a stretcher or something. My body never did figure out how to respond. I still trip over my own shadow."

Mason had a hard time believing that Grace was clumsy. And he had to admit that he was surprised at her modesty. Grace Gordon was one pretty woman. And that throaty voice with the hint of a British accent was quite a turn-on. And those endless legs . . . "Oh, come on, you look a lot like your mother, who, um, just happened to be a famous fashion model. Didn't you ever want to follow in her footsteps?"

Grace took a sip of her ale. "Oh, don't get me wrong, I love fashion, but to this day I struggle with wearing heels, making following in her footsteps rather difficult," she said, and nudged him to make sure he got the joke. "There was brief talk of me doing some modeling for BGC, my mother's company, but I can tell you that having me walk down a runway would have been a total disaster. And I know I resemble my mum, but I'm not the stunner that she still is at fifty-five. And she isn't vain or anything, but she has that certain . . . you know, *thing*, like Audrey Hepburn. Just so effortlessly classy." She leaned closer. "Plus, don't tell my mother, but I have a weakness for junk food," she whispered.

Mason had to grin at the horror laced in her voice. "So what's your biggest weakness? Cheeseburgers? French fries?"

"Just about all of it," Grace continued in a stage whisper. "I brake for the Golden Arches." She shook her head and sighed. "Sophia is like my mother. They eat, you know, *clean*, or whatever."

"Did you just roll your eyes?"

"No!"

"So you're the black sheep of the family?"

"Well, I think Garret wins that dubious honor. Or at least he used to until he married your sister, Mattie. But, yes, sort of, I suppose. I just can't . . . always *behave*, you know?"

"Well, like I said, from what I know of Sophia, you two seem to be opposites." Mason took another drink of the ale, liking how it took the edge off. He'd been so stressed lately that in an odd way this little unexpected break felt kind of nice . . . well, as long as there wasn't any damage. "She seems almost shy whenever I go into the bistro for breakfast."

"Yeah, Sophia was always quiet and studious, while I ended up in detention at least once a week."

"And what were you being punished for?"

Grace pulled a face. "I tended to be late for class. But mostly because I couldn't shut up. Isn't that a bunch of rubbish? I mean, what crime is there in talking? Can I help it if I have the gift of gab?"

"Maybe you had more fun than Sophia. Ever think of that?"

"Ha! Sweet little Sophia is a prankster with a wicked sense of humor. No, it's just that the quiet ones get away with everything. For example, if there was something broken, I would get blamed instead of my sister. She's got those big brown doe eyes that make her appear so innocent. And she had Garret wrapped around her little finger. Still does, the little minx."

"So you were always being wrongly accused?"

She flicked a glance at him. "Well, no . . . I was almost always to blame . . . you know, clumsy and all that, but I at least deserved the benefit of the doubt, wouldn't you say?" She took a long pull from her bottle and then gave him a sideways look. "Oh, I just bet you're the good egg too. Strong, silent type. Hard worker. Dependable." She gave his knee a little shove. "Come on, fess up. I'm usually pretty good at reading people right off the bat."

"Think so, huh?" Mason thought he could read people too, but Grace was a bit of a mystery that he found himself wanting to explore. He chalked up his instant attraction to being so busy with the brewery that he had neglected his social life; being with her laughing and flirting had him realizing that he missed the company of a woman.

And it wasn't easy to make Mason laugh, at least not lately.

"Well?"

Mason shrugged and took a swig of ale, thinking he'd like another bottle after this one.

"Thought so." She nodded slowly.

"Don't be so quick to judge," Mason said, but in truth Grace had pretty much nailed his personality. Birth order had something to do with it—he was the oldest. "I might have a few surprises up my sleeve."

"I'm not judging. I despise judgmental people. Oh wait, is that being judgmental?"

Mason chuckled. "Really? Then what are you doing?"

"Assessing, maybe."

"Oh, sizing me up, huh?"

"Let's go with getting to know you. You're avoiding the question, Mason."

"Do you really think I'm that boring?"

"Hey, those were all good qualities that I mentioned." Grace gave his knee another nudge, harder this time, making him think that the porter was kicking in. "I didn't say anything about you being boring, now, did I?"

"Not in so many words."

"I didn't say it in any words. Are you kidding? I'm fascinated by the whole brewing process. Especially those giant teakettles out there."

"Ah, that's the mash tun and boiling kettle."

"The who and what kettle?"

"It's where the malted barley is soaked to release the sugars. This is important because the sugars are what the yeast eats during fermentation. When people refer to a malty beer, it really means it's a sweet beer." He liked the direction of this conversation much better.

"Eats? I have this vision of little yeasty things gobbling up the barley like Pac-Man." She did an imitation of chomping with one hand.

Mason laughed. "You have quite an imagination."

"Gets in the way of normal thinking sometimes."

Mason chuckled and took a swig of his drink. "I somehow get the impression that there's nothing normal about you." He gave her knee a nudge this time. "Am I right?"

"You would be right on the money. I just had a similar chat with my mother."

"Ah, thought so."

Grace chuckled. "But, seriously, this is interesting stuff, Mason."

"Really?"

"Yeah, I mean it. When I know how something is produced, I have a better understanding and appreciation for it. Do go on."

"Brewing beer dates back over seven thousand years. I could give you the whole history, but then you really would think I'm boring."

"We might not have to go that far, but I would love a tour of the brewery sometime."

"I can arrange that. I happen to know the owner."

Grace laughed softly. "Well, you were right about one thing. This chocolate porter packs quite a punch, especially on an empty stomach. Last thing I ate was my not-good-for-me cheeseburger and fries. And that was, like, ages ago."

"Does that mean you're ready for another one?"

"A cheeseburger? Do you have one in your pocket?"

"Let me check . . . ah no. But I can get you another ale."

"You're reading my mind, but not until the tornado warning is lifted. Let's not tempt fate twice. I can wait."

"Well, I can't." When Mason pushed up to his feet, Grace joined him. "What do you think you're doing?"

"Coming with you, of course."

"No, you're not."

"Um, watch me." She took step closer, clearly meaning business.

"What about the flying cows?"

"I'll take my chances," she announced firmly.

"Are you always this bossy?"

"Yes, without fail."

"Okay, then, take my hand. I don't want to have to fish you out of the fermentor."

"You mean that big vat of frothy stuff?"

"Yeah." Mason reached over and took her hand. "Enough said."

Although he didn't mean for there to be anything personal about the touch, Mason liked the feel of her small hand protectively tucked within his grip. He really didn't think they were in much danger, or he wouldn't go out into the main building, and the storm sounded less fierce than it had a while ago. The flashlight illuminated the way to the fridge, where Mason located two more chocolate porters. He handed one to Grace. "I need both hands, so stay close, okay?"

"I get lost easily, as you already know," Grace said, and looped her arm through his. "I'm staying glued to your side through this maze of beer-brewing stuff."

Mason didn't mind one bit that she had her arm hooked with his as he weaved his way past the machinery. "Well, I'll be happy to get you up to the bistro or wherever you're staying tonight. If your car is too wet, I'll toss your luggage in my truck."

"Thank you. I was going to stay with Sophia while I visit, but she has to get up at the crack of dawn to work at the bistro. I'm a night owl and I tend to play my music fairly loud. And as already mentioned, I talk way too much for her liking. I love Sophia to pieces and we get along famously for the most part, but we are on totally different schedules. Even though she offered, to be fair to her I'm going to rent a cabin here at the marina. I would drive the poor thing crazy."

"One of our cabins on marina property, I guess. Danny takes care of the rentals."

"Oh, I suppose so. My visit was sort of last-minute after my rather unexpected career move, so I don't have a lot of details nailed down."

"We'll get it figured out." Mason stopped by the bathroom door. "I think we can sit here and lean against the wall. The worst seems to be over." He sat down and patted the space beside him.

"That's a relief." Grace joined him and then opened her ale. "I hope the electricity comes on soon."

Mason blew out a sigh. "Me too. I'll find out which cabin you're staying in and take you there. The keys are over at the office, where I got the dry clothes. Your cabin will be within walking distance of the bistro, I'm guessing."

"Good, I don't mind walking. I did a lot of hoofing it while living in London."

Grace's comment reminded Mason how very different their backgrounds were and that after her stay in Cricket Creek she would likely be moving back to London. But just when he thought he'd better keep his distance, her leg brushed against his, and damn if he didn't want to lean over and plant a kiss right on her pretty mouth. Must have been the kick of the strong chocolate porter, the intimacy of the storm, the muted, thick darkness, and that sexy voice of hers making his mind go places it shouldn't have. "So when will you go back? I guess you have a job waiting in London?"

"I'm actually in between jobs at the moment."

"Oh, I'm sorry. That's too bad."

"Thanks, but not really." Grace shrugged. "Once the challenge is over I get bored. I don't like staying in one place too long either. I liked traipsing all over Europe, exploring. I don't like the feeling of being tied down, I suppose. You?"

"Other than a couple of years away at the University of Kentucky, Cricket Creek has always been my home."

"A couple of years?"

"Much to my parents' dismay, I dropped out of college to go on the pro bass-fishing circuit."

"You can make a living catching fish?"

"If you're good at it." He rested his wrists on his bent knees, letting his beer bottle dangle between his legs.

"And were you?"

"Yeah," he said quietly. "It was pretty much my dream to go pro from the time my father taught me how to cast into the water."

"You were hooked?"

Mason chuckled. "Good way of putting it. Of course, growing up on a marina helped me hone my skills. The water has always been my playground." Just thinking about it made him want to get out in his boat. He took a swallow of ale.

"So why did you give up on your dream?" she asked quietly.

Mason toyed with the swing top on his bottle. He didn't usually like talking about giving up competitive fishing, but there was something about Grace that had him opening up. "The recession hit Cricket Creek hard. The town relies a lot on tourism, and the shops up on Main Street struggled for a few years. Some even closed. With no extra money to spend boating and fishing, the marina was hit hard too."

"Oh, that makes sense. But why did you have to quit pro fishing if you were making money at it?"

"My dad's health. The stress of hanging on to the marina did a number on his heart. I had to come home to help out. I didn't want my family to lose the marina. It's been in our family for years. My family means more to me than fishing."

"But the marina seems to be thriving now, right? If you don't mind me asking, why didn't you go back out there and chase your dream?"

Mason inhaled a deep breath.

"Sorry. I shouldn't pry. I guess I am a . . . what did you call it?"

"Busybody. Hey, no, it's okay. Being a busybody goes hand in hand with living in a small town," Mason said lightly. "News and gossip travel like wildfire." He'd never really talked about how much it bothered him to have to quit or the girlfriend who'd dumped him when he gave up his career. He didn't want his parents to feel guilty that he had been on the cusp of hitting the big time. But for whatever reason, he didn't mind talking about it with Grace. "By the time I got back onto the competitive circuit, the technology had changed. I was pretty far behind the young guys trained by coaches on college fishing teams."

"They have college fishing teams?"

"Yeah, and in a lot of high schools now too. It's a fast-growing sport, relying a lot on GPS technology that helps find fish and mark locations. Bait is important, and even that is becoming something of an art. It's all about color and how it moves through the water. Fish, especially bass, can be damned picky."

"I just think of worms when it comes to fishing."

"All of the bait in pro fishing is artificial. I made a lot of my own, and if a certain kind of bait won a tournament, well, selling the design could make you a ton of money. Trust me—it's much more than casting a hook into the water."

"So did you try to get back into it at least?"

"At the insistence of my father. I was back on the tour for a year and lost a ton of money, lost my sponsors, which included the use of a bass boat. Unless I wanted to sink my own past earnings into trying another year, I was done. Entry fees and the cost of traveling along with upkeep on a bass boat is an incredible amount of money."

"So you invested in the brewery instead."

Mason nodded. "It was a hobby I had for a long time. I knew, for whatever reason, I had a knack for it. And what can I say? I love a well-crafted beer."

"I think that anytime you get to be creative and love what you do, it makes work so much more fulfilling."

"And by living in Cricket Creek I can still help out at the marina. My parents have come back home for the birth of Mattie and Garret's baby, but they will still winter in central Florida. They have lots of friends down there now, and they fish in a co-ed bass-fishing club that travels all around the state."

"It sounds like your parents have a great marriage and have fun together."

"Oh, like everyone else, they have their moments, but, yeah, you're right. I can't even imagine them not being together."

"Rare these days."

"I suppose." Mason shrugged. "I guess you're right,

but there seems to be a fair amount of happy couples in Cricket Creek. Maybe it's the small-town lifestyle and old-fashioned values ... oh, hey, I didn't meant to infer that that if you're from the city—"

"It's okay." Grace put a brief, gentle hand on his knee. "I get what you're saying. No offense taken. So go on."

"Plus, I'm still needed here too." When Grace fell silent, he gave her little nudge. "What, no more questions?"

"I'm just sorry that you had to quit fishing when you were so close to fulfilling a lifelong dream. Does it bother you?"

Mason hesitated to talk to her about such personal things, but whether it was the chocolate porter or her company, he felt himself confiding in her. "Well, yeah, I admit that it gets to me now and then, but I didn't like all of the time spent on the road. Fishing tournaments meant lots of travel, sometimes for weeks on end. When you're not winning, it becomes a grind. So does living out of hotels and campers. Then again, maybe I just didn't have the courage to go out there again after a year of failure."

"I know we've just met, but I'm not buying that last part. I think you like being home around your family. While in London, Mattie talked about how close you all are. By the way, I adore your sister. I'm so happy that she and Garret found each other."

"Thanks. I'm happy for them too. Yeah, truthfully, even during my successful years I was always ready to come home. I suppose I like feeling grounded," Mason said, thinking that he couldn't imagine just wandering around all over creation the way that Grace said she did.

"To me, grounded means being trapped in one place. I mean, it even sounds horrid. Planes are grounded. Naughty kids are grounded. That word scares me."

"It's not punishment if you want to be there. There's something to be said for putting down roots. Blooming where you are planted, as my mother called it. I guess what I'm saying is that no matter where I roam, Cricket Creek will always be my soft place to land. Home."

Grace fell silent, as if mulling that notion over in her head.

Feeling as if he was getting too personal, Mason said, "Well, at any rate, I'm sorry that Cricket Creek welcomed you with a raging storm. Hopefully, you'll have better weather for the rest of your visit. How long do you plan to stay?"

"I'm not sure, actually."

"So your plan is no plan?"

"You sound horrified," Grace said with a light chuckle. "No plan often turns into an adventure."

Mason took a drink of his ale, and then nodded. "I've always had to be a planner. For me timing is everything. In pro fishing you have to be at the right place at the right time to catch fish. Brewing beer is all about timing too."

"So will you only sell your ales locally?"

"Yes. I already have interest from several Cricket Creek restaurants to carry the ale in addition to having the taproom here. Mattie is going to acquire a liquor license and have a happy hour at the bistro, at least on a limited basis. I hope to have the Cricket Creek Cougars baseball stadium eventually have some of my beer on tap. I want to do some seasonal ales too."

"Sounds like you're starting to put a marketing plan together. What is the brewery called?"

Mason nibbled on the inside of his lip. "I'm not entirely sure yet. I think I'll just go with something simple like Mayfield Brewing Company." At her silence he chuckled. "Not thrilled, huh? Or maybe something to do with fishing or relating to the marina in some way. I don't know, but I have to make a decision pretty soon. It's been driving me sort of crazy. I can't seem to make up my mind. I guess the marketing end of the operation wasn't something I put as much thought into as I should have. I just wanted to brew beer."

"If you brew it, they will come?"

Mason laughed. "Yeah, that's the gist of my plan. I just don't like that end of the business, I guess."

"Oh no, that's the exciting part," Grace said, and seemed ready to say more, but just like that the lights suddenly came on. The machines started clanking, startling Grace so much that she jumped and grabbed his arm. "Oh my goodness!"

"Let there be light." Mason laughed at her reaction. He tapped his bottle neck to hers. "Welcome to Cricket Creek, Grace Gordon."

"Thank you. I know I'm going to love my visit here. I have to say it's already been quite the adventure so far."

"Well, I certainly hope the rest of your experience here isn't quite so traumatic."

"Oh, no worries. I thrive on adventure. And trust me—most of them are unexpected."

"I want to hear more about your adventures while you're in town," Mason surprised himself by saying.

"Hey, just provide more of this ale and I'll be glad to fill you in." She raised her eyebrows. "I could be your official taste tester."

"Will you work for beer?"

"Absolutely."

Mason laughed. "You're hired."

He tilted his head to the side and listened. "I think the rain has let up. Do you want to get the keys to your cabin or head up over to the bistro first?"

"Let's get the keys while I give my phone a charge. My mother is going to be wild with worry if I don't call her soon. And then I'll phone Sophia and Garret to let them know that I've finally arrived."

"Sounds like a plan. Let's go."

3

Charmed by Chocolate

WHEN THEY VENTURED OUT INTO THE NIGHT, MASON pointed the beam of his flashlight here and there. "Other than some fallen limbs, there doesn't seem to be any damage." He looked down at his phone and blew out a sigh.

"Everything okay?"

"Yeah, I just got a text from my mother, basically saying the same thing. A little bit of cleanup tomorrow and everything should be back to normal."

"Where do they live?"

"My parents live on the far side of the marina, closer to town. They like being able to walk everywhere. We'll know more in the morning, but probably a few shingles blown off some of the cabins, but nothing to be concerned about."

"That's good. I do have to admit that I was getting a bit worried for a minute there," Grace said as she followed him across the front lawn to the main road.

"I could tell."

Grace gave him a lift of her chin. "What? I thought I held it together pretty well."

"You did. I'm just teasing. I'm good at teasing—just ask Mattie."

Grace thought he'd be good at flirting too, if he put his mind to it, especially if he utilized that smile that he kept in reserve.

"Watch out for puddles."

Grace looked down at the wet road and had to hop over a puddle directly in front of her. "Good call. Wow, it's really dark out here away from city lights." Grace had the urge to reach out and hold Mason's hand while they walked down the road. Other than the beam of his flashlight cutting through the night, they were in total darkness. But then they rounded the bend and Grace could see lights that reached out into the river, seeming to float on top of the water. "Oh, is that the marina over there?"

"Yes, doesn't it look sort of peaceful?" Mason asked, but slowed down, as if knowing she might be just a little bit wary of her surroundings. "And so quiet after the stormy weather. But I like the lingering smell of rain in the air."

"Quiet? Are you kidding?" Grace edged a little bit closer to him, hoping he didn't notice. "I hear all kinds of . . . *noises*."

"Like what?"

"Well, something just howled." She looked skyward. "Not a full moon, so I suppose we don't have to be wary of werewolves. So what do think was behind the howl? And all of that . . . rustling?"

"Well, let's see." Mason slowed to a stop and tilted his head. "Coyotes."

"Coyotes?"

"An owl hooting. Deer bedding down, maybe. Raccoons scurrying around for food."

"Should we be worried?" Grace lowered her voice to a whisper.

"You mean worried like we might be attacked?" There was an edge of humor in Mason's voice that made Grace stand up taller.

"I'm not scared. Did you forget that I thrive on adventure?"

"It's been my experience that when people say they aren't scared is when they're terrified."

"Well, I'm not terrified," Grace boasted, but in truth she wanted to grab the flashlight from him and have a look around.

"What are you, then?"

"Maybe, like . . . just a tad unnerved. But calm. Wait." She put a hand on his arm. "What was that loud splash?"

"The Loch Ness monster," he said in a low whisper.

"Right . . . and Bigfoot hangs out in the woods and eats beef jerky," Grace said with a laugh, but there suddenly seemed to be noises coming from everywhere, closing in on them. "Lions and tigers and bears . . . oh my!" But she liked the feeling of her heart pounding a little bit harder. Her day had turned into quite an event, and except for the frustration of getting lost, Grace liked her life that way.

"How did you know?"

"I follow him on Twitter. He's quite clever, actually . . . hashtag *I'm so misunderstood*."

Mason laughed. "You're funny—you know that?"

"What? I was being completely serious."

Mason started walking again, steering her away from another puddle. "I find that hard to believe."

"That I follow Bigfoot on Twitter?"

"No, that you are able to be completely serious."

"I have my moments." Although she knew that Mason was teasing, he'd hit a bit of a tender spot with her. Because Grace tended to joke around, she wasn't always taken as seriously as she wanted to be in the corporate world. And in all honesty, women still had to work harder than men. But she'd recently proven her worth in a big way when she'd sold Girl Code Cosmetics for a staggering amount of money. Who knew that playing with her mother's endless supply of makeup as a child would lead to founding a line of her own products? She'd learned from her mother that confidence and enthusiasm sell, but more than anything else, Grace loved the excitement of launching a new product. Ah, but now she felt a bit lost, wondering what challenge to tackle next. Although Grace wasn't close to her father, she knew that she'd inherited his savvy sense of business, the difference being that she would never allow making money to rule her life.

"Watch it walking across the dock," Mason warned her. "With the water being choppy, the walkway will be unsteady and move up and down."

"Oh great." The short walk across to the main building suddenly seemed a mile long. "Why aren't there railings? People like me need railings." The water looked murky and smelled like fish. Grace certainly didn't want to fall in. "Oh boy, here we go." She put her arms out to her sides like airplane wings. At least there were lights along the way.

"I won't let you fall in." Mason chuckled, and then offered her his hand. "Hold on."

Grace gratefully grasped his hand. "I might take you with me. Just fair warning."

"Not gonna happen."

"Whoa, this thing really is moving up and down." Grace clung to Mason's hand as if there were piranha schooling around in the water ready to gobble her up as soon as she took the plunge. The poststorm wind kicked it up a notch, blowing the hair that had once again escaped from her clip across her face.

Mason looked over his shoulder to where Grace followed him, nearly plastered up against his back. "You can walk beside me, you know."

"Too close to the edge."

"You okay?"

"Sort of." Her trying-to-keep-her-balance gait was like a toddler learning to walk.

"We're almost there," Mason said, and when they stepped off the dock, Grace breathed a sigh of relief.

"Thank goodness." She followed Mason over to a

building to the left side of the dock. While he paused to unlock the door, she looked around. Several rows of boat slips lined up on the other side of the building. Lights strapped to poles along the dock illuminated the marina, and she thought the sight was quite pretty. A bit farther away, Grace could see a few houseboats huddled beneath a big roof and another building jutting out into the water. She could see that some of the houseboats and cabin cruisers were lit up. "Do people live on the houseboats?"

"Some of them, at least during the summer and into early fall, depending upon how the weather holds up. I live on mine year-round."

"Really? You live on a boat?" Grace tried to decide whether she would like the feeling of living on the water or not. Perhaps the gentle bobbing up and down would put her to sleep at night, something she struggled with on a regular basis. Then again, perhaps it would keep her awake.

"Yep, for the past few years." He glanced at her before sliding the key into the lock. "It was easier for me to button up a boat when I went on the road instead of maintaining a house. And it makes commuting to work pretty easy."

"Do you like it?"

"It's okay for now." Mason shrugged. "I'd like to build a cabin somewhere on the property someday, I guess. Or maybe a rambling farmhouse with lots of land to play around on. I've been so focused on the brewery that I haven't really thought about it much. Right now, I just want to get the brewery up and running."

"Well, this is a really pretty setting. For the brewery as well. Having the marina in the background is just perfect." A variety of boats both big and small bobbed up and down, and the sound of water lapping against the hulls sounded almost musical, making Grace think that it looked as if the boats were dancing. The thought made her laugh.

"What's funny?"

"I just thought that the boats looked like they were doing a little dance. I think it's a combination of being a bit slap-happy from the drive and those chocolate delights you fed me."

"Porter. Manly chocolate porter."

"Right, there's nothing made of chocolate that women wouldn't want." She turned back to where he was unlocking the door and noticed two big wooden barrel planters spilling over with cheerful flowers on each side of the entrance. "Aren't those just so very lovely."

"That was Mattie's doing before she was put on bed rest."

"Oh, poor dear. I bet it's difficult to keep her down," Grace said as she followed him inside.

"Oh boy." Mason blew out a sigh and flipped on the light. He stepped aside and gestured for her to enter the building before him. "You got that right. Having her baby in danger is the only thing that could keep Mattie off her feet. She's none too happy about it, and I have to say that Garret has been really patient and at her beck and call. She really hates not being able to work at the bistro. And it's really great of Sophia to step up and help." He shut the door and smiled.

"Luckily, unlike me, she's an excellent cook. I guess your parents are helping too."

Mason nodded. "They are—well, at least until the cold weather hits, and then they will head back to Florida. Although I'm sure they will extend their stay to spend more time with their grandchild. My mother has been very vocal about how much she wanted grandbabies."

"My mother is over the moon too. It's wonderful that everyone has pitched in for Mattie."

"Shane McCray and his wife, Laura Lee, helped out while Garret and Mattie were in London, but they've been doing some traveling, so their time is limited."

"Holy cow, do you mean the country music singer?"

"You like country music?"

"I do."

"Yeah, he and Laura Lee donated what would have been their salary at the bistro to Mattie's literacy charity. Shane got a kick out of being a short-order cook. He still helps out when he can. Pretty cool dude, huh?"

Grace nodded. "And he invested in your brewery."

"He was actually going to have more of an active role, but Shane also helps out at Sully's South, a Bluebird Café kind of venue where songwriters showcase their music. For a guy who came to Cricket Creek to retire, he's really busy. And he still performs for charity events and for the troops."

"I love his music."

"I have to say that I'm a bit surprised that you're a country music fan."

"I love a wide variety of music, and country is one of them. I enjoy the story in the lyrics. Remember that my father is American."

"You don't sound even half-American."

"That's because I've spent the last few years almost entirely in London and abroad, except to visit Sophia in New York."

"So you've remained close." He walked across the room and turned on another light.

"Yeah, and Garret is a good big brother. He attended lots of make-believe tea parties for me and Sophia. I've always adored him. He went through a bit of a troubled time, but I had faith in him. And I know you're close to your siblings. Mattie said so. Is your brother, Danny, involved in the brewery?"

"Just building the bar and maybe some other carpentry work I might need. He might bartend here and there just for fun. But Danny has his hands full with the daily business of running the marina. He does a little fish guiding here and there, but now that Jimmy Topmiller is living here, guiding and setting up a few tournaments, he has some time to do other things. My friend Colby is going to help me bartend and later maybe take on a role in sales and delivery. Danny's friend Avery Dean might come to work for me too."

"It takes a village."

"Yeah, and my mom is going to help out babysitting once Mattie can come back to the bistro. Everybody will pitch in. That's how we do it round here."

"We'll all be so glad when the baby girl has arrived. My mother cleared her schedule so she can have an extended stay here. It's going to be quite nice to have all of us together for a few weeks." Grace smiled just thinking about it. "Oh, this is a cute little shop." She looked around. "Has a little bit of everything."

"After my parents moved to Florida, Mattie put her touch here and there. Funny, we always considered her kind of a tomboy, but she blossomed with Garret. Wait until you see Walking on Sunshine Bistro."

"Mattie showed me pictures. I love that she got some of her inspiration for the bistro while living in London with Garret."

"My little sister really surprised us all. Before she decked it all out, Walking on Sunshine Bistro was called Breakfast, Books, and Bait."

"An interesting mix of offerings, I must say. Bait? Really?"

"Artificial bass bait. It's gone from the bistro. We only sell it here now." Mason pointed to a display of fishing-related gear and walked over toward an office. "The local fishermen liked being able to buy bait while waiting for breakfast. Now the bistro attracts a wide variety of customers."

"What about the books?"

"Mattie still has the books at the back of the bistro. It's used books that are donated or exchanged. All sold for a buck. The proceeds go toward a literacy program in Cricket Creek."

"What a lovely concept. I'll have to check out the selection while I'm here. I enjoy a good read now and then."

Grace followed Mason through boating accessories to a small grocery section tucked to the side. She eyed the rack of snacks with a bit of guilty longing. "What on earth are pork rinds?"

Mason walked over and tossed her a bag, which of course Grace failed to catch. "Deep-fried pork skins." He arched one eyebrow in silent challenge.

Grace felt a flash of delight. "Oh right, they're called pork scratchings in England. Don't mind if I do." Grace pulled the bag open and took a crunchy bite. "Mmm, tasty."

Mason folded his arms across his chest and gave her a long look. "Interesting."

"What, that I eat them? Of course I would love something this rotten for you. And don't get me started on bacon. I do believe I'd eat a shoe if it was wrapped in bacon."

Mason shook his head. "Here I thought pork rinds were a Southern food ... well, I use the term *food* loosely."

"A delicacy, you mean."

He gave her that killer grin again. "If you say so. Have at it. But in reality pork rinds are low-carb and not as unhealthy as you might imagine."

"I feel a tad better, then, not that it would matter in the end. Do you fancy one?" She held a fat, curly pork rind up to him in polite offering.

"No, thanks."

"Wait—are you only into healthy food?" From the looks of him Grace could believe it. He appeared as solid as a rock. She'd like to squeeze one of those biceps to find out—oh yes, she would.

Mason hesitated and then said, "No, not really. But craft beer pairs well with certain meals, much like wine, so I've become a bit of what Mattie calls a foodie, even though the term makes me feel silly."

"You don't say."

"Your turn to be surprised?"

"I happen to like surprises." She reached into the bag for another pork rind. "So can you cook too?"

"Sure can." Mason nodded. "I honed my skills over a campfire. I can cook anything from beef stew to brownies."

"Seriously? Brownies? I can barely manage s'mores. Oh, now I want one. So how is it that you're such a proficient campfire cook?"

"I used to conduct overnight fishing trips, and I wanted the food to be something to remember. So, do you like to camp out?" He gave her a look that said he couldn't quite imagine her sleeping beneath the stars.

"I haven't done a lot of it, but I did a white-water rafting trip in West Virginia that lasted three days. I had to be pretty hardy for that."

"I'm impressed."

"Don't be. I fell out of the raft twice." She held up two fingers. "But I loved it . . . well, except for the night noises and complete darkness. When you're a city girl, thick, black darkness can be quite scary, not that I wouldn't give it a go again. Being a bit frightened is part of any adventure, wouldn't you say?"

"I have to agree. It's all about the adrenaline rush."

"No doubt! Well, I'm certainly impressed by your campfire cuisine."

"After mastering a campfire, cooking in the kitchen is a breeze. How about you?"

"Not so breezy." Grace really didn't want to explain that she'd grown up with a cook in the house. Her mother enjoyed cooking but didn't have the time. Of course, Grace could have been like Sophia and watched meals being prepared, but Grace was always too antsy to sit around the kitchen island for any length of time. "I'm always on the move, so I never really put much effort into fixing my own meals. Why cook when you can unwrap a cheeseburger?"

Mason made a face.

"Oh, stop. Fast food is a guilty pleasure, but I know my way around fine cuisine." She tilted her head. "But in truth, what I love the most is discovering hole-in-the-wall restaurants that serve up amazing local dishes. Getting lost in the middle of nowhere has its rewards."

"Wine and Diner up on Main Street serves up comfort food with a gourmet twist. I'm sure you'll enjoy the menu there."

"Sounds lovely." Grace nodded, hoping he might offer to take her there, but he started walking toward the office again.

"The food is really delicious. It used to be Myra's Diner, you know, Southern comfort food like pot roast and meat loaf."

"Chicken-fried steak? Mashed potatoes?"

Mason nodded. "The best."

Grace groaned. "Stop, you're killing me. So the diner changed hands?"

"Sort of," he said, while looking through some notes on the desk. "When hard times hit, Myra's niece came back from Chicago, where she was a chef at some big-time restaurant downtown. Jessica was supposed to only help get the diner back on its feet but ended up taking over, so now it's a blend of old-fashioned favorites and Jessica's specialties. Jess married Ty McKenna, a major league baseball player who now coaches the Cricket Creek Cougars."

Grace shook the bag and located the biggest pork rind. "While she was in London, Mattie told me about some of the movers and shakers who moved to Cricket Creek over the past few years. Including, of course, my mother's ex-husband, Rick Ruleman."

"We sure were blown away when he moved here." Mason stopped what he was doing and looked at her as if suddenly remembering her connection to the famous rock-star legend.

"I know." Grace nodded. "If you had told me a few years ago that Rick would have ended up starting his own record label catering to country and bluegrass music, I would have laughed in your face."

"I can understand why you would feel that way," Mason said, but Grace sensed him pulling away from their earlier easy bantering. "I can't imagine . . . ," he began, but then stopped and nibbled on his bottom lip.

"Imagine what?" Grace quit crunching and looked at him, even though she was pretty sure what was coming.

"Nothing."

"In my experience, *nothing* always means a great big *something*," Grace said lightly, trying to bring back some humor, but Mason didn't even crack a smile. "So what is your *something*?"

After another slight hesitation, he said, "I'm just a country boy, Grace. I guess it just hit me that you grew up around really famous people. And . . ." He trailed off again, but Grace knew that he wanted to say something about being wealthy.

"So?" She tapped her foot, waiting, and then felt silly and stopped tapping. "Go on, then."

"I don't know." Mason shoved his fingers through his hair. "Why are you getting mad at me? You forced it out of me."

"I'm sorry. It's just that people tend to get the wrong impression about my lifestyle. I get kind of touchy about it. Not your fault."

"I didn't mean anything by it. I really like Garret and Sophia too. But I understand what you're saying. When I knew who Garret was, I wasn't exactly thrilled when he started seeing my sister. I don't have to tell you about Garret's player reputation, which was splashed all over the tabloids. I didn't want my sister to get hurt by the rich son of a rock star out to have a good time."

"Things aren't always as they seem," Grace said with an edge of defense in her tone.

"I get that now." Mason sat down on the edge of the desk and crossed his ankles. "I'm not a judgmental person, and I was completely wrong about your brother. And Rick doesn't look anything like he did back in his leather-and-long-hair rocker days, so I don't think of him from back then. I guess for a moment I just forgot about all of that, not that it matters. So will you give me a break?"

"Your arm or leg?"

"My nose," Mason said, and gave her a small grin.

"I'd probably swing and miss."

"Okay, then." Mason stood up and took a step closer. He tapped the bridge of his nose with his finger. "Go ahead."

"No, thanks, you don't deserve it." Grace lifted one shoulder and then looked down at the pork rinds, which were holding less appeal. She seriously needed to get rid of that chip on her shoulder.

"Good, because I think you'd pack quite a punch if you connected."

"Well, you know, I get it. And Garret didn't help matters by all of his shenanigans caught by the paparazzi. He egged it on just to get his father's attention, and of course worried my mother to death. But we didn't live the kind of pampered, reality-show-worthy lifestyle that people imagine." While she knew that her upbringing was anything but normal, her mother had made sure that she and Sophia worked their tails off, not only to become successful, but also to be just good, caring people. In truth, after her divorce from Rick Ruleman, her mother modeled for only a couple of years, to earn enough money to start her own business. Becca never expected one swimsuit poster to make her into a household name, and to this day she still hated when it was mentioned. Grace's father hated when it was mentioned even more. At least Mason was too young to have had the poster hung up on his bedroom wall. "Let's just drop the subject, shall we?"

Mason raised his hands in surrender. "Like a hot potato."

"Oh, there you go mentioning food again!"

Mason laughed and the mood lightened. "Well, I have to say that it's really cool to have a recording studio in Cricket Creek. We're getting all kinds of talent in from Nashville, thanks to Garret. And even though we don't get the *Sing for Me* competition here on a local television station, we were able to view it on the Web and had watch parties on the big screen at Sully's Tavern."

"Really? That's so wonderful. Does Garret know?"

"Of course." Mason seemed to find what he was looking for on the cluttered desk. "We're really proud of him."

"Me too." Mason's straightforward admission put a lump in Grace's throat. Even though her mother never spoke poorly of Rick Ruleman, Grace grew up resenting him because of his lack of interest in Garret's childhood. Grace's own father had been missing in action in her own life, so she understood some of Garret's void, but she never had to endure having her father's crazy exploits splashed all over the tabloids—most of them with starlets half his age. Desperate for his father's attention, Garret had tried his best to outdo his father in the public eye. Classic but sad. "It's good to see Garret getting recognition for his talent rather than his antics."

Mason looked up from the note he was reading. "Danny is on the wild side too. Always doing some fool thing that drove my parents crazy. Still does, now and then."

"I guess there has to be one in every family." The fact that Garret and Rick had mended their fences and Garret was a talent scout for My Way Records was nothing short of a miracle. But for Grace, the best part, other than Garret's marriage to Mattie, was that Garret had made it as a judge on *Sing for Me* on his own merit, not on the coattails of his father.

"Okay . . ." Mason started looking through some keys dangling from hooks on a big board behind a desk. "Mattie also told me that Sophia is an amazing hairstylist sought after by celebrities. So what is she doing cooking and waiting tables at the bistro?"

"To help out, but she also needed a break from the stress of being in a high-end salon in New York City. She specialized in brides . . . Can you imagine?" Grace shuddered.

"And your mother designs clothing that Mattie says isn't fancy but for the everyday person, and she's coming out with a cute line for babies."

"Mattie has told you quite a lot."

"She's confined to bed rest. When you visit, she holds you captive."

"I would be the same way."

Mason gave her a look that said he believed her. "But seriously, you come from a talented family, Grace."

"Thank you."

He unhooked a key from the grid. "So what's your talent?"

"Talking."

"Oh, come on." Mason glanced over his shoulder and laughed, but Grace wasn't really joking all that much. Sure, her Girl Code line of edgy cosmetics was pretty damned cool, but it was her ability to sell that made the product take off. She also knew the value of finding the perfect niche in the marketplace, which more often than not meant finding a demographic that was being ignored or neglected. "Elaborate for me."

"Sales and marketing is my thing, which equated to being really good at persuasive speaking."

"Hey, that's a talent, in my book."

"Thank you. I like your book." And his book had a very nice cover.

Mason chuckled. "Okay." He looked at the selection of cabin keys again and then turned to her. "Danny has you in cabin twenty-three up by the lake."

The tone of Mason's voice had her asking, "Is that not good?"

"Well, Mattie and Garret's cabin is right over there."

He pointed to the left. "And the bistro is up on the hill. Danny has you up in the wooded area overlooking the lake. Pretty setting and conveniently located."

"Where's Sophia's cabin?"

"Sophia is actually staying in the only high-rise in Cricket Creek. It's just down the road near the baseball stadium. She wanted to be close to town and shopping. Of course, that's an option for you too, but I can't help you with that one."

"Oh, now that I think of it, she mentioned that. What are my other options?"

"I do have something that you will think is either cool or a pain in the butt."

The tone of his voice captured her interest. "What?"

"I have a cabin over by the covered slips that's actually built on a slab out on the water. It used to be the main office until we built this bigger one with the shop. You have to walk on the dock to get to it or use a boat, but you might find it fun to be surrounded by water. There's a back deck with patio furniture and a grill."

"I'll take it."

Mason grinned. "I kind of thought you would." He tossed her the keys and she surprised herself by catching them.

"Good catch."

"Lucky catch."

"Let's get you settled in and then locate Sophia," he said. "If she's not at the bistro, I'll take you over to her apartment."

"Thanks. Hopefully she's charged her phone and I can finally get in touch with her."

"Your phone should be charged now too. We'll stop back at the brewery, get your phone, and grab your suitcase. I just need to close things up here," he said, but then his cell phone rang. "Excuse me." Fishing it out of his pocket, he said, "Oh, it's Mom, probably wondering if you're settled in yet." Mason answered, "Hi, Mom . . . whoa, wait a minute, slow down . . . what? Mattie's in labor? But isn't it too soon?" He glanced over at Grace, and her eyes widened. "Yeah . . . I still have Grace with me. No . . . no, we'll be right there."

"Oh my God!" Grace grabbed his extended hand. A moment later they were out the door.

4

The Road Less Traveled

BECCA GORDON DROVE DOWN THE WINDING ROAD A good ten miles per hour over the legal limit, but she didn't care one bit that she was speeding. She was on a mission. Getting to Cricket Creek in time for the birth of her first grandchild had her taking the next bend like a NASCAR driver. The rear tires of the rented sedan skidded into the gravel off the side of the road, but she gripped the steering wheel tighter and carried on as if she wasn't terrified to drive so fast.

The plane ride from London had seemed to take days to land, with the hardest part not being able to use her cell phone to keep up on the progress of Mattie's labor. Because she was nearly a month early, they had put her on meds to keep the contractions from progressing. Garret was a complete wreck with worry, and although Becca had said words of encouragement to him, she was worried sick too.

Becca looked at the GPS on the dash of her car and wanted to weep. She still had nearly thirty minutes to go! God, how she wanted to be at the hospital holding her son's hand! At the straight stretch of road she gave the accelerator a bit more of a push and watched the red needle of the speedometer hit ninety. "Oh . . . I should slow down," Becca whispered, but when the GPS indicated that she had eaten up some of the travel time, she kept going. She wasn't one to break rules, but out on this country road, surely no one would care. Except for a big green tractor she'd passed a few miles ago, she seemed to be the only one on the road anyway.

And then she saw blue lights in her rearview mirror.

"You've got to be kidding me." In a panic, part of Becca had the wild urge to go faster to outrun the cop, but when he put his siren on she knew she'd better pull over. "Damn the luck!" Letting out a little squeal of frustration, she slowed down and eased the car off to the side of the road. She couldn't care less about getting a ticket, but just wanted to get to the hospital. Of course, just as the officer was striding her way, she got a text message from Garret saying that they were going to take the baby via cesarean section. Becca inhaled a shaky breath and sent a message back that she would be there soon, and then rolled the window down when the officer reached the side of her car.

"Do you know why I pulled you over, ma'am?"

"Yes," Becca said, "I was speeding, but—"

"So." He pushed his mirrored aviator glasses up the bridge of his nose. "Do you know how fast you were going?"

"Yes, ninety, I think, but—"

"I need to see your driver's license, proof of insurance, and registration," he said in a no-nonsense tone of voice.

"Please listen, you don't understand."

"I understand that you were speeding."

"I know, but . . ." She fumbled around for her purse. "It's . . . this isn't my car," Becca said, nearly in tears. She handed him her driver's license with shaking fingers. "I'm so sorry for speeding, but I've flown in from London and I desperately want to get to the hospital in Cricket Creek for the birth of my grandchild. My dear

Mattie went into early labor. They're doing a C-section and my son is worried sick. Please, can you … can you just let me go? I promise to slow down, but I must get there—"

"Wait." The officer abruptly looked up. "Mattie Mayfield?"

"Well, Mattie Ruleman now, but yes."

He handed back the license.

"Follow me," he said in that same don't-mess-with-me tone.

"Are you taking me to jail?" Becca's heart thudded. She'd never been in trouble for anything, not even a parking ticket.

The officer chuckled, but even that sounded stern. "No, I'm giving you a police escort. I know a faster shortcut to the hospital."

"You'll do that for me?" Becca wanted to jump out of the car and hug him.

"I know the Mayfields well. I go way back with Mattie's father. This is how we do things in a small town. Are you ready?"

"Yes, sir." Becca nodded, and kind of wanted to salute.

"But listen." His smile faded. "Be careful. I'll go as fast as I can."

"I'll stick to you like glue," Becca promised, and a moment later she was flying down the road following the police cruiser. He made a turn down a bumpy back road, but Becca didn't care that she was kicking up dust like a scene from *The Dukes of Hazzard*. This was the kind of adventure that would terrify Sophia, she thought, but Grace would be holding on tightly and laughing.

Becca heard her phone ping but didn't dare look anywhere but at the winding road. When a big barn loomed ahead of her, she thought for a wild moment that they were going to drive straight through the opening, scattering chickens and busting through bales of hay. And dammit, she was going to do it! But the squad car veered to the left and Becca found herself on a narrow road cutting through a cornfield. "Dear God!" Becca could have reached out the window and picked an ear of corn if she hadn't had a death grip on the steering wheel. Another left turn had them on a paved two-lane road driving past farms and grazing cows. At least she thought they were cows. Everything was a blur.

A few moments later they pulled into the entrance to a hospital.

Becca came to a screeching stop behind the police car at the main entrance. The officer got out and hurried to her side. "The visitor parking lot is to your right. I have a call to respond to or I'd go in with you."

"I can't thank you enough."

"No need to thank me, ma'am. My job is to serve and protect." He tipped his hat. "Give Mattie my best," he said and then pointed a stern finger at her. "But no more speeding."

"You don't have to worry about that." Becca pulled into the parking lot and then took quick strides up to double doors that parted for her to enter. Digging inside her giant purse, she located her cell phone and called Garret.

"Mum, hey, love, where are you? They're prepping Mattie for . . . for . . . the C-section." His voice cracked a little bit, and Becca understood. The thought of Mattie undergoing surgery and worry about the baby were tearing Garret apart.

"Darling, I'm in the lobby."

"Good . . . good." She heard his sigh of relief and said a silent thank-you to the kind cop who'd gotten her there in record time. "I'll send Grace down to get you. Sophia is on her way too. She's closing up the bistro."

"Okay, I'll wait right here," she said in a voice much more calmer than how she felt. Becca had learned a long time ago how to control her emotions. She'd always been a calming factor in the lives of her children, and when she did lose control, she did it in private. Her life had been full of ups and downs, but the one thing that would always be consistent was her unconditional, total love for her three children. Absolutely nothing else in the world meant more to her. And she was going to be a grandmother!

As soon as Grace stepped off the elevator, Becca rushed over and enveloped her daughter in a tight hug. "Oh, Gracie, please tell me that everything is going to be okay."

"Better now that you're here. Oh, but, Mum, I'm worried."

Becca pulled back and put her palms on Gracie's cheeks. "Darling, how is Garret really holding up?"

Gracie's eyes misted over. "Fine when he's with Mattie. He holds her hand and strokes her head. But, Mum, he's dead on his feet. He's been worried sick. Garret loves Mattie so much, and of course he's fretting over the baby too ... our Lily." Gracie's smile trembled at the corners.

Becca put a hand to her chest and felt the rapid worried beat of her heart. "Oh, I simply adore that name." She took Grace's hand and they walked toward the elevator. "Let's get up there and bring this baby into the world," Becca said, and then turned when they heard Sophia's voice calling out to them.

"Mom! Grace! Wait for me!" Sophia jogged as fast as her short legs would carry her, and a moment later the three of them did a quick group hug. "Any more word about Mattie, Grace?"

"No." Grace shook her head. "Only that after Lily was showing some signs of distress, that's when the doctor decided that they needed the C-section. Apparently they held off as long as they could."

Sophia inhaled a deep breath and nodded. "Oh boy. I didn't know it was possible to be so worried or to love a child so much who I haven't had the chance to hold yet."

Becca reached over and squeezed Sophia's hand. "Well, they seem to be on top of everything here, right?"

Ever since she'd had her tonsils taken out as a child, hospitals made Becca feel anxious. The antiseptic smell still made her stomach lurch.

"Oh, the staff has been wonderful." Grace nodded firmly. "And there's a whole crew of friends and family up there waiting and praying."

"Is Rick here?" Becca asked.

"He was a while ago." Grace nodded and exchanged a brief glance with Sophia. "With Maggie."

"Good," Becca said as they walked over to the elevator. She pushed the button. There had been a time when she didn't want to be in the same room with Rick Ruleman, but those days were thankfully over. When Rick's music had turned from soulful ballads to hard-core rock and roll, Rick became a man she no longer knew, and she'd pulled away from the marriage, not wanting to live that kind of lifestyle or expose Garret to it. Looking back, though, she realized she'd come between Rick and his son, hampering their relationship, and although Becca had few regrets in her life, that was certainly one of them. While she thought she'd been protecting Garret at the time, she should have found a way to keep the father-son bond that they both needed.

Becca glanced at her daughters, so different from each other, but they loved each other fiercely. Although it had been ill-fated, she didn't regret her marriage to Marcus Gordon, because the union had resulted in Grace and Sophia. Her life had been full of success and sacrifice, but she'd not quite mastered how to find the right balance between the two. But Becca hid her disappointments and heartache well, only shedding tears on her pillow. She began each day with a smile of determination, never allowing the world to see a moment of weakness.

The elevator doors opened and they stepped aside for a man to exit. He gave Becca a glance, and the slight hesitation and then the widening of his eyes said that he recognized her. Ah, the damned swimsuit poster had been both her salvation and her worst enemy. Pinup models weren't taken seriously, and it had taken her a long time to prove that she knew her way around the business side of the fashion industry. The popularity of the poster had landed her several commercials and a guest television spot here and there, even though her acting skills were suspect. Now, nearly thirty years later, Becca was always surprised when she was still recognized.

"That guy totally knew who you were." Grace gave her a nudge with her elbow, and then pushed the button for the third floor.

Becca rolled her eyes as the doors closed with a soft *whoosh*. "From the poster that will live on forever and ever."

"Mom, I don't know why you hate it so much," Sophia said. "The one-piece swimsuit is modest by today's standards. I think it represents a more refined era, showing more class and less skin. You were beautiful and classy then and even more so today."

"I agree with Sophia. I am and will always be so very proud of you. We all know how hard you've worked."

"Thank you, my sweet girls." She curved her arms around them both and squeezed.

Becca found it darkly amusing that she was an object of envy. The public assumed that because she'd been married to Rick Ruleman and then Marcus Gordon that she was swimming in unearned money. The truth was that Rick's fame had skyrocketed after their marriage ended. Marcus Gordon had insisted on a prenup, leaving her with very little after they divorced twenty years later. But Becca didn't care. Her success in the fashion industry was hard-earned and her own doing, and she wouldn't have it any other way. Money, she'd taught her children, was a commodity, and not what life was all about. While Grace and Sophia embraced her belief, it had taken Garret longer to learn what was most precious in life.

When the doors opened, all three of them rushed into the waiting room. Garret hurried over to greet them with hugs.

"God, Mum, I'm so glad you're here."

"Me too, love. The flight seemed to take forever. So fill me in."

Garret took a step back and raked his fingers through his shaggy blond hair. "Mattie is being prepped for the C-section right now. I just popped out to see you. I have to wash up and get in the scrubs." He leaned over and gave her a kiss on the cheek. "Lily will be here soon," he said with a smile, but Becca could see the lines of worry bracketing his mouth. "You just missed Mattie's parents and brothers. They stepped out for a quick bite to eat in the cafeteria but should be back up here soon."

"It's wonderful to have so much love and support," Becca said and then put a hand on his arm. "Everything will be fine, Garret. Now, go on in there and let Mattie know we are all out here pulling for her. I'm ready to start spoiling my granddaughter."

"It won't be long now." Garret nodded and then gave Grace and Sophia a quick hug before hurrying through two double doors leading to the operating room.

Once he was out of sight, Becca took the hands of her daughters and squeezed, drawing strength from holding on to them. "It's been way too long since we've been together," Becca said. "That's got to change."

"I agree." Grace nodded and then sat down in a beige chair.

"Think you can slow down long enough to stay here for a while?" Sophia asked Grace as she sat down beside her.

"Ha, isn't that kind of like the pot calling the kettle black?" Grace asked her sister.

Sophia splayed her hand across her chest and leaned forward. "Personally, I love the slower, small-town pace."

"Yeah, but for how long?" Grace asked. "And what about your career?"

Becca took a seat across from her daughters. "Sophia, are you thinking of moving to Cricket Creek?"

Sophia pressed her lips together and then lifted one

shoulder. "I wouldn't go that far. I mean, I do enjoy working at the bistro, and I've come close to mastering Mattie's biscuits and gravy." She smiled. "And the regular breakfast crowd is a hoot." Her smile softened.

"What else?" Grace asked.

"I don't know what you mean," Sophia said, but the sudden color in her cheeks indicated otherwise.

"It's about a boy!" Becca said and rubbed her hands together. "What is it about this town that people find love and move here?"

"Must be something in the water," Grace said, and then eyed the water fountain.

"It's not!" Sophia protested. She shook her head so hard that her ponytail swung back and forth.

"In the water?" Grace said.

"It's not about a guy," Sophia said, but started twirling the end of her hair, a tell sign since she was a kid.

"Right," Grace said. "What's his name? And if you don't tell me, I'm going to pinch you."

"Mom! Are you seriously going to let Grace bully me?"

Becca laughed, enjoying this trip down memory lane. "Yes, I want to know too."

"There's . . ." She paused and blew out a sigh.

"Oh, come on," Grace said.

"Okay, there's this cute guy, Avery Dean, who comes in the bistro on a regular basis, and he flirts a little bit, but he hasn't asked me out or anything like that."

"You should ask him, then." Grace gave Sophia's knee a nudge.

Sophia shifted in the fake leather chair and nudged Grace back. "I'm not as bold as you. And I haven't heard about any guys in your life lately."

"I've been too busy with Girl Code." Grace shrugged, but when Mason Mayfield walked into the room, Becca noticed her daughter's eyes widen just fraction. Grace tried to act calm, but a quick intake of breath had Sophia nudging her sister.

"And then again, maybe you've been holding out on

us," Sophia whispered. "No wonder you chose to stay at the marina instead of with me."

"Oh, stop," Grace whispered back. "I've only been here three days."

"By how he's looking at you, you've made them count."

"Right, he gave me a glance, and now he's chatting up that nurse over there. Mason just kept me safe during the storm and helped me get settled in."

"If you say so."

Becca followed the conversation like she was watching a tennis match. But she had to agree with Sophia. Something had passed between Grace and Mason with just one short look, and they might not be aware of it, but the lingering glance spoke volumes to anyone watching.

"I like my little cabin surrounded by water. Look, I love you, sis, but we would have driven each other up the wall."

"I'm guessing you're still a night owl, listening to music loud enough to wake the dead instead of keeping the normal hours of regular people."

"Getting up at the ass crack of dawn isn't normal, Sophia. It's simply inhuman. Am I right, Mum?"

"A matter of opinion."

"I can't help it if creative inspiration comes to me late at night with music thumping through my veins."

"So is Mason a night owl like you, Grace?"

"I wouldn't know!"

"Oh, look, he's coming this way," Sophia said.

"Shh, he's going to hear you." Grace reached for a *People* magazine and started flipping through it.

Becca watched Mason as he approached. He walked in that laid-back country-boy style and was good-looking in a rough-and-tumble sort of way. He wore faded jeans like he'd been born in them, and his cowboy boots clicked on the floor.

Magazine forgotten, Grace couldn't take her eyes off him.

"Hello, Ms. Gordon. Glad you made it here okay," Mason said in that smooth Southern drawl.

"Thanks, Mason. I am so glad to be here too! But do call me Becca."

"I'll try to remember to do that," he said and then turned to greet Sophia and Grace. "Good to see you, Sophia. Mattie told me yesterday that your biscuits and gravy rival hers."

"Not hardly. I'm just a stand-in. But she's a sweetie for saying so."

"Hello, Gracie," Mason said. "Everything in the cabin still workin' okay?"

"Splendid so far."

"No sign of the Loch Ness monster yet?" Mason asked with a crooked grin that Becca thought was quite charming.

"No, but one can only hope," Grace replied lightly. "Bigfoot tweeted that it's National Chocolate Chip Cookie day."

"Really? Who knew?"

Grace tilted her head. "Hey, if Bigfoot says so, it must be true."

Mason chuckled but frowned when his phone pinged. "Excuse me, ladies."

When he was out of earshot, Becca said, "That was interesting. He calls you Gracie?"

"Mum . . ."

"Inside jokes already?" Sophia asked. She bit her bottom lip and looked at Grace expectantly.

"I'm not going to pay one bit of attention to either one of you." Grace started flipping through the magazine again.

Becca picked up a magazine and held it up to her face to hide her smile. Her visit to Cricket Creek, Kentucky, was going to be quite interesting.

5

On a Wing and a Prayer

𝒯HE MOMENT THAT MASON HELD TINY LILY IN HIS ARMS, he was a goner. He cradled her as if she were made of spun glass and said silly baby things to her in a soft, high voice that should have felt ridiculous but didn't. Her pink Cupid's bow mouth, perfect nose, and blue eyes fringed with long lashes captivated him. He couldn't stop staring at her angelic face. "I'm so glad you're home." Emotion, a tenderness like he'd never felt before, washed over him in waves, and damn if he didn't have to blink back moisture forming in his eyes. Swallowing hard, he ran a gentle fingertip down her cheek, thinking that in all his years, he'd never felt anything so very soft.

"You gonna give me a turn?" Danny asked from where he sat on Mattie and Garret's sofa. After an extra week of staying in the preemie ward, this was Lily's first day home. Still small, she swam in the newborn nightgown, making Mason's heart melt. "Seriously."

"No, I'm never giving her up," Mason said, but when Lily started to whimper and root around, he looked over at Mattie, who grinned. "What does she want?"

"I'm afraid you can't give her what she's looking for, Mason."

"Oh . . . okay," Mason relented, but when Mattie started to push to her feet, he shook his head. "Don't you dare. I'll bring Lily over to you." He eased carefully to his feet and gingerly made his way across the living room to the sofa. Slowly leaning over, he placed Lily in her mother's outstretched arms. When she started unbuttoning her blouse, Mason backed up and Danny stood up. "We'll give you some privacy," Mason said.

"I'll put a blanket over—"

"I've got to get going anyway," Mason said gently. "My beer needs my attention."

"I'll be over this weekend to work on the bar," Danny said.

"Sounds good."

"Is the Belgian blonde ready for consumption?"

"Yes, and I'm anxious to try one."

"Save a few for me," Danny said.

"I can have only a few sips while I'm nursing," Mattie said, and then stuck out her bottom lip.

"I'm going to pop in the kitchen to say bye to Mom. Then I gotta bounce too. I promised to help out Sophia at the bistro."

"Cooking?" Mattie asked with a grin.

"Hell no," Danny said, and then his eyes widened when he looked at Lily. "Sorry."

"It's okay." Mattie laughed. "She can't understand English yet."

"Still . . . ," Danny said. "I need to watch my mouth around her. To answer your question, nope, I'm just gonna help take out the trash and mop the floor and stuff."

"Thank you, Danny. I don't know how to repay all of the help Garret and I have gotten over the past few months."

Danny pointed at Lily. "She is all the thanks we'll ever need."

"Oh . . . Danny." Mattie sniffed hard. "She's precious,

isn't she? Garret falls to pieces every time he looks at her."

"She's gonna have us all wrapped around her little finger," Danny said. "How are you ever gonna put her in time-out?"

"Mom managed to send me to my room often enough."

"Yeah, but you were a troublemaker."

"I was not! You just blamed me for everything."

"Sorry. If I had known back then that you would give us Lily, I wouldn't have been such a shit."

Mattie chuckled. "I should have given you a heads-up."

Mason smiled at the exchange between his brother and sister. While he still had pangs here and there about not being on the pro-fishing circuit, it suddenly hit him in the gut that he was glad to be home instead of on the road for weeks at a time. He supposed he should be thankful for unanswered prayers.

"See you later, Mattie," Mason said, but then followed Danny into the kitchen to say good-bye to his mother, who was cooking up a storm.

"Mom, you do realize that only two people live here, right?" Danny said with a chuckle.

"You know I never learned to cook small," she said as she skinned a potato.

"Where's Dad?" Mason asked.

"Helping Garret put the crib together. The bassinette is good for now, but the crib needs to be assembled. When Lily decided to make her appearance early, Mattie and Garret weren't quite ready. That boy can sing so pretty, and the lullaby he wrote for Lily brought me to tears, but he's helpless when it comes to puttin' things together."

"We all have our talents," Mason said.

"Really?" Danny asked. "I'm still looking for mine." Although Danny chuckled, Mason knew that his brother was a little bit at loose ends with his life. Working at the marina was all Danny had ever known, but he had a talent for carpentry that he needed to put to use more often. Mason hoped that after people saw the amazing bar Danny was building, he would get more requests for similar projects. "Maybe I'll join the circus."

Danny was rewarded with a potato peeler being pointed at him. "Now, you just hush. You're plenty talented, Daniel Jay Mayfield."

"If you say so."

"I know so. The rocking chair that you built for Mattie is simply beautiful. So just stop with that nonsense."

Danny raised his hands in surrender. "I was just jokin'," he said, but Mason wasn't buying it. "I'd better get up to the bistro and help Sophia. I know that Shane and Laura Lee stopped in this morning and helped cook breakfast, but I don't want Sophia stuck with the cleanup on her own."

"I'll walk out with you," Mason said, and they gave a last good-bye to their mother.

"So, you sweet on Sophia?" Mason asked as they walked to their trucks.

Danny waved him off. "No, nothin' like that. She's like a little sister to me. Cute as a damned button, though. Plus, she's got a thing for Avery Dean."

"Really?"

"Avery pops in for breakfast nearly every day. Flirts until Sophia blushes. And I've noticed that she always gives him a little extra of everything."

"Isn't he engaged to Ashley Montgomery?"

"Not anymore."

"What happened?"

Danny shrugged. "Don't really know. It just suddenly . . . ended. Avery has been closemouthed about it. He was pretty tore up for a while, but he seems to be getting over it."

Mason fished his keys out of his pocket. "Huh. That's too bad, I guess."

"I dunno. Guess it wasn't meant to be. So what's up with you and Grace?"

"Nothin'. Why would you ask?"

"Dunno. The way you look at her, I guess."

"Well, she's a damned pretty woman, but I've got bigger fish to fry."

"What do you mean?"

Mason propped his boot up on his bumper. He gave Danny a level look. "This goes nowhere."

"Okay." All humor left Danny's eyes. "You got my word."

"I'm struggling financially with the brewery. The damned machinery cost more than I expected, and when I got it late, it pushed back the brewing process. I don't want to ask Shane for more than his initial investment, so I'm left with a nut I don't know that I can cover. I might have to shut the whole thing down."

"No way."

Mason nodded. "When that storm hit, I was scared shitless that there would be damage that I couldn't fix. The insurance deductible would have buried me, Danny. It's already high because we're in the flood zone." He shoved his fingers through his hair. "I'm not sure what I can do to save it."

"Get another investor. What about Jimmy Topmiller?"

"I don't know if I want to ask."

"He's got to have a shit ton of money from his pro-fishing days. The dude won every tournament possible, and he still drives a beat-up pickup truck. Probably one of those guys who has the first dime he ever made."

"Doesn't sound like he would want to risk it either."

"Yeah." Danny blew out a sigh. "Guess you got a point."

Mason closed his eyes and shook his head. "I know I can make it if I can just hang in there, but at the moment it's not looking good. Bills started piling up all at the same damned time, tugging me down like quicksand."

"Man, I'm sorry. I had no clue."

"Keep it under your hat. With the stress of Lily's birth, I didn't want to throw anything else at Mom and

Dad. You know that Dad might look healthy as a horse, but he still has heart issues."

"Hey, I'll keep it to myself. Mason, I wish I could help in some way."

Mason looked at his younger brother and shook his head. While lots of people thought that Danny was just a screwup, Mason knew better. Danny had a heart of gold and would give him the shirt off his back. Unfortunately, it was all Danny had to offer. "Maybe I'll come up with an answer. And just getting it off my chest to you has helped. Sorry to burden you with this, Danny."

"Are you kidding me? I'm kinda pissed that you didn't say something sooner." Danny came over and gave Mason a quick, hard hug and a slap on the back. "Hey, we managed to save this marina with a lot of work, creativity, and a little bit of luck. Something will come up. I can feel it right here," he said, and pounded his chest with his fist.

"I hope you're right. It would suck, because I'm a damned good brewmaster." He didn't mention that after he didn't return to the world of bass fishing, losing the brewery would feel like two failures in a row. And that didn't count a broken engagement.

"You've got a lot of people champing at the bit for the first beer tasting."

"Well, I perfected the chocolate porter. No easy feat. Uppity city girl Grace even liked it."

"She doesn't seem uppity. Sophia sure isn't."

Mason shrugged, not willing to admit how much he liked her. Having his heart broken once was quite enough. "Whatever."

Danny looked like he was going to say something else, but thought better of it. Good. He didn't need another lecture about moving on. "Hey, I've got to get going. But if there's anything I can do, let me know. If it's just to bend my ear or maybe get out on the water . . . seriously, anything. Just give me a shout."

"Will do." Mason gave Danny a slap on the back and then hopped up in his truck. He put the keys in the ignition, but then paused and gripped the steering wheel. He was thirty-two years old, and while he was proud of doing his part to keep Mayfield Marina afloat, he was starting to feel the pressure of taking on the brewery. Of course he knew it was a risk. But he'd been good at tournament fishing by taking risks and fishing in places others veered away from. He'd thought he'd done all of the research, crunched all the numbers. And Danny was right. He had people anxiously waiting for the beer-tasting party, restaurants willing to have his product on tap. He was so damned close . . .

And hanging by a wing and a prayer.

After checking on production at the brewery, Mason decided that he needed pizza from River Row Pizza to go with the Belgian-style blonde that was ready to tap. Another blonde popped into his head, and he thought about asking Gracie to go up to the pizzeria with him, but then squashed the idea. He was suddenly in a crappy mood and should probably eat alone on the back deck of his boat and do a little brooding. One thing he was good at was brooding. Maybe he'd listen to some music and stare out over the river, hoping for an answer to come his way.

Mason pulled into the parking lot of Wedding Row, a pretty strip of bridal-related shops built just a few years ago. The thought hit Mason that he could have been married by now, maybe had a child or two, but just weeks before their wedding, Lauren decided that small-town life wasn't for her after all and she gave him his ring back. Of course he didn't buy into her reasoning completely. It wasn't just that she missed living in Lexington. She also missed her debutante lifestyle. He'd proposed at the height of his pro-fishing career, when he was poised to make it to the top, but when he'd taken the break to help out at the failing marina, his relationship with her crumpled like a beer can in a compactor. Mason hadn't expected their engagement to hinge on his career or living in Cricket Creek, but he supposed in the end he'd dodged the bullet. His parents had stuck it out through thick and thin, and that was the kind of love that he longed to have in his life. Sure, he wanted to be successful, but Lauren was only after money and a pampered lifestyle, and when times got tough, she bailed.

Still . . . the pain, though dull now, raised its ugly head now and again. And it was pretty damned frightening to think he'd put his love and trust in someone who was so shallow. Why hadn't he seen though her?

"What the hell is wrong with me?" Mason leaned forward and turned the radio up louder, trying to drown out his sudden emotions, which he usually held in check. Oh great, the song was Darius Rucker singing about kids and family.

Beautiful Lily popped into his mind, and he felt a sharp pang of longing. While he and Danny joked about not wanting kids, Mason was a big fat liar. He wanted a family. He wanted a little boy to take fishing and a little girl to spoil with everything pink and pretty. Mason grinned, thinking of Mattie. Okay, maybe he wanted a little girl to take fishing. And he wanted a good woman by his side.

Maybe this mood was all about wanting to kiss Gracie Gordon. Mason smacked the steering wheel. No, the gorgeous half Brit would do her thing here in the small town and then head back to London and whatever it was that she did over there. Getting involved with her would be damned stupid. And he was done being stupid. Not only that, but he liked Garret a lot and he didn't want to do anything to ruin their friendship. Mason and Danny had been super protective of Mattie, and he was sure that Garret felt the same way about Grace and Sophia. Having a fling with Garret's half sister while she was in town for the birth of her brother's child would fall into the being-really-stupid category.

Mason tuned his mind to pizza. River Row Pizza was by far the best pizza he'd ever consumed, and he started to think of toppings to get his mind off . . . other things. Owners Tony Marino and his nephew Reese brought their Italian cuisine expertise from Brooklyn, and if the pizza wasn't enough, Reese's homemade desserts were, as Mattie put it . . . to die for. Mason didn't indulge all that often, but tonight he felt like ordering the works. Plus, River Row Pizza was one of the restaurants eager to serve his craft beer. This was business, he reasoned.

Mason drove slowly past the shops overlooking the river. The brick storefronts resembled old-fashioned Main Street in downtown Cricket Creek even though they were fairly new construction. He'd been in some of these shops with Lauren. Designs by Diamante was where he'd purchased her engagement ring. Mason inhaled a breath and picked up the pace. More shops had opened since then, including a bakery specializing in wedding cakes, and in spite of the crappy memories, Mason had to admit that the shops were pretty and he was glad to see expansion and that business seemed to be thriving.

Gas streetlamps would light up soon, and pots of plants dripping with flowers decorated the sidewalk. He drove past a bridal shop, the jewelry store and florist, and just about anything a bride needed to plan her wedding. Mason sighed, thinking that his mind-set hovered between *that ship has sailed* and *sure he still wanted a family*, depending upon his mood.

Tonight the mood was . . . what? Slowing down, Mason eased the truck into a parking space. He was in the mood for pizza and left it at that. No more thinking about the past.

When Mason entered the restaurant, he was hit by the tantalizing aroma of garlic and marinara sauce underlined with fresh-baked bread. He inhaled deeply, catching a hint of sweetness, meaning Reese must be creating one of his decadent desserts. The hostess greeted him, but he opted to go to the bar and order takeout while relaxing with a cold beer.

Tony Marino pushed through the double doors leading to the kitchen and spotted Mason. "Well, hey, stranger."

"What's up, Tony?"

"Me, half the night. Trish decided in a moment of insanity that we needed a puppy to give Digger some company."

Mason laughed.

"When will the beer be ready?"

Mason's grin faded. "I'm getting there. I hope to have the beer tasting sometime soon." If he could keep the production going, he thought darkly.

"Sweet. We'll be there with bells on. So what will you have tonight?"

"Takeout. Large hand-tossed supreme pizza, but leave off the green peppers. Oh, and a tossed salad with your house dressing."

"Got it. Want a beer while you're waiting?"

"No doubt. I'll take a Kentucky Bourbon Barrel."

"Always a good choice," Tony said, and placed the beer snifter in front of Mason. "I'll go place your order."

"Thanks." Mason took a sip of the bourbon-infused ale and rolled it around in his mouth. "Good stuff." Aged for at least six weeks in freshly decanted bourbon barrels, the smooth yet robust beer had gentle undertones of vanilla and oak. Mason loved it. He paged through the *Cricket Creek Courier* while he savored the ale, wondering if he should place an ad for the beer tasting or if advertising would bring in too many people. While he knew how to brew an excellent beer, the marketing end of the business was still somewhat of a mystery. Because of the marina, the Mayfield name was well-known, and friends and family would spread the word, but in order to make a profit, he needed to land large sales quickly, without overextending his limited facility.

Eventually, Mason wanted to conduct tours and maybe even teach a home-brewing class. He took a sip of the ale and sighed, thinking that he needed more hours in the day, and an extra set of hands would help. The ale helped him feel mellow, relieving some but not all of his stress.

"Here you go," Tony said. "Piping hot."

"The pizza smells so good. I don't know if I can make it home without a slice."

Tony chuckled and patted his midsection. "Yeah, good thing I run most days or you'd have to roll me in and out of here every day. Tessa put a turtle cheesecake in the bag with your salad, on the house. Take some of it over to Mattie and give her and Garret our congratulations."

"Wow, thanks a lot. Reese's cheesecake is the best. How's your sister doing?"

"Really good. She's champing at the bit for Reese and Gabby to have children."

"And Trish? Are you still in newlywed bliss?"

"Are you kidding? I'm always in trouble for something," Tony said, but then grinned. "Actually, she's busy writing for the *Courier* but just started working on a novel."

"Good for her! Tell Trish I said good luck."

"It's fun getting to see her fulfill her dream," Tony said, and the soft smile said how much he loved his bride. "And I'm sure she'll want to do some articles about the brewery. Do you have a name yet?"

"I'm sure it is great to see her get to fulfill her dream," Mason said as he reached in his wallet for his debit card. "Nah, I can't seem to come up with a name I like yet."

"I'm sure you'll come up with somethin'," Tony said in his booming Brooklyn accent.

"Hope so." After paying the bill, he thanked Tony again for the cheesecake and headed to his houseboat, eager for a slice of the pizza.

6
This Kiss . . .

FEELING ANTSY JUST HANGING AROUND THE CABIN, Grace had offered to help out at the bistro during the lunch rush, but ended up staying there the rest of the afternoon. Who knew that waiting on customers and bussing tables would be so exhausting? As she walked home, her feet ached and the small of her back throbbed. If she felt this way after a few hours, what must it be like to do a double shift? While Grace worked hard at whatever project she put her mind to, she had a new respect for people in the service industry.

Grace could really go for a deep massage. She moaned just thinking about it, then eyed the long distance across the dock to her cabin and pulled a frown. While she really did love the solace of being surrounded by the water, the long trek on tired feet was a bit of a pain tonight. And she was starving.

"Oh, dammit!" Grace stopped in her tracks when she realized that she'd left her takeaway meal back at the bistro. A lovely pastrami and baby Swiss on fresh marble rye with homemade potato salad and chips on the side. Her stomach grumbled in protest, but when she turned and saw the hike back up the hill to the restaurant, she shook her head, wondering if it was worth it.

Of course it was, she thought, and hiked back across the dock. She was passing the covered slips when she realized the lights were turned off at the bistro, indicating that Sophia had already locked up. "Bollocks!" Grace stomped her foot and then winced.

"What's all the cussing about, Gracie?"

Gracie? Grace turned and spotted Mason standing on the back of his boat. Since when did he call her Gracie, and why did she like it so very much? Wait . . . he appeared to be eating something . . . a slice of pizza maybe. *Score.* "I left my dinner up at the bistro," she said in a pathetic little feed-me voice.

"You're in luck. I have a whole pizza over here, a giant salad, and dessert. Oh, and a Belgian blonde IPA that's my best ever."

"So why am I in luck?" she asked lightly, but was already heading his way.

"Because I want you to join me," Mason shouted.

"Are you quite sure?" she asked politely, but picked up her pace. "I don't want to impose," she said.

"I never say anything I'm not sure of," Mason said when she reached the back of his boat. He held out his hand for her to step onto the deck. "Careful." His hand felt warm, and she was reluctant to let go. "Plus, I heard that you worked your tail off at the bistro this afternoon. You deserve the best pizza on the planet."

"Really?" Grace tilted her head. "I'm pretty much a pizza lover, I'll have you know."

"Then you're gonna love me."

"Oh, no doubt," she said. "Love the pizza," Grace added breezily, but her heart skipped like a rock across the water. She'd secretly hoped that Mason would stop in the bistro or pop over to her cabin to check up on her. The best she got was a text message asking if she needed anything. Yeah, she needed for him to press her up against the wall and kiss her senseless. She needed that sexy mouth on her neck while she slid her hands beneath his T-shirt.

"Yeah, you'll love the pizza," he said, but the low, sexy tone of his voice coupled with that Southern drawl slid over her skin like velvet. "Have a seat and try a slice."

"Now you're speaking my language," she said in a nearly steady voice.

"I have to confess that I don't always understand your language."

"It's called English."

"Right."

"Hey, you have an accent all your own, you know." And she could listen to it all day long. All night long . . . Try as she might, over the past few days she couldn't get the sexy country boy off her mind. Well, maybe it was because she hadn't really tried. Grace enjoyed thinking about Mason. She liked thinking about his whiskey-smooth voice, his intense blue eyes, and his killer smile, which didn't pop out nearly often enough.

"Do I have sauce on my face?"

"No . . . why?"

"You were looking at me funny."

Oh no . . . busted. "That's because I have low blood sugar and I'm about to faint." She fanned her face.

"Well, hellfire. Then grab a slice of pizza and sit down before that happens." He pointed to a table attached to the deck and then turned and bent over to open a small fridge. As always, Grace took the opportunity to admire his jean-clad butt. There was a little hole in the back pocket that intrigued her.

When he straightened up, Grace quickly opened the cardboard box and slid a slice of pizza onto a paper plate, hoping she hadn't been caught ogling. Grabbing a napkin, she sat down on the wide seat spanning the back of the houseboat. Grace usually wasn't one to get so caught up in a man's bum, but there was something about his that captured her attention. Did he do, like, a thousand squats a day or something?

"Presenting my Belgian blonde," Mason said, and put a swing-top bottle beside her pizza. I'll be right back with a glass."

Grace nodded, wanting so much to go into the houseboat and have a look around. She took a bite of pizza and chewed. Oh ... oh yeah, this pizza was superb. The dough was crisp on the bottom and chewy in the middle, with just the right amount of delicious edge of crust. The ingredients—a generous amount of them—tasted fresh, and the sauce was simply divine. Oh, and the tons of cheese was the kind that stretched with each bite, so you had to roll the strings around your tongue. Yeah, her kind of pizza.

A moment later, Mason arrived with two pilsner glasses and offered her one. "What do you think of the pizza?"

"Brilliant. Everything. All of it." She dabbed at the corner of her mouth, nodding before taking another healthy bite.

"The best ever?"

"If not, close enough. I'm going to have to work extra hours at the bistro to keep from needing elastic waistbands."

Mason chuckled. "And don't forget I have dessert."

"No ... just ... no." She polished off the slice of pizza and took a drink of the beer.

"How do you like the beer?"

"Excellent. Smooth ... citrus and ..." She took another sip and added, "Pear. Maybe just a hint of coconut? What makes it taste like that?"

"The Belgian yeast. It actually goes best with chicken and sharp or peppery cheese, but I wanted to try it."

"I like it a lot." She held up the glass, tipped her head sideways, and looked at the beer. "Pretty golden color too, if that means anything."

"Actually, it does," Mason said and seemed pleased at her observation. "Thanks, I'm really glad that you are enjoying it."

"Why do you seem so surprised?" Grace asked. She held up her glass. "Beer as good and complex as this is an adventure in and of itself," she said, but then hoped he didn't think her comment was silly or that she was trying to kiss up to him or anything . . . although the kissing part held some appeal.

"I agree with you." Mason sat down across from her and propped one boot up against the side of the boat.

"Is that the shape of things to come?"

"What?"

"You agreeing with me," she joked. Although he tried to grin and his stance appeared relaxed, there was a certain tension about him that hung in the air. Maybe he wanted an evening alone and she'd imposed. The thought made her fall silent, and she decided that she needed to finish another slice of pizza and then give him room to brood. The beer really was excellent. Mason knew what he was doing, so his brewery should be a success. This was his home turf, and so far everyone in Cricket Creek seemed to like and respect the Mayfield name. Grace picked a banana pepper off her pizza and popped it in her mouth. The tartness made her mouth pucker, so she took a bite of the crust to counteract the pepper. Ah . . . better. She picked off a mushroom and stole a glance at Mason, wondering if she should stay silent or come up with some meaningless chatter. Judging by the faraway look on his face, she opted for chewing a bite of crust instead of talking.

Mason sipped his beer and gazed out over the water, the pizza on his paper plate forgotten. Grace wondered if she tiptoed away if he'd even notice, but then again she wasn't good at tiptoeing, and being on a boat might complicate a stealthy escape. Should she clear her throat? Crack a joke? Break into song? She took another bite of the crust, unsure.

"Do you always eat your pizza like that?"

"Like what?" So he'd been paying attention to her after all.

"Picking off individual ingredients and then going backward."

Grace looked down at her pizza and shrugged. "I guess I don't do anything quite the normal way."

"Interesting." Mason slid Grace a look that made her feel the need to fan her face.

"So what were you brooding about, Mason?" She put her pizza on the plate and tilted her head in question.

"I wasn't brooding."

"Okay, thinking about, then."

"How much I want to kiss you."

The slice of pizza slid from her plate and landed on the table.

"Did I just surprise you?"

"Yes."

Mason gave her a look that said he wasn't sure if he was glad or sorry for voicing his desire. He scrubbed a hand down his face and then took a drink of his beer. "Sorry, but that was out of line."

"I like surprises, remember?"

Mason shook his head and gazed back out over the water. "Forget it," he said softly.

"Why? Was it the Belgian blonde talking?" Though she asked in a joking tone, Grace was actually serious. She wanted to kiss him too, but not if his desire was fueled by the ale and any woman would do.

"No." Mason shook his head slowly. "It's the British blonde who has been in my brain since the moment I met her."

Grace's heart thudded. "So kiss me, then."

"No."

"Why not?"

Mason brought his foot down to the floor with a clunk. He put his glass down on the table and finally looked over at her. "For a whole bunch of reasons. You're my sister-in-law, Grace. If we start something and it goes south, it affects the whole family."

Okay, he had a valid point, but she still wanted to kiss him. "Go on."

"You're in Cricket Creek for a visit. A visit means you'll leave, and not just a few hours away but across the damned ocean. So we know where this will end up before we even get started."

He was right, but kissing him stayed in her brain and refused to budge. "But I'm here now."

"For how long?"

"I dunno, really. I'm not entirely sure if I'm going back to London or not." She wasn't sure of anything except she wanted to kiss him.

"That's even worse."

"How so?"

"Because it could lead to false hope," he said, and something in his eyes communicated that he'd been hurt before, so it gave her pause. Grace couldn't relate, because she'd dated but never really felt as if she were in love. "And for the life of me I can't believe I'm saying this stuff to you. I must be out of my mind."

"Care to tell me about her?"

"Who?" he asked casually, but glanced away.

"The woman who hurt you."

"We were engaged." Mason shifted to look at her and lifted one shoulder. "In the end we wanted different things out of life," he answered quietly, but she sensed there was more to his simple, direct answer.

Grace thought of her parents, though, and understood. "But you must have loved her."

"I thought I did. What about you, Gracie? Have you ever been in love?"

"No," she said, and the admission gave her an odd feeling in her gut.

"I have to say that I'm surprised. You seem so full of . . . I don't know . . . big emotion? Life?" He looked as if he wanted to say more, but then fell silent again.

Grace wasn't sure how to respond. She often wondered why she'd never fallen in love. She supposed it was because of her need to travel—to roam and to start new projects as soon as the previous one was complete—that perhaps she never even gave herself a chance to experience true love. But since coming to Cricket Creek, she felt . . . different. Being in the same place with Garret, Sophia, and her mother made her feel settled. But how long would this feeling last before she felt restless?

Grace knew that she needed a project or investment here or she would go out of her gourd with boredom. And it wasn't about money. Grace never dreamed that she'd become a millionaire before the age of thirty, and now she didn't even know what to do with it all. Working on a shoestring was somehow much more thrilling. And while she enjoyed developing the edgy makeup chockfull of long-lasting, eye-popping pigment, she loved the marketing end of Girl Code most of all. For Grace, finding an overlooked slice of the marketplace crying out for a product was like panning for gold and finding a big nugget.

"Sorry. I've made you uncomfortable."

The sincerity in his voice made Grace smile. He was truly upset. "There's no need to be sorry, Mason."

"I've told you something that I should have kept to myself."

"Well, if it makes you feel any better, I feel the same way."

"That I should have kept my feelings to myself?"

"No, silly. That I've wanted to kiss you since the night of the storm. It's only been a few days, but somehow seems like ages. I suppose it's because with the birth of Lily, so much has gone on that the passage of time seems a bit off, don't you agree?"

"Yeah."

"Well then . . ." She nibbled on her bottom lip, waiting.

"And we could, you know, kiss, and no one would be the wiser. Just . . . a little kiss. To get it out of our systems. Who knows? Maybe it will be a big dud after all of the thinking about it. You wanna find out?"

"You make a good point," she said in what she hoped was a practical tone, even though her heart was thumping like a bass drum. "I mean, with a kiss behind us, we could carry on and I'll quit staring at your bum every time I get the chance. Well, I'll probably still do that. Here's wishing for a dud and a good laugh."

"Wait—you've been checking out my ass?"

"It's a really nice one, by the way."

Mason tilted his head back and laughed. "Well, thank you."

"No problem." She waited, but when he didn't mention the kiss again, she felt the need to escape and stood up. "Do you mind if I use your loo?"

"What? Oh, you mean the bathroom."

"Yes."

He pointed to the door. "To the left as soon as you go inside. And by the way, it's called a head on a boat."

"I'll remember that." Grace went inside the houseboat and looked around. A fully equipped kitchen gave way to a dining area that expanded to a living room. Deep brown leather furniture, masculine yet stylish, seemed to fit Mason's personality. A rustic wood coffee table was strewn with beer-brewing-related magazines and books. It appeared as if there was a master bedroom at the other end. A spiral staircase led to an upper deck. She wanted a real tour, but for now she needed to use the loo and gather her scattered wits.

After washing her hands, Grace gazed into the small mirror. Should she leave now or see this thing through? She narrowed her eyes at her reflection, changed her mind five times, and then opened the door.

Mason stood with his back to her, putting away the leftovers in the fridge. "We forgot to eat the salad," he said.

"I always start with calorie-laden stuff first. Who wants to fill up on salad when you have pizza?"

Mason lifted up a cheesecake swirled with turtle goodness on top. "Yeah, especially when you need to leave room for dessert."

Grace looked at the delicious work of art and groaned. "Would you like a slice?"

"Yes, but I really shouldn't." She held her hands up to ward him off.

"What's the fun in that?"

"You make a lot of good points."

"Thank you for noticing." He turned around to cut a small slice.

"I notice a lot of things."

"Are you checking out my butt again?"

"Of course. Some habits are hard to break."

Mason laughed and then turned around with a plate and fork. "I've never met anyone quite like you."

"Is that a good thing?"

"Yeah. And you've made a difficult night into something fun." When he walked toward the sofa, she followed, knowing she was setting herself up for trouble.

After sitting down next to him, she asked, "Want to talk about what's bothering you?"

"I want to eat cheesecake." He pressed his fork through the dessert, but instead of putting it in his mouth, he offered a bite to her.

Grace hesitated. There was something so intimate about being fed. She shook her head.

"Go on. You know you want to."

"Okay ..." She opened her mouth to accept his offer and let the silky texture roll over her tongue. Caramel, chocolate, and pecans finished off the bite of heaven. "Oh ... mmm ..." She could only shake her head and make noises of pure bliss.

"Yeah, Reese Marino makes some kick-ass desserts." He put a bite in his mouth and nodded. "He and his uncle own River Row Pizza and Pasta."

Mason fed her another bite and then she put her hand up. "It's too rich. I might go into a cheesecake coma."

"Wouldn't want that to happen." Nodding, Mason put the plate down on the coffee table.

For a moment they were silent, and Grace knew why.

She didn't want the night to end, but they were sitting on his sofa in a room bathed in soft light above the stove in the kitchen. The beer and pizza made her feel mellow and a bit drowsy. She wanted to lean against him and snuggle. Maybe watch some television.

Yeah, right.

She wanted the kiss.

And she wanted him to press her against the cushions and . . .

Don't go there!

"I should whistle off."

"I have no idea what you mean."

"I should go," she said softly.

"Oh." He nodded. "I'll walk you to your cabin."

"You don't have to do that," Grace answered in a not-very-convincing tone.

"I should, you know, in case the Loch Ness monster decides to make an appearance."

"Okay," she said, trying to feel relief that they'd dodged some sort of sexual-tension bullet, but longing and disappointment misted over her like the morning fog on the river. She pushed up to her feet, and they got as far as the kitchen door when Mason pulled her into his arms, lowered his head, and kissed her.

Grace melted into a lingering, luscious kiss that had her wrapping her arms around his neck and sinking her fingers into his hair. His mouth . . . warm; his lips . . . firm; and his tongue worked a seductive magic that had her clinging to him, wanting, needing more.

And Mason gave it.

He pushed her up against the wall and pressed his lips against her neck, kissing and nibbling until warm chills slid down her spine. Needing to feel his skin, she tugged his T-shirt from his jeans and ran her hands up his back. His skin felt warm and oh so smooth, and the thought went through her head that she wanted to explore every inch of him with her mouth.

Mason eased his hand up to her rib cage just below

her breasts and then kissed her again, deeply. She could feel the steely hardness of his arousal and she pressed closer, moving against him. She'd never felt such white-hot desire, and the need to have him naked, skin against skin, was overpowering.

But of course she shouldn't.

Couldn't.

Wouldn't.

Summoning up the last shreds of her resistance, Grace pulled back. She put her forehead against his chin, taking shallow breaths while clinging to his shoulders. "Well, my wish didn't come true," she said with a weak laugh. She pulled back and looked up at him.

"And what was that?" Mason asked in a velvety voice that slid all the way to her toes.

"That you sucked at kissing and I could get kissing you off my mind and be content to just ogle your bum," she joked, but had to look down so he couldn't see the desire remaining in her eyes.

Mason chuckled, and she liked the rumble of his laughter against her hand. "Thanks . . . I think." He tucked a finger beneath her chin and tilted her head up. "So what do we do about this, Gracie? Fight it or give in?"

Grace looked up into his gorgeous blue eyes, which were so sincere. He ran a gentle fingertip down her cheek and she fell a little bit in love with him right then and there. "I might sound cliché, but this really is complicated, isn't it?"

He nodded. "Maybe we should sleep on it."

"You had to put it that way, didn't you?" Grace asked with a groan.

Mason leaned in and gave Grace a brief kiss that made her want to grab his shirt and pull him in for more, but she didn't.

"All right, girl, I need to walk you home." The smile he gave her was tender, and she melted just a little bit more, but she nodded.

"Okay," Grace responded softly. She straightened up

and took a step away, needing to put some distance between them. She sensed that there was still something on his mind that was bothering him. Grace wasn't going to ask, but she couldn't help herself. "Is there something wrong? Anything I can help with? Other than kiss you, that is."

"Nope." Mason shook his head.

"No to both questions?"

"There you go bein' a busybody again." He turned and walked out onto the boat deck.

Grace followed. "And there you go avoiding the question."

Mason leaned one hip against the railing and gave her a long look.

"Well?"

"You don't give up, do you?"

"Uh . . . no." It was true. Not giving up was precisely why she had in excess of a million dollars from the sale of Girl Code Cosmetics. And then it hit her. Grace knew that look of panic when the walls start closing in on a business. Her mother had gone through it several times. Grace certainly had struggled financially with Girl Code in the beginning, nearly losing her investment several times before it finally took off. She put a hand on his arm. "Mason, we're like family now. You can talk to me."

"Don't say that. I just kissed you."

Grace inhaled an exasperated breath and blew it out. "It's the brewery, isn't it? Give it to me straight. I won't tell a soul."

A muscle worked in his jaw, and he glanced away.

Grace squeezed his arm. "Go on, then."

Mason finally nodded. "I had everything perfectly planned out, but I was sent some of the wrong machinery, which put me behind schedule." He shrugged. "I had unexpected roof issues and had to replace the entire thing. I'm hanging on by the skin of my teeth, Gracie." Leaning over, he gripped the handrail. "I knew doing this was a risk. I had sleepless nights thinking about it. But . . ."

"It was your dream."

"My fallback dream, but yes."

She squeezed his arm again, and he turned to smile at her. And that's what did it. The smile. "I can help you."

Mason frowned. "What are you gettin' at?"

"Well . . ." Gracie raised her eyebrows and nibbled on the inside of her lip for a moment. "I developed an urban, edgy line of cosmetics called Girl Code." She tilted her head sideways and continued. "Wende Zomnir, cofounder of Urban Decay, paved the way for high-voltage makeup. Before that we had lots of pinks and reds and beige, but purple, my personal favorite, was pretty much left out of the color wheel. And like craft beer, it's not just about the product but the names. They came up with crazy fun names like Roach Smog, Oil Slick, Acid Rain."

"You're kidding me."

Grace shook her head. "Hey, it worked. You have to create a great product, but marketing is where you get sales. They launched their line in 1999 with ten lipsticks and twelve nail polishes. In 2000, Moët Hennessy Louis Vuitton purchased Urban Decay."

"Wow, I might be a country boy, but I know who that is."

"Exactly."

Mason sat up straighter, clearly interested. "So tell me about Girl Code. What does that term even mean?"

"Allow me to enlighten you." Grace raised her index finger and nodded slowly. "Girl Code means you have to obey certain rules or guidelines, if you will, so as not to be kicked out of your community of girlfriends. For example, you must never date a friend's ex or someone she was into." She wagged the finger. "And never diss a friend's boyfriend, even if he is a complete wanker. Inside jokes are not to be explained to outsiders. If a friend is drunk, never allow her to drunk dial her ex. Oh, and if a girlfriend is telling a story, never say, *Me too*, and steal her thunder. I can go on and on, but do you see where I'm going with this?"

"I get the picture." Mason tossed his head back and laughed. "But what does this have to do with makeup?"

"Well, Girl Code palettes, meaning a box of color-coordinating shades of makeup, have names like Girls Night Out—in other words, bold colors to go out clubbing and dancing. "Let's Do Lunch is lighter, more subtle shades meant for the afternoon. The Hangover palette contains concealer, lotions, and remedies for under-eye puffiness. Do you get it now?"

Mason nodded slowly. "Yeah, I do, but my biggest problem right now is financial. All of that marketing took some money."

"Absolutely. Money for development and pitching until I turned blue in the face. I know where you're coming from because I scrimped and scraped, barely making ends meet. Finally, Sophia urged me to give samples of my product to high-end hair salons, and little by little, it worked. I soon had too many orders to handle, which is another problem with a small business. Huge success can also become a problem unless you prepare for it." She snapped her fingers. "And just like that I had a crazy offer to buy me out."

"Wow. It can happen that quickly?"

"Yeah, at first I didn't want to sell because there was so much more I wanted to do with the line, but the offer was so crazy big that I had to accept."

"I am really happy for you, but what does this have to do with me?"

"Mason, I have this money just chilling in the bank. I need an investment. Why not invest in your brewery?" Grace tilted her head and saw hope in his eyes, but then male pride shut it down.

"No."

"Why not?"

"Because what if it still fails? Doing business with friends or family can get dicey."

"You run a family business. You know the ropes by now."

"But you don't know anything about brewing beer."

"I've seen your facility. I've tasted the beer. Of course, I would want to sit down and see some numbers and get my accountant involved, but I'm looking for a new project. I'd love to do the marketing end to get you up and running." She snapped her fingers. "And this would keep me in Cricket Creek near my family for at least a bit longer." She raised her palms skyward. "I think it's brilliant." Reaching over, she pointed her fingertip into his chest. "And like I explained, I just happen to be a marketing genius."

Mason gave her doubtful frown. "I don't know . . ."

"Put everything together and we can meet in a day or so. Fair enough?" She stuck out her hand and gave him a challenging arch of her eyebrow.

Mason hesitated and then shook her hand. "Yeah, fair enough."

7

Upside Down

$\mathcal{B}$ECCA SAT ON THE BACK DECK OF HER CABIN LISTENING
to the Beatles while sipping a cup of tea. The late-
day sun dipped low in the sky, previewing what was sure
to be a gorgeous sunset. Ever since the birth of Lily,
Becca felt a sense of calmness, like all was finally right
with her world. The birth of her grandchild made her
rethink what she thought were wrong choices in life. Every step of the way, every fork in the road, led her to
right here and now. If she hadn't married Rick Ruleman,
she wouldn't have had Garret. And if she'd never met
Marcus Gordon, she wouldn't have had Gracie and Sophia, and now sweet baby Lily to shower with love.

Knowing that she wanted an extended stay in Cricket
Creek to bond with Lily, Becca had put the wheels in
motion for her semiretirement from her clothing company. Still the major stockholder of BGC, she would
have to return to London now and again for meetings,
but with modern technology she could do most of her
correspondence via conference calls.

Becca had been winding down for months now, and
she didn't miss the long, meeting-filled days, not even a

little bit. She'd proven herself and was finally financially secure, so it was high time to stop and smell the roses. Although she had to admit that she was having a blast working with her designers on the children's clothing line, called, of course, Lily. Funny, she thought, how one tiny human being changed her priorities.

As soon as Mattie felt up to returning to the bistro, Becca had promised to help babysit. Between her and Miranda Mayfield, little Lily would be well cared for. Mattie's brother Danny was adding on to the bistro, creating a playroom off Mattie's office where Lily would eventually nap and play with a sitter. Mattie would run the restaurant but could also spend time with her daughter. But until then, the grandmas got to help out. Or Nan, as Becca wanted to be called.

Thinking she'd like another spot of tea, Becca stood up, only to have the engine roar of a fishing boat disturb her peace. She didn't like the way the boat created a huge wake, and she felt like waving an angry hand for the bloke to slow the hell down. Standing up, she shaded her eyes and knew that the boat belonged to the man living in a cabin directly across the lake. According to Mattie, he was Jimmy Topmiller, former fishing pro who filled in as a fishing guide at Mayfield Marina now that Mason shouldered the responsibility of his brewery. Intrigued, she'd Googled her neighbor's name, and sure enough, he'd been one of the top bass-fishing anglers *ever*.

Jimmy Topmiller had a line of bait with his name on it, along with a whole slew of fishing-related products he endorsed. He had to be wealthy, Becca supposed, but while she was out walking a couple of days ago, he'd gone bumping along in a beat-up pickup truck, kicking up enough dust to all but make her choke. Perhaps he'd lost his earnings gambling or in bad investments—not that she cared. She was simply curious. And if the gazillion pictures of him holding up giant fish were any indication, Jimmy Topmiller was good-looking, if one went for that rugged, outdoorsy type . . . and of course she did not. Did she? Well, that might not be quite fair. She'd never really spent any time with someone in his profession. She reminded herself that her urban son fell in love with a small-town girl who now embraced living in London for weeks at a time. Did she—or rather, should she—really have a type? Expanding her horizons could lead to an adventure, she mused, while recalling the steamy love scene she'd just read. Maybe she needed to step up her game and make love beneath a waterfall or in an elevator, like the spunky heroine in the novel. "Game?" she whispered. "What game?"

Becca frowned at the water now wildly lapping against the shore. "Becca Gordon, maybe you need to get your groove back." The dock connecting to her back deck bobbed up and down, and the pussy willows did a little hula dance. She supposed that the man wasn't doing anything wrong, exactly, but he seemed to be disturbing the peaceful surroundings with his noise and waves. And it had to hurt when he hooked those poor fish. She'd seen him do it yesterday. He'd been fishing right up around her very dock, casting nearly onto her back deck, under and over things with amazing precision. She'd pretended to be concentrating on her juicy romance novel, but behind her big Gucci sunglasses, she'd secretly been watching him as he fished.

Becca had almost lost interest until he'd hooked a big fish innocently swimming around beneath the lily pads and yanked the poor thing up into the air while it struggled to get free. She'd given him a good stare down. He'd responded with a tip of his baseball cap and continued to carry on right next to the cabin as if he owned the bloody lake. But since she didn't know the protocol of where one was permitted to fish, she kept her fist at her side instead of raising a little hell.

Not that she was a hell-raiser. Becca kept her cool under the worst of circumstances. Just don't mess with her children, because then all bets were off. After watching Jimmy Topmiller roar back across the water, she picked up her teacup and headed inside.

The cabin was quite nice, she thought, as she entered the interior. Mattie had made sure that there were some lovely touches here and there in anticipation of her arrival. Becca ran her hand over the smooth surface of the polished coffee table, which Mattie said was built by Danny. The Mayfields were quite an interesting, talented family.

Rather than confront Jimmy again, Becca was considering reading while soaking in a nice long bubble bath when her cell phone rang. Picking up her phone, Becca smiled, seeing that the caller was Sophia.

"Hello, darling, what's up?"

"Grace and I are going to Sully's for a light dinner and a martini or two. Sully's makes the very best lemon drop around. Would you like to join us?"

"Tonight?" Becca glanced at the digital clock on the microwave. "Sophia, it's nearly seven."

"Oh, come on, are you going to turn into a pumpkin? Don't tell me you're already in a robe and fuzzy slippers."

"I'm not," Becca said defiantly. That wouldn't happen for at least an hour or so after . . . oh boy, she really did need to get out. "I'll be there at eight o'clock sharp."

"Okay, if you get there before us, grab a high-top table near the bar. That way we can watch the cute country boys shoot some pool. Maybe even join them."

"You play pool?"

"How do you think I put myself through cosmetology school?"

Becca was rendered speechless until she realized that Sophia was pulling her leg. "You little minx." While Sophia hadn't picked up much of an English accent, she could deadpan with the best of them. "I'll see you at Sully's in a little while. I could use a nice, crisp martini."

"You'll thank me later."

"I'm thanking you now and I'll thank you later."

Becca hurried into her bedroom and started pushing through her closet. When she'd had to leave London so quickly, she'd tossed random clothing into her suitcase and now she didn't know if she had anything to wear to go out for cocktails. Everything was just too casual. She finally found a little black dress that by some miracle had made it into her suitcase. "Yes!" And she had some strappy heels that would do nicely. Add a beaded bag and she had her outfit. "Perfect for a night out on the town drinking a lovely martini."

After freshening up her makeup and pulling her hair up into a French twist, she located a pearl necklace and matching earrings and thought she looked quite slinky. With a smile, she sprayed on some Chanel No. 5. A moment later she was out the door and on her way. "Early," she said with a shake of her head. The older she got, the earlier she arrived; years ago she'd thought it classy to arrive late to make her entrance. "It's good to be punctual," she said, and then realized she hadn't a clue where she was going. *Oh no . . .* "Siri?"

"How can I help you?"

"Directions."

"Where would you like to go?"

So polite, that Siri. "Sully's." Oh, wait. Restaurant? Café? Becca nibbled on her lip, trying to remember.

"I cannot find Sol-ease."

Becca rolled her eyes and was about to call Sophia when she spotted a sign up ahead on the left. "Sully's . . . Tavern, not Restaurant and Lounge? Could that be it?" Well, there were plenty of nice taverns in London, so she must be in the right place. Becca pulled her rented SUV into the parking lot and noticed that it was pretty packed. "No valet," she mumbled and parked as close to the entrance as she could. The heels she wore were not wearer friendly.

As she walked up the sidewalk, she looked down at a text message from Garret that included a picture of Lily taking a bath. "Oh, so cute!" she said, nearly bumping into a group of people in front of her. They parted and a guy in a cowboy hat opened the front door for her.

"After you, ma'am."

"Thank you." Becca stepped inside, but then pulled up short. This was . . . oh dear, a bloody honky-tonk. She looked to the left and spotted pool tables and wanted to put the heel of her hand to her forehead. Country boys . . . pool tables, just like Sophia had said. What had she been thinking?

Oh, dear God . . .

The place was pretty busy, mostly with guys playing pool and darts, and old-fashioned pinball pinged and clanged in the far corner. Country music blared from a jukebox. A group of women were doing some sort of complicated-looking line dance with lots of spins and boot slapping. Becca sucked in a breath. There wasn't a high heel in sight.

Becca didn't mind being here. She loved little hideaways and pubs, but not when dressed to the nines. Her Chanel seemed to slice through the aroma of deep-fried food and beer — not unpleasant, but she felt completely out of place.

And people immediately noticed her. She felt as if she were back on the runway, with all eyes upon her. A cold bead of sweat rolled between her shoulder blades, and she knew she had to move, but she felt frozen to the spot.

Although Becca had the urge to turn and hightail it out the door, she lifted her chin and headed over toward the bar, praying that Sophia and Grace were already here and had a lemon drop waiting for her, which she planned on tossing back in record time.

Becca's heels clicked across the slightly uneven hardwood floor, while the crowd parted for her like the Red Sea. Of course all of the tables were taken and her daughters were nowhere in sight. Go figure. With a thumping heart she pretended not to notice people staring and slipped onto the only vacant barstool, between two big men who crowded her personal space. She gave a brief smile to the man on her right. Looking a bit nervous, he smiled back and touched the bill of his baseball cap to her before turning his attention back to his pint of beer.

The stares weren't malicious, just curious, kind of like when looking at an animal at the zoo with quiet compassion, thinking the poor thing needed to be in its true environment. Sophia and Grace were going to have a field day with this one. Maybe she should take a selfie straightaway and get the laughter out of the way.

A big bear of a bartender lumbered her way. "Welcome to Sully's. What can I get you?" he asked in a booming voice, and a moment later she saw recognition register in his eyes.

Please don't mention the damned swimsuit poster, she silently prayed.

"Oh, hey, you're Garret's mother, right?"

Becca swallowed her sigh of relief and gave him a big smile. "Why, yes, I am. How did you know?"

"Pictures on Garret's Facebook page with your beautiful new grandbaby. Said I'd never do that Facebook stuff, but my wife, Maria, talked me into it."

"Ah, the wonders of social media."

"Yeah, both good and bad. I'm still learning how to use it all. I'm friends with Garret, so I saw the pictures. Garret showcases some of his artists here on open mic night, and we do outdoor concerts on the stage out back." He jammed his thumb over his shoulder.

"Oh." Becca nodded. "How lovely. I'll have to attend."

"Congratulations on the grandbaby."

"Why, thank you."

"And by the way, I'm Pete Sully."

"Becca Gordon." She reached across the bar and shook his hand. "Nice to meet you. Oh, come to think of it, Garret has spoken of you. Your wife is a songwriter." Some of the pieces were coming together. "An *amazing* songwriter who has written quite a few big hits."

"Thanks, yes, she is," Pete said with pride in his voice. "Garret works with her and Shane McCray up at Sully's South, a showcase for songwriters. After Rick brought My Way Records here, Cricket Creek is starting to become well-known in the music industry. Being so close to Nashville helps."

Becca nodded. "I never would have thought that Rick would go back to his bluegrass roots, but I'm so glad he did."

"And you must be so proud of Garret."

Becca felt her eyes mist over. "You'd better believe it." She leaned forward. "I'm supposed to meet my daughters here, but I'm a bit early"—she rolled her eyes—"and way overdressed. I must confess that when I was told that you make the best martinis on the planet, I assumed this was a more like a cocktail lounge. The mention of pool tables and country boys went right over my head. I suppose I zoned out after I heard *excellent martini.*"

Pete tossed his towel over his shoulder and laughed. "Well, you were right about one thing. I do make a killer martini. And sounds like you need one. What kind would you like?"

"Lemon drop, please."

"Coming right up."

"Thanks!" Oh boy, could she really use a cocktail right about now. Once the girls arrived, they'd have a good laugh about her attire and carry on. While Pete mixed her drink, she took a discreet look around and noticed a tall, wide-shouldered guy walk up and take a seat at the far end of the bar where it angled back toward the wall. There was something vaguely familiar about him, and when he glanced her way, she realized that it was the dust-kicking, wave-making fisherman who lived across the lake from her.

Becca wasn't quite sure whether or not to smile at him, but she got her answer when he frowned ever so slightly, as if in disapproval of her, and then averted his gaze. Well . . . of all the nerve! Silly, but she wanted him to look her way just so she could toss a frown right back at him. But he didn't and thankfully her drink arrived, demanding her undivided attention.

Pete placed her lemon drop martini down with a flourish. "Enjoy!"

Becca looked at the sugar-rimmed glass with the curl of lemon zest and sighed. "Oh, this looks lovely." She took a taste, noting that it was deliciously cold without a smidge of ice floating around. The tang of the lemon was softened by the sugar. Licking her lips, she nodded. "Oh, Pete, this is perfectly blended. You are a talented mixologist!" She took another sip. "Oh yes, this is brilliant."

"Thanks." Pete beamed at her. "I take making drinks seriously."

Becca raised her drink in salute. "It shows."

"I'm glad you approve." He handed her a menu. "Give me a holler when you want something else."

"I will." After a few sips she reached inside her clutch for her cell phone, thinking she needed to text Sophia and check on when they would be arriving. Oh, she had missed one from her. She read the message. "What?" she said, drawing a look from the man on her left. They weren't coming! Grace wrote that she was up to her eyeballs researching something, and Garret suddenly had to stay late at the studio, so he'd asked Sophia to bring dinner to Mattie. Becca sighed. Well, she couldn't fault Sophia for that. She briefly wondered what Gracie was researching, hoping whatever it was wouldn't take her away from Cricket Creek anytime soon.

Oh well, the martini was hitting the spot, and she decided to go ahead and look at the menu. She tapped her toes to the music and decided to make the best of the evening. It did feel good to be out, even though she wished her fairy godmother would appear and wave her wand, changing her cocktail dress to jeans and . . . ? Becca looked around at what the other women were wearing. Cute T-shirts and blouses and cowboy boots! Wouldn't boots be fun? She started to dream up what could be a Cricket Creek line of clothing. Maybe she could open a little shop up on Main Street, something with the Becca Gordon spin on it.

Becca decided she'd have to head into town tomorrow and do some shopping. Without meaning to—at least that what she told herself—her gaze landed back on Jimmy Topmiller. He was talking to Pete, giving Becca the opportunity to check out his profile. Okay, he was even better looking in person, she thought grudgingly. And when he propped his elbow up on the bar she noticed his tanned, muscled arm stretching the limits of his short-sleeved Western-cut shirt. His voice floated her way, deep and rich, with a slight Southern twang. The discussion was about fish, and Jimmy held his hands apart, indicating the size of one he'd caught, most likely the one from her dock. She remembered watching him fight to catch the fish. She just bet he would be pissed if he knew that she'd been rooting for the fish to get away.

Becca was about to look away and give her attention to the menu, but Jimmy suddenly tipped his head back and laughed at something Pete said. For some reason, the sound of his laughter made her smile. Odd . . .

And then, as if feeling her gaze upon him, Jimmy looked her way. Becca's instinct was to quickly bury her nose in the menu, but when he frowned slightly again, as if she somehow offended him, she lifted her chin a notch just to show him. But she'd forgotten that she was still smiling, and to her horror she realized that the look she gave him must appear . . . inviting!

Dear God.

And then Jimmy Topmiller did something that hadn't happened to Becca since secondary school.

He snubbed her.

The nerve!

Even though she'd been a model, Becca never considered herself to be a vain woman. Perhaps her confusion was because, like Gracie, she'd grown tall seemingly overnight and always felt gangly and uncertain through secondary school, towering over the other girls and most of the guys, as well. She was not one of the cool kids, and it was quite a shocker when she was suddenly thought to be beautiful.

Although she had to admit that her success later in her twenties was almost a how-do-you-like-me-now feeling. But even though she had a knack for fashion, she'd never really understood why she felt comfortable on the runway or on the covers of magazines.

Becca didn't know the reason, but Jimmy Topmiller's blatant brush-off made her furious. *Who cares?* she thought, but for some unknown reason she did. And because she did, his dismissal made her even angrier. If her martini weren't so delicious she'd like the satisfaction of tossing it in his face! For someone who prided herself on keeping her cool, her unexpected flash of fury left her feeling unsettled.

Becca whipped her menu open, nearly knocking over her martini. She bumped the man next to her just as he was taking a drink of his beer. He spilled some of it down his chin. "So sorry," she said, hoping that Jimmy didn't see her getting flustered.

Over the top of the menu, Becca flicked a discreet glance his way just as a female bartender approached him. Because his beer was nearly full, Becca realized that the cute bartender wasn't waiting on Jimmy but flirting with him. Leaning forward, she touched his hand lightly and did a hair flip. And while Jimmy didn't exactly flirt back, he certainly didn't brush her off. Becca frowned, wondering why on earth she cared, and then it hit her all at once that she missed having a man in her life.

Not someone rude like *him*, she thought, and turned her attention back to the menu, hoping that she could find something healthy. To her horror, she realized that she'd been holding the menu upside down.

Now the trick was how to turn it right side up without anyone noticing.

8

The Games People Play

EXCEPT WHEN FISHING COMPETITIVELY, JIMMY TOPMILLER considered himself a pretty laid-back kind of guy. He let very little get under his skin, but if there was one thing that got to him, it was uppity rich women. While he knew he was being completely unfair to judge someone simply because of his or her station in life, he had a huge chip on his shoulder when it came to people like Becca Gordon, and for good reason. A reason he didn't care to think about right now, and so he pushed it to the back of his brain, where he kept it locked away most of the time.

Becca Gordon had already riled him up by glaring at him every time she spotted him out on the water fishing. He didn't usually roar up and down the lake and adhered to the no-wake zone, but when she stood out on her back deck with her hands on her hips and the sunshine glinting off her blond hair, he felt the need to piss her off. And although flipping his bait in and around docks was a smart way to catch bass, he chose to cast near Becca's cabin simply because she didn't want him around. Well, too bad. She didn't own the lake. When she'd been walking along the road a few days ago, he deliberately kicked up some dust just to mar her long-legged perfection.

Jimmy knew his behavior was nothing short of juvenile, but he couldn't seem to help himself when it came to annoying his uppity new neighbor. What pissed him off more than anything was that he was undeniably attracted to her. And he didn't want to be drawn to her, because she represented everything he detested. After she'd moved in across the lake, he'd asked Danny Mayfield about her and found out that she was Becca Gordon, Mattie's mother-in-law. Danny went on to explain that Rick Ruleman was her ex-husband but that they were cool with each other. Becca was also the mother of Sophia, the cute little cook standing in for Mattie at the bistro. But something about Becca nagged at him, and after doing some research, he knew why. While not in the limelight lately, Becca was at one time a supermodel with a swimsuit poster that had rivaled Farrah Fawcett's famous red swimsuit pose. And she'd married Marcus Gordon, some sort of business tycoon, whom she'd also divorced. Or maybe he'd divorced her. She had high maintenance written all over her. Jimmy shook his head when he glanced her way. What a typical rich-princess lifestyle, trading in one rich husband for another one. His own parents had adored each other, and Jimmy was certain they'd still be happily married had his father not died tragically at the age of thirty-five. And the reason his father had perished still chapped his ass.

Jimmy found out that Becca had, among other business ventures, gone on to start her own successful clothing line. Impressive, he supposed, but hey, it's pretty damned easy to make money when you start out with piles of it. Because his father had worked for the wealthy, Jimmy had witnessed enough of that kind of over-the-top lifestyle during his childhood, and he steered clear of it. And he was going to steer clear of her . . .

But hot damn, when he'd walked into Sully's and saw Becca sitting there in that fancy black dress with those endless legs crossed, he'd all but swallowed his tongue. She had her hair pulled back in some fancy twist that reminded him of a classy movie star. He knew she had to be near his age, somewhere in her fifties, but that didn't stop every guy in the place, both young and old, from checking her out, making him want to go over there and . . . *and what*?

Protect her slammed into his brain and refused to budge, no matter how hard he tried. Not even having Angie, the cute-as-hell bartender, flirt her ass off with him could chase away the fact that Becca Gordon sat just a few feet away from him. And when she spoke in that accent of hers, he thought that he could listen to her talk all night long.

Of course, *that* particular image took his brain on a journey that had him thinking he just might need to order a shot of bourbon. But then Jimmy looked down at his Kentucky Ale, wondering how a few sips of beer could make him not think straight. Maybe a shot of bourbon wouldn't be a smart move after all. And when she'd smiled his way, it took every ounce of resistance not to go over there, shouldering everyone else out of the way, and offer to buy her a drink.

But then again, no one else in the joint seemed to have the courage to approach her. Oh, Jimmy had the courage, but he just didn't want to give her the satisfaction, and he took delight in snubbing her when she'd smiled his way. But after he'd given her the brush-off, she seemed to get both furious and flustered at the same time. Well, maybe his disinterest would take her down a notch or two, even though he was sure she had a lot more notches to go before feeling humble. And when she'd pretended to read the menu while holding it upside down, it was all he could do not to burst out laughing.

Jimmy knew the moment she realized that the menu was upside down, because her eyes widened and she gave a little glance right and left to see if anyone else had noticed. Then she'd silently put the menu down, picked up that ridiculous purse, and headed toward the ladies' room. Of course, Jimmy noticed that every guy watched her progress across the floor in her fancy-ass high heels. She passed behind him on her way to the hallway, giving him an enticing sniff of her perfume. How in the world did she walk on heels that high? He saw a couple of women give her the stink eye and for a brief moment thought they were being unfair. And then he told himself that she deserved it, coming into the bar dressed to kill and sucking up all of the male attention from the local gals out on the town.

While Becca was gone, another martini suddenly appeared at her spot. Jimmy ground his teeth together, wondering just who'd bought it for her. While Sully's Tavern was a pretty tame local watering hole, Becca was clearly out of her element. Even though Pete kept everyone in line, there were occasions when a scuffle would break out. And having someone like Becca in the place could shake things up. Jimmy wondered what she had been thinking, sashaying into a honky-tonk all by herself, dolled up like she was going to a formal event.

When Jimmy heard Becca's heels clicking down the hallway from the bathroom, he braced himself for her appearance. Deciding he wouldn't give her a glance, he reached for a handful of snack mix from the bowl in front of him. He munched for a minute, but when she failed to appear, Jimmy leaned back and looked into the hallway, wondering just what the hell had happened to her. Had someone approached her?

She stood off to the side with her back to the wall, just visible to him through the doorway. She stared down at her feet as if she'd lost the power to walk, and it took Jimmy a minute to figure out that she'd somehow managed to get one of her silly spiked heels stuck in between the floorboards. She started wiggling her trapped foot harder, but without any luck. Her close proximity to the wall must be making it difficult for her to bend forward and loosen her heel or remove the shoe.

Jimmy turned and took a gulp of his beer, telling himself it wasn't his problem and that someone would gladly come to her rescue. Who wouldn't want to put their hands around Becca Gordon's ankle? Well ... not him.

But when she failed to appear, Jimmy's legs took on a life of their own, and he suddenly found himself standing beside her. "Need some help there?"

"No ... I'm fine," she answered tightly.

Her attitude should have been enough to send him walking away, but what the hell was she going to do? "Clearly, you're not. Do you want me to loosen your heel for you or undo your shoe or something? How did you manage to get stuck like that?"

"I stepped aside for someone to pass and my heel sank into a crevice next to the wall."

"Well, let me help you."

"No, I've got this."

"I don't think—"

Becca gave her foot a huge tug. Her heel popped free and she tumbled forward, right smack into his arms.

"Whoa, there." After she pitched forward and sideways, Jimmy's hands found her waist, trying to hold her steady. She grabbed for his shoulders and her cheek landed against Jimmy's cheek, almost as if they were slow dancing. Her skin was silky soft and she smelled like ... damn, like heaven.

"Would you kindly let go of me?"

"So much for being an angel."

"What?"

"Um, sugar, you're clinging to my shoulders, by the way."

She pushed at him, making her back smack up against the wall. She glared at him as if the whole thing was somehow his fault.

Typical.

Jimmy let go of her waist and held his hands up in surrender. "Seriously, I was only trying to help."

Her expression softened. "I know. I'm sorry. I'm just so embarrassed."

Jimmy was caught off guard by her easy admission. "About getting your shoe caught? Sugar, just wait a while. This is a bar. Pretty soon some way more embarrassing things are going to happen."

"Worse than coming into a honky-tonk bar wearing a cocktail dress?"

He wanted to touch her cheek but didn't. "Yeah, trust me."

Becca gave him a little smile that trembled ever so slightly. She tried to hide it with a chuckle. "Well, I'd walk back over there with what's left of my dignity, but in my stubbornness I broke the heel."

"Let me help," Jimmy said, wondering if anyone in the bar was curious as to what was going on in the hallway. When she gave him a look that said that she wasn't sure that she wanted his assistance, he leaned in next to her ear and said, "Becca, please allow me to help you out."

"You know my name, do you?" she asked in that sexy British voice of hers.

"I think everyone in here knows your name," Jimmy replied in a tone that made her tilt her head to the side.

"I highly doubt that."

"Um, you happen to be famous."

"In this small town? Because of a silly poster from a million years ago? I do believe that you are more famous than I am, *Jimmy Topmiller*, world-class bass pro angler."

Jimmy felt a jolt of surprise and was rather pleased. "Do you even know what that means?" Jimmy asked and could tell by her blank look that she wasn't quite sure. He could also tell that she wanted to take a step back and put some distance between them, but her back was up against the wall. And damn if he didn't want to place his hands on either side of her and lean in for a smokin'-hot kiss. And it pissed him off that he wanted her with an intensity that he hadn't felt in a long time. "Well?"

She lifted one shoulder. "Catching, you know . . . fish."

"Right, that's what I do."

"Isn't it, though?"

Technically, she was right, but it irritated Jimmy that people thought that competitive tournaments were all about luck. In reality, bass fishing took tons of research and endless hours of practice. You had to be an expert boater, racing like a NASCAR driver over the water to spots nearly impossible to navigate. "Right," he answered with a sigh, and looked away. He needed to get back to his barstool.

"Just why do you have a stick up your arse where I'm concerned? What did I ever do to you?" she asked in a low tone. "You don't even know me."

Her candor surprised Jimmy. "I know your type, sugar." He knew he was being rude, but her comment about his fishing got under his skin.

"Excuse me?" She was trying hard to give him a dressing-down, but the accent took away some of the heat. Everything she said sounded so proper. Then she leaned over and slipped her shoes off, giving Jimmy a sweet glance of her cleavage. He should have looked away, but he didn't. And since when did fancy pearls seem so very sexy? When she stood in her bare feet, she was only a few inches shorter than his six foot four. Ah . . . those long-ass legs. "Would you kindly step aside?"

"Gladly," he said, but he wasn't glad at all. When she started to walk away, he wanted to haul her back and . . . *Stop it!*

"Thank you." With her head held high, she padded on bare feet back over to the bar, slipped onto her stool, and proceeded to take a sip of her fresh martini.

Jimmy went back to his seat and plopped down, ignoring curious stares from those who knew him well. Pete gave him a what-the-hell-just-happened look, but Jimmy merely shrugged and then rolled his eyes. He ordered some hot wings, even though he knew he'd pay with heartburn later. He didn't care. That was the kind of mood he was in . . . all because of Fancy Pants over there.

Becca, who was quiet earlier, suddenly became animated and had a captive audience. Maybe it was the alcohol kicking in, or it could be that she was one of those women who could adapt to any situation. Perhaps it was the accent that had everyone hanging on her every word. For whatever reason, she seemed be settling in at Sully's. At one point she even got up and danced with the group of women who had given her nasty looks earlier. She had them laughing. Jimmy wondered if it had anything to do with the martinis, but a look her way indicated that she was nursing her second one. She ate a giant salad with grilled chicken and let Pete know that she appreciated that he had some healthy options on the menu. Everyone was soon charmed.

Ha, but not him.

Becca didn't even glance Jimmy's way again. He told himself that he didn't care, but when some young guy, most likely fueled by alcohol and dares, approached her for a dance, Jimmy wanted to step in and tell the kid to get lost. It was stupid. Why the hell did he even care?

The fact that Jimmy couldn't get Becca off his mind made him want to do something to piss her off, and so when she went to the bathroom again, he motioned for Pete.

"I want to cash out and I want to pay Becca's tab."

"Okay." Pete slapped his towel over his shoulder. "You want her to know?"

"Yeah, let it slip." Jimmy somehow knew it would get her goat.

"You got it." Pete gave Jimmy a grin. "You sweet on her or somethin'?"

"Hell no. She lives across the lake from me and gets under my skin."

"Right. So you showing her who's boss by paying her tab? That really makes a lot of sense, Jimmy."

Jimmy shrugged, not sure what he was doing. He handed Pete his debit card. "Just do it before she gets back."

"Okay." Pete nodded. "You got it."

After leaving Sully's, Jimmy headed over to his truck, wishing he could see Becca's face when she found out that he'd paid her bill. He somehow knew she'd be ticked off instead of pleased. Women like her wanted to be in control, and he'd just taken that away from her. *So take that, Becca Gordon.*

Just as Jimmy was getting into his truck, he heard his name called out in a British accent. Grinning, he stopped, prepared to get chewed out by Becca Gordon.

"Jimmy, wait!" He turned around and watched Becca limping his way with her one broken heel.

"Yeah?" he asked when she finally made it to his truck.

"I wanted to thank you for paying my tab. How nice of you," she cooed, and gave him a big smile.

Jimmy blinked at her. "You're . . . welcome."

"Pete didn't want to tell me, but I got it out of him."

Jimmy nodded, wondering if she was onto him or not.

"Well, I'm off. I just wanted to catch you and express my surprise and gratitude. Here, for some reason, I thought that you didn't really like me. Silly me, right?"

"R-right."

"I'd like to return the favor by inviting you to dinner."

"I . . . uh . . ."

"A week from Thursday good for you?"

Caught off guard, Jimmy could only nod.

"All right, then." She gave him a bright smile, turned on her good heel, and limped away.

Jimmy watched her progress, trying to figure out what had just happened. By the set of her shoulders, he knew that she'd just gotten the upper hand. Ha, so what was she going to do? Serve him something horrible like a salad or something? Well, he'd get her back and bring some insanely decadent dessert and guilt her into eating it. Yeah, he'd show Miss Swimsuit Model. "Two can play this game," he mumbled, even though he wasn't quite sure what game he was playing. But he was damned sure gonna win.

After he arrived at his cabin, he went out onto the back deck, telling himself that he wanted some fresh air and to do a little stargazing. Heading out there had nothing to do with looking across the lake to Becca's cabin to see if her lights were on and to be sure that she'd made it home safely. No . . . he just wanted to enjoy the warm summer evening.

Jimmy grabbed a bottle of water, sat down on a lounge chair, and gazed up into the inky black sky. Stars glittered like diamonds on velvet. Next to being in a boat on the water, stargazing was his favorite way to relax.

After a few minutes, music drifted his way, something soft and sultry, and he realized he wasn't the only one enjoying the beauty of the night sky. For a moment Jimmy allowed himself to wonder what it would be like to be sitting with Becca on her deck, listening to music and getting to know each other. But then he shut that notion down. She wasn't even close to being his type of woman. And before long, she'd hightail it back to London and do whatever kind of fancy-pants fashion-designing thing she did for a living. Going to her cabin for dinner would be completely insane.

Jimmy shoved his fingers through his hair, thinking he'd have to find a way to get out of it. He had more than a week to come up with an excuse of some sort. But then he thought that she was most likely banking on him being a no-show. Well, maybe he'd just have to call her fancy-ass bluff. And except for tossing a salad, she most likely didn't know a thing about cooking anyway. Yeah, watching her fumble around in the kitchen was bound to be damned humorous and way too good to miss.

9

If You Could Read My Mind

MASON SHOOK HIS HEAD WHEN HIS PHONE PINGED again. He read another text from Gracie and blew out a sigh. "You've got to be kidding me."

"What now?" Danny looked up from where he was putting the finishing touches on the bar in the taproom.

Mason swung his leg over a barstool and sat down. "You're not gonna believe what Gracie just suggested."

Danny chuckled. "So she's Gracie now?"

Mason shot his brother a look. "It's . . . just . . ."

"What?"

"She seems like a Gracie to me, okay? Don't start jumping to conclusions. She's just been driving me nuts this past week." In more ways than one, but Mason wasn't about to let his brother know that he thought about Gracie day and night . . . especially night.

"Did you really expect her to be a silent partner?"

Mason scrubbed a hand down his face. "No, I knew that she wanted to help on the marketing end of launching the brewery. Marketing is her thing."

"Nothing wrong with that, right? We both know that marketing isn't your thing."

"Yeah, but I don't agree with all of her suggestions. Dammit, Danny, what have I gotten myself into?"

Danny waved his arm in an arc. "Saving your business, for one thing."

"Yeah, but now Gracie has her nose in my business." Mason jammed a thumb into his chest so hard that it hurt.

"Are you forgetting that it really is her business now too?"

"No." And Mason wasn't forgetting how thoughts of their hot kiss kept him up at night . . . and awake too. "And believe me, I'm grateful. And you know that she came along just in the nick of time. Without her investment I might have had to shut things down." He let out a groan and looked up at the ceiling.

"So what's got you so riled up?"

"She wants to call the operation Broomstick Brewery and have a witch riding on a broomstick as the logo! And . . . *get this*, have the ales called goofy witchcraft-related names. Like Love Potion, Spellbound, Black Magic, and Witches' Brew. She insists that we need to tap into the female market and that this marketing plan will work." Mason rolled his eyes and continued in a mock British accent, "We can have several soft openings on weekends leading up to a huge Halloween grand-opening party."

"What did you reply?"

"The same thing I've been saying to all of her crazy-ass out-there marketing plans for the past week. No damned way!" Mason sputtered. He wanted for Danny to jump on the outraged bandwagon, but his brother gave him a long, measuring look. "Oh, come on . . . what? You can't possibly be buying into any of this bullshit."

Danny shrugged. "I mean, she made over a million bucks convincing women to wear weird metallic shades of eye shadow and lipstick. I did some research on Girl Code. You might want to take her suggestions seriously."

"This is about my craft beer that I've spent years perfecting. I take *that* seriously."

"It's also about making money, Mason."

"Yeah, I get that, but not at the expense of my integrity."

"Mason, crazy names for craft ales is all part of the fun, and you know that. You gotta admit that we've laughed at a bunch of them. Remember the beer fest in Cincinnati we went to last year?"

"Uh . . ." Mason had to grin. "Some of it."

"We laughed our asses off at some of the names of breweries and beers. Remember, Hoppy Ending from Palo Alto Brewing Company? The Great Big Kentucky Sausage Fest? Citra Ass Down? Java the Nut? Mason, we even made a list of our favorites."

"And your point?"

"It's a crowded market and you have to stand out with fun names and a kick-ass label. I hate to say it, but I think she has a valid point. And deep down you know it."

"Okay . . . okay, I get that, but you've got to be shitting me. Broomstick Brewery?" Mason shook his head. "Over my dead body."

"Over your dead, broke body."

Mason groaned and then sucked in a breath. "No, I can't do it."

"Look at the bright side. Not only did Grace put up some serious cash, but she's a marketing genius. You should be thanking your lucky stars instead of fighting this angle."

"I know, but why can't the name be something to do with the marina or fishing? Why not just something simple like Mayfield Brewing Company? I mean, I built the brewery out of the boathouse."

"Mayfield sounds more like milk than beer."

"Boathouse Brewery, then. Not witches! What guy is going to order a beer called Love Potion?"

"I think that's Grace's main point. She's going after women. Chicks will eat this up with a spoon."

"I'll be a laughingstock, Danny!" Mason raised his hands in the air. "Come on, back me up on this."

"Look, I'm just saying that you need to have more of an open mind. And you gotta remember that Cricket Creek draws lots of tourists. You want the brewery to appeal to them too."

"Since when did brewing a great craft beer have to appeal to everyone?" Mason grumbled. "This started as a simple concept, and I don't want to turn it into a three-ring circus. Broomstick Brewery . . . what the hell?"

Danny closed his toolbox and turned to face Mason. "I have to say that I think her idea is pretty damned creative. I mean, guys don't care what the beer is called—only that it tastes good. Women need more stimulation than that, kinda like in bed. Not everything is as straightforward as you want it to be, bro."

"Since when did you become an expert in every damn thing?"

"Come on, Mason. Look what Mattie did with the bistro. Before it was Breakfast, Bait and Books. Not a very appealing name if you're not a dude. Now that Mattie made it all pretty and everything, switched up the menu, and added the patio, the place is packed with regulars and tourists too. And the regulars still come. With the bistro being so close, you and Mattie can feed off each other, but not if this taproom is all about guy shit." Danny shrugged. "It depends upon what you want, I guess."

"Apparently not."

"Don't be so stubborn." Danny walked around the bar and slapped Mason on the back. "Look, I gotta bounce. I promised Dad we'd do some night fishing for crappie. If we catch a mess, I'll bring you some. We'll grill out and drink until we solve all the problems of the world. You'll come up with a solution."

"Sounds good," Mason said. But after Danny left, he leaned over and gripped the edge of the bar. After a moment he blew out a sigh. What Mason didn't tell Danny was that although he maintained controlling interest, Gracie had insisted upon being head of marketing, something he'd signed off on in their contract. He'd been that desperate. Although Gracie wasn't exactly his boss, he'd pretty much given her free rein over marketing, so he didn't have much of a choice. What he could do was give her the cold shoulder until she hated being around him. Then maybe she'd throw in the towel and let him run the business the way he saw fit and not with some gimmicky bullshit that made him want to bang his head against the wall. Yeah, that was a good plan. The silent treatment would drive animated Gracie Gordon insane.

"Hello, there."

Mason swung around and faced the woman who was turning his world upside down in more ways than one. Why did the mere sight of her make his heart race? Oh yeah, because he was super pissed at her. That was the reason. "Gracie," he said tightly.

"Don't sound so excited to see me. It might go straight to my head like that chocolate porter of yours."

Mason's scowl didn't seem to faze her. She wore white shorts and a blue tank top that *did* faze him. Her skin had a golden glow, making him think she must have been sunbathing while conjuring up all of her crazy ideas. He tried not to imagine her in a bikini, but his brain failed to cooperate. Nothing on his body cooperated where Gracie was concerned.

"The bar is amazing. Danny is a talented carpenter." She ran her hand slowly over the wood and smiled before looking his way. "Lovely."

Mason couldn't argue with her observation, so he nodded.

"How's the Russian imperial stout coming along?"

"Aging in the secondary."

"Excellent." Gracie nodded, but he had to wonder if she knew what he was talking about. "I think we should name that one Black Magic. What do you think?"

Mason deepened his scowl as his answer, but she ignored it.

"All right, then, take a look at this." Grace pulled her iPad out of a case and placed it on the bar. "I had the artist who designed my cosmetic-line labels come up with some creative beer labels. They're really cool."

"About that . . ."

"We need to get this marketing plan up and running to create interest. I'll manage the Web site and Facebook page. We should get some hype going, don't you think?" She angled her head at him and waited.

"No."

"Mason, we need to do a few soft openings until you can build up inventory. But we still need to get some Facebook and Twitter followers. Are you open to doing a blog? Seems to be a popular way to get the word out in this industry. Some of them are really clever and informative."

"I'm too busy brewing beer."

"Do you think you could speed that process up just a teensy bit?" She put her thumb and index finger an inch apart.

"I'm running at full capacity," Mason answered in a short tone. "You can't speed up brewing beer without ruining the outcome. It doesn't work that way."

Grace nodded slowly. "That's all right. I had a similar issue with Girl Code. When demand outweighs the supply it just creates the need to have it even more, you know? Human nature, I suppose."

His silence didn't stop her from rambling on.

"I'm also looking into having a gift shop off to the side of the taproom. And of course the witches theme is going to just rock there."

Mason gave her a look that said how much he thought it didn't rock, unless you considered rocking his boat.

Nonplussed, she rattled on while he pretended not to be interested. "People wearing T-shirts are free advertising. Oh and baseball caps seem to be huge around here. We might consider giving a shirt or hat away with the first purchase of beer. Or maybe other giveaways when you like our Facebook page. People love free stuff. I'm going to have brochures for Mattie to hand out at Walking on Sunshine Bistro."

Mason couldn't take it any longer. He raised both hands, palms up. "Stop."

"What's the matter?"

"I'm not cool with the whole Broomstick Brewery thing, Gracie. Not at all. In fact, I pretty much hate it."

Grace lifted one bare, tanned shoulder and gave him a brief smile. "I knew you wouldn't be thrilled, Mason. But I've done tons of research, and reaching out to women is going to grow your popularity way quicker than relying on appealing just to men."

"I don't know that I really buy into that."

"Well, like I said, I happen to have done the research to back up my claim," she said with a little bit of a sharp edge to her tone. Good, he was getting under her skin. "Did you know that in a recent Gallup poll, women in their twenties and thirties now prefer beer to wine?"

No, he didn't know that, and he had to admit that it surprised the hell out of him. "You mean like Bud Light. Generic domestic beer. That's not who I'm after."

"I get that, and no. Would you kindly allow me to continue?"

He crossed his arms over his chest.

"Did you know that there's an international club called Barley's Angels for women who love craft beer? Clever, right? And did you know that they conduct classes on how to pair beer with food? We could create a local chapter and do some of the same kind of thing here. Mattie said she would enjoy doing some of the classes at the bistro."

Mason opened his mouth to interrupt, but Gracie was on a roll.

"Did you know that there's an organization called WEB, which stands for Women Enjoying Beer? The CEO, Ginger Johnson, founded the company for the sole purpose of marketing beer toward women. After all, we do make up over half of the population." She arched an eyebrow. "And American women make nearly eighty-five percent of the purchasing decisions, especially when it comes to food and drinks."

"You've got it all figured out." The edge to his voice didn't even begin to slow her down.

"When I get involved with a marketing project, I jump in with both feet. I just get chock-full of energy, and I can't slow down." She put a hand on his forearm. "Look, I know this isn't what you envisioned for the brewery, but you were only thinking about brewing an amazing craft beer. That won't change. The only thing we're doing is reaching out to an eager demographic that's been pretty much ignored by the craft beer industry. It works, Mason. My mother saw the need for affordable high fashion and carried sizes geared to the average woman, and it went over like gangbusters. Just look at what Mattie did with the bistro. She has the same regulars but now has a much bigger clientele. You told me so yourself. You can still have darts and pool tables and that corn hole whatever-it-was game, but you need to add something more for the girls."

"Okay, so you've done your so-called research." Mason pulled away from her. "I know you have an investment, but in the end this is just a project for you, Gracie. Once you're bored, you'll move on, and then I'll be stuck with a brewery named after witches."

"You don't know that I will move on."

"I do know that, because you flat out told me." And it bothered him for more reasons than he cared to admit. "This is just playtime for you, but it's the rest of my life."

Hurt registered on her face, making him want to take the words back. But there was even more at stake than the brand of his brewery. Try as he might, and even though he was pissed at her for swooping in and taking over marketing with such bold moves . . . he still wanted her. No, not just wanted her. He was drawn to her in a way that scared him. Even though Mason had been going through a tough time with trying to save the marina, he'd still been blindsided by Lauren's cold breakup with him. He knew he'd been partially to blame with his moods, but in his mind, if you loved someone, you helped them through a difficult time rather than bailing like she did.

"This isn't a game to me."

Mason knew that this was where he should apologize, but he remained silent. Getting involved with someone likely to leave once she was bored would be plain stupid. Kissing her had been insane, because ever since he'd held her in his arms, it was all he could think about as soon as she walked into the room. He was thinking about it now and it pissed him off even more.

Gracie gave him a lift of her chin. "I'm not one bit intimated by your crossed arms or your icy glare. Your whole broody thing rolls right off my back. I've worked with diva fashion models and bullheaded businessmen who wrote me off as a dumb blonde. My mother dealt with the same thing. Your little pout means nothing. Zero." She curved her finger to touch her thumb. "Nada."

"I don't pout," Mason insisted, and then realized that was exactly what it sounded like he was doing. "Look, when we first discussed your investment, I hoped you were going to be more of a silent partner. I thought that this was going to be an investment, something you needed as a tax write-off or something, and you would go on about your merry way. I shouldn't have agreed to having you take over marketing. At least not in such a big way. I just didn't think you would get this involved or do this much research."

Grace raised her arms above her head. "Why would you think . . . ," she began, and then her eyes widened. "Oh . . . right, the dumb blonde thing raised its ugly head. I guess you thought that I made my money riding on my mother's coattails. Played around with makeup like I was playing around with Barbie dolls. Or maybe Daddy funded the whole thing for me." She shook her head really hard. "Well, for your information, I created Girl Code with my own hard-earned money. My mother made it clear to all of us that we needed to work our tails off and create our own success, just like she did. My father, who loved money more than his family, had a pre-nup that left her with virtually nothing after she finally left. Of course, it's hard to leave someone who was never there to begin with."

"Gracie . . ." Damn, he felt like such an ass. He knew it was his plan to piss her off so she would back off, but still, this was too much. He hated seeing Gracie this upset.

"In fact, Garret had to *overcome* living in the shadow of Rick Ruleman and finally prove how talented he truly is after all these years. Having famous parents isn't always what it's cracked up to be."

"Gracie, I—"

"You have a lot of bloody nerve."

"You put words into my mouth."

"I could see how you feel about me in your eyes." When Gracie tilted her head, her hair slipped over her shoulder. Mason remembered how silky it felt when it brushed against his face. She was wrong about one thing. She didn't have a clue as to how he felt about her.

"Really?" Mason asked softly. "So you think you can read my mind?"

"Yes," she answered just as softly.

Mason took a step closer. "So what am I thinking?"

"That you want to kiss me again."

Mason looked at her mouth and felt desire so damned strong that he could barely keep from pulling her into his arms. She surprised him at every turn. He wanted to deny it, but even if he did, she'd see right through the lie. "And if you're right?"

"Then you should do it."

Mason swallowed hard and stood as still as a statue. Any movement would be to touch her, to kiss her . . . and so he shook his head. "No."

"Why not?"

"Because of all of the reasons I already mentioned. You've said that you feel the need to wander, explore. You get bored. Gracie, Cricket Creek, Kentucky, is my home and always will be. Getting involved with you would be . . . stupid."

"Well, I hate to tell you, but you're already involved or we wouldn't be having this conversation."

Gracie was right, but he wasn't going to let her know it. "No, I'm preventing a lot of heartache for us both. You should thank me."

"All right, then, you've made yourself crystal clear. This will remain strictly business." Grace reached over and picked up her iPad. She stuffed it back into her case and hefted her purse over her shoulder. "I want to make a few things of my own clear, though. I invested in this brewery for a few reasons. Solid reasons. I was looking for a challenge, something different. I also needed an investment."

"I know," he said in a gentle tone.

Gracie gave him a quiet, rather sad smile that hit him in the gut. "But there is a lot of that kind of thing out there. This wasn't a whim. I really did dive into the research. I wasn't going to just toss my money away. But it's not the main reason I chose to invest in your brewery."

When she fell silent, he looked at her. "Are you going to enlighten me?"

She licked her bottom lip. Her chest rose and fell as if she was holding back emotion. "I wanted to help and . . ."

"And what? Are you going to finish?"

"No. I'm going to leave," Gracie said, but paused long enough to give him the opportunity to stop her.

He wanted to. God, he wanted to.

But he didn't.

10

Born to Run

BLINDED BY TEARS, GRACE WISHED THAT HER EYEBALLS had windshield wipers so she could see straight. Filled with a whirlwind of emotion, she wobbled as she walked across the endless floating dock, clinging to her purse and iPad for fear of having them fall into the river. Of course, if she fell in, all would be lost. She wasn't exactly sure why she'd become so undone. That Mason hated her marketing plan was a given, but she was quite certain she was on the right track, and so he could just bugger off on that one. Grace had learned from her mother that success was more than a great product. Her mother's early designs were magnificent, but the market was small. Filling a need was the way to approach the market. Mason would soon find that out. Grace was used to naysayers, and it only made her want to prove them wrong even more. Part of her tenacity stemmed from her desire to be taken seriously and squash the notion that she was a rich girl playing around in the business world. She'd known she had something special and marketable with Girl Code, and in truth, her struggle with getting her company off the ground taught her more than if the road to success had been a smooth one.

When a stiff breeze made the dock move up and down, Grace planted her feet firmly and got her bearings before proceeding. No, she knew that her explosion of emotion came from Mason hitting too close to the mark. Avoiding their attraction would end up saving heartache for them both. There was only one problem. She couldn't remember ever feeling this strong pull of attraction to anyone—especially this quickly—and to not explore where it could lead just seemed like such a loss.

But Mason was right.

Grace somehow made it to her cabin, tossed her things onto the sofa, and then flopped down in a heap of noisy sniffing, crying, and cursing. She put phrases together that didn't even make sense, punctuating each sentence with a stomp of her foot. A pillow, innocent of any wrongdoing, went flying across the room, nearly knocking over a lamp. She looked for something else to throw and then remembered that this wasn't her place . . . and since when did she throw things anyway?

But she suddenly wanted to do something crazy to blow off steam. She inhaled a couple of deep breaths, trying to think of something maybe like . . . like . . . doing a cannonball into the river! Wait—were there snakes in the river? Would a turtle bite her in the bum? Would catfish nibble at her toes?

Was there really a Loch Ness monster?

"Okay, scratch the cannonball idea," she mumbled. Maybe she should head to Sully's and finally get the lemon drop martini that she'd missed out on with her mother. Ask for one the size of her head. Perhaps she should call Sophia and pour her aching heart out to her sister, who was a good listener.

Or then again, maybe she should just sit right there and feel sorry for herself, which was utterly ridiculous because she had so much going for her, especially at the moment.

Didn't she?

Grace squared her shoulders. After all, at the age of twenty-eight she'd sold Girl Code for more than a million dollars and she'd been serious when she told Mason that she'd developed and financed the company on her own. Convincing the bank to lend her start-up money hadn't been easy, but she'd had her ducks in a row and learned to pitch from her mother. She had a loving and supportive family, and now they had Lily. And for the first time in forever, she was in the same place with them all ... not counting her father, who was never around anyway. She did love him and missed him, but in a rather abstract way.

So why in the world did she feel so lost?

At lonely, uncertain times like this, Grace wished she had a loyal dog like Rusty, the Irish setter, who belonged to Mason but spent most of his time hanging around the bistro with a little doggie girlfriend named Abigail. They were so cute together, like something out of a Disney movie. Right now Rusty would have his head resting on Grace's leg, looking up at her with sympathy in his soulful eyes while she patted his head. Abigail would jump onto her lap and lick her hand. Yeah, maybe she needed a dog. "Or a cat or a gerbil ... any bloody thing!" she wailed. "Okay, enough!"

Crying was pretty foreign to Grace because she was such an upbeat person, but the warm tracks of tears streaming down her cheeks felt oddly freeing. Licking her lips, she tasted salt, and she wondered if she would carry on crying or if at some point the tears would simply stop once the well was dry.

Oh, the mysteries of life ...

Grace inhaled a shaky breath. While she understood Mason's reluctance to embrace the Broomstick Brewery idea, she had crunched numbers with her accountant in addition to doing marketing analysis. There might not be another craft brewery in Cricket Creek, but there were lots of them in nearby Lexington and Louisville, with the number growing steadily. Craft breweries and related businesses in recent years generated more than $160 million in tax and revenue just in the state of Kentucky. While the popularity continued to grow beyond expectations, Grace also knew that the market was saturated. At some point something had to give, and only the strongest would survive. Plus, the big dogs like Budweiser weren't happy about craft breweries taking a big chunk out of their profits and were doing everything possible to make distribution difficult, including buying up ingredients necessary for brewing.

Mason wasn't going to be able to make much of a profit with just local distribution. Cricket Creek wasn't big enough, even with the baseball stadium. Having a venue that big certainly helped, but it was seasonal. No, Mason was going to have to expand to a regional level. While he was creative and smart, marketing wasn't his strong suit, and that's where he needed someone like her. Why couldn't he see that? She wasn't the damned enemy.

Grace realized that male pride was getting in Mason's way. He didn't like her swooping in and taking over—and she got that loud and clear—but he would soon see that she was a godsend. The quality of his beer would speak for itself. Broomstick Brewery was simply a marketing tool. At least she hoped so.

Grace also knew Mason was fighting his attraction to her because she'd admitted she would leave at some point. But Grace believed in honesty, and sadly, she knew that day would come and more likely sooner than later. Mason was doing the sensible thing by not kissing her again, getting them both involved in something doomed from the start. Another fat teardrop slid down her cheek and landed with a splash on her hand. If it hurt this much not being with Mason this early in the game, she couldn't begin to imagine what it would feel like to fall completely in love with him and then have to leave him.

Unless she stayed.

That seductive thought slid into her brain and hovered there, circling and floating, making her want to reach up and grab it. God, how she wanted to hang on to the possibility of staying and cling to it.

"No, no . . . no." With a sigh, Grace looked up at the ceiling and then shook her head. "That would never happen," she said in a broken whisper. She'd gotten the roaming gene from her father, who wasn't a bad man, just not a family man. Was she just like him? The thought made her shudder.

Grace thought about how amazing it felt to hold Lily in her arms, and for the first time she suddenly felt a hollow pang. She wondered if this was her biological clock ticking in response to the baby smell and the feel of holding sweet Lily?

Grace closed her eyes and swallowed. Could she ever put down roots? What did Mason call it? Bloom where you are planted? Or would she have to uproot and carry on?

Marco Cosmetics was already after her to come up with a Girl Code line of urban nail polish, and although Grace had turned them down, if they sweetened the pot she knew she might cave in and do it. She'd already been thinking about wild shades and jotting down kick-ass names for the polish. Once an idea wiggled its way into her brain, she was helpless not to see it through, or it drove her to distraction. Grace craved constant change and challenge . . . It was part of what made her tick and would wage war with her biological clock. People who roamed weren't meant to get married or to have children.

Or fall in love?

No, she didn't think that anything or anyone could ever keep her in one spot without having her going completely stir-crazy. She treasured her freedom. Didn't she? Okay, if she was honest with herself, perhaps not completely. Grace sighed, thinking that the charm of this small town must be getting to her. Sophia had as much as said the same thing. And there could be compromise.

Mattie and Garret were a shining example of how to blend two very different lifestyles together.

"Okay, then, this is getting you a big fat nowhere." Feeling sorry for herself wasn't in Grace's nature either, so she pushed up to her feet and headed to the bathroom to wash away the tracks of her tears. "Just look at you," she said after viewing the black mascara running down her face. "You're one hot mess, Grace Gordon." After scrubbing her face and patting her cheeks dry, she picked up her tablet and decided she'd listen to some music and maybe do a bit more research. No matter how much Mason didn't like it, she was determined to make the brewery a success in the best way she knew how. It wasn't just about protecting her investment, but also about helping Mason see his dream come to fruition. But she didn't want to let him know that her investment had anything to do with wanting to help him personally. Part of the emotional tug was that he was a Mayfield. Grace had gotten to know warmhearted, loving Mattie in London. Mattie's stories of the antics of her brothers had entertained Grace but also gave her a glimpse into the close-knit Mayfield family.

But it was Mason who drew her in like some magnetic force that she couldn't control.

When he walked into the room, Mason commanded her full attention, something that was difficult to do. A brush of his fingertips, a lingering look, the sound of his voice, stroked her senses in a way that she'd never experienced. And they had kissed only . . . once. What would it feel like to be naked in his arms with his mouth exploring her body, inch by inch?

"Oh dear Lord." Grace grabbed a bottle of water and headed outside onto her back deck. A stiff breeze and gray clouds rolling across the horizon indicated a storm warning, but she didn't care if it poured down rain. The wind caressed her face and lifted her hair, bringing the earthy scent of the river and woods her way. She inhaled deeply, thinking she would miss having nature wrapped all around her once she headed back to the city.

Grace turned Pandora on to the Billy Joel channel, her go-to guy when she was in a mood. Like the storm brewing, her mood was an odd mixture of anger, disappointment, and something she couldn't quite put her finger on. Oh yeah . . . desire. After a long sigh, she gave her bottle of water a look and decided she needed a glass of wine. Crossing her fingers that she had a bottle of her favorite red, she went back inside and located a nice Cupcake merlot. After pouring a glass, she looked at the bottle and decided it might be the kind of night to consume the entire thing, and so she picked it up and took it with her.

The first glass of wine made her feel mellow. She sat back in the lounge chair and looked out over the water, letting her mind wander here and there. After consuming her second glass, she started singing along with Billy to "Only the Good Die Young." She sipped and sang, carefully avoiding a look in the direction of Mason's houseboat. Who cared if he was home or not? Who cared if he hated her marketing plan? Who cared if she was falling in love with him?

"What?" Grace sputtered.

She sat up straight, nearly sloshing red wine over the rim of the glass. "Now, just hold on." She inhaled a deep breath and carefully placed her glass on the small table beside her lounge chair. Okay . . . the important word here was *falling*. She was *falling* for him. Not in love . . . yet. She would just have to stop the *in love* part from happening. She could do that, right? "No." She shook her head, knowing that falling in love didn't work like that . . . or at least she didn't think so. All she knew was that she'd never felt like this before, and she needed to put on the brakes.

The trick was going to be doing her job in an efficient, impersonal manner and leaving how she felt about him out of it. "This requires a list." Grace picked up a pen and stared at the blank sheet of paper. "Okay . . . okay, I've got one." She wrote number one and circled it. "Do not think about kissing him. Stop ogling his very fine bum. Do not be sucked in by his killer smile or his sweet Southern drawl." She tapped the pen against her teeth. "Aha." She nodded slowly. *Stay at least five feet from him so you can't get a whiff of his aftershave. Do not think that his broody, sulky demeanor is somehow sexy. Above all else, stop falling in love with him!* Grace tossed her pen down and dusted her hands together. Ha, piece of cake. She took a big gulp of wine in celebration.

In fact, Grace was so pleased with herself that she was starting to get hungry. Thinking that some fruit, cheese, and crackers would go nicely with her wine, she stood up and walked through the double doors, nearly bumping into . . . "Mason!" Grace shrieked. "You scared the day-lights out of me!" She backed up in order to adhere to her five-feet-away-from-him rule. She'd already caught a whiff of his aftershave, and she already had kissing him on her mind. "Damn."

"Sorry. I knocked, but I was drowned out by your duet with Billy Joel. I know I shouldn't have come in, but the door was open, so—"

"Why are you here?" Grace bluntly interrupted, and then turned Billy Joel off.

Mason shrugged. "I couldn't resist your singing. Your voice carried across the lake."

Grace narrowed her eyes at him, digging deep for the not-thinking-about-kissing-him rule, number one. Of course he had the nerve to look super hot in a plain black T-shirt and basic Wranglers. "Since when do you crack jokes?"

"I was serious." Mason took a step forward and Grace took a giant step back, nearly out the door.

"My singing is pretty horrible."

"Yeah, it is."

"You didn't have to agree with me." She tilted her head to the side. "So did you come here to laugh at me?"

"No."

"Give me singing lessons?"

"No, although you could use some."

"Ha, very funny." She narrowed her eyes. "What, then?"

Mason shook his head. "Okay, I confess. I *can* resist your singing." When he smiled, Grace closed her eyes and fisted her hands at her sides, mentally going through her list of rules. She was on number three when he said, "What I can't really resist is *you*, Gracie."

"No!" Her determination to stick to her list was only so strong. Opening her eyes wide, Grace turned and fled out the door, which of course didn't lead to an escape because she was surrounded by water. Unless she opted for a cannonball into the river, she had no place to go. When a gust of wind picked up her list of rules from beneath the pen, she lunged for it. "No!" The list fluttered away like a bird in flight before taking a nosedive into the water once the wind died down. "Oh, bollocks!"

Mason hurried over to stand beside her. "Was that sheet of paper something important?"

"Extremely."

"Do you want me to go in after it?"

Grace gave him glance. "Into the water? Are you quite mad?"

"Angry?"

"No, mad as in crazy."

"I ran out into a raging storm, remember? I don't mind jumping into the river, but the current is taking your extremely important paper away fast." Mason gripped the railing, clearly willing to take the plunge. "Speak now."

"No! Don't!" The knowledge that he would jump into the river on her behalf made her want to break all of her rules at once, beginning with kissing him. "Perhaps it wasn't nearly as important as I thought." She gazed at Mason while her brain warred with good sense and potent desire. Good sense was losing by a long shot. "Mason," she began, but he shook his head.

"Don't."

"Don't what?"

"Say anything."

Grace gave him a slight smile. "Unfortunately, that

doesn't usually work for me." She longed to take a step closer and put her hands on his solid chest. She wanted to bury her nose in the soft cotton of his shirt . . . and most of all she wanted to be in his arms kissing him.

"You drive me insane, you know."

"Wait—do you mean that in a good or bad way? Because it can go in either direction," she tried to joke, but her voice came out soft and husky.

"Both."

Grace tried to look away, but those blue eyes of his held her pinned to the spot. Her heart thudded and good sense left the building for good.

"And you're totally ruining my careful plan."

"Hey, the Broomstick Brewery idea will work," she said, trying to steer this visit toward business and get back to her rules. "I'm quite sure of it."

"Maybe."

She arched an eyebrow.

He sighed. "Okay, probably, but I'm not thinking about or going to talk about the brewery right now."

"So what plan are you referring to, if not a business plan?"

"My grand plan was to give you the cold shoulder so you'd get pissed off at me and stay away."

"What kind of bizarre plan is that?"

"Well." He shoved his fingers through his hair and gave a short chuckle. "The plan was designed to protect me from getting hurt. See, if you stay away, I can't kiss you." He reached over and ran a gentle fingertip down her cheek, which made her want to tilt her head into his palm—but she wanted to look into his eyes and grasp just what he was trying to tell her. "And . . . ," he began, but hesitated, as if not sure if he should divulge the rest of his plan.

"Carry on. I must know the rest."

"My plan would keep me from falling for someone who has no intention of staying."

Grace's heart thudded and she thought of her own set

of silly rules floating down to feed the catfish. So they'd both been trying to stay from each other. Grace pointed to the river. "That paper had a list of rules concerning pretty much the same thing. I think we're on the same sad page."

"Really?"

"I suppose so, yes."

"Interesting, but Danny had a better idea." The sideways look he gave her made her feel warm all the way to her toes.

"Are you going to share Danny's little tidbit with me?"

Mason looked at her for a heartbeat and then nodded. "Danny told me to give you a reason to stay, Gracie."

"Oh." She glanced away so he couldn't see how close to the mark he'd just hit. "Is that so?"

"Maybe that's all you ever needed."

Mason's statement startled her. Could he be right?

"You make a strong point." Unable to stop herself, Grace put her hands on his chest. She felt his warm skin through the shirt. He felt solid, strong, and real in a way that no man had ever felt to her before. He wasn't playing games but being honest. God, he was such a good guy, and she didn't want to hurt him. "But, Mason, I can't give you any promises. I know my nature, and—"

"Hey." Mason put a fingertip to her lips. "I'm not asking for any promises. Just a chance. Forget about the brewery right now. Why don't we give this thing between us a fighting shot? In case you haven't noticed, a lot of so-called visitors end up moving to Cricket Creek, Kentucky."

She smoothed her hands over his chest. "So your brother changed your mind?"

"He gave me a different point of view. But no, you changed my mind. After you left, I wondered how I could be crazy enough not to kiss you. What in the Sam Hill was I thinkin'?" He looked at her mouth as if it were the most interesting thing on the planet, and then gazed into her eyes. "Seriously."

"I don't know who Sam Hill is, but he's a smart man."

Mason laughed and then dipped his head and kissed her.

Grace melted into the kiss, and when he pulled her closer, the whole five-foot rule blew all to pieces and fell like warm confetti sprinkling over her body. Make that warm, wet confetti. Oh wait, it was raining! Thunder boomed and the sky cracked open.

Laughing, Mason grabbed her hand and pulled her into the cabin. "What is it with us and thunderstorms?"

Grace joined in his laughter as they all but tumbled inside the cabin. She danced around when the cool air-conditioning hit her. "I don't know, but I sure want to get out of these wet clothes. How about you?" She started backing up toward her bedroom while crooking her finger at him.

"Gracie!" Mason shouted just as she tripped over her forgotten running shoes.

With a yelp she went down hard on her bum.

"Oh my God! Are you all right?"

"Well, I guess that's what I get for trying to be sexy and lure you into my bedroom." She shoved her hair out of her eyes and winced.

When Mason extended his hands, Grace allowed him to haul her to her feet. "Just to give you a heads-up, you don't have to lure me anywhere. You've already caught me, hook, line, and sinker. How about that for using fishing terms?"

"So all I have to do is reel you in?"

"Pretty easy, huh?" he asked, but then without warning he swooped her up into his arms.

"Mason!" She wrapped her arms around his neck and held on. "What do you think you're doing?"

"Um, sweeping you off your feet. Is it working?"

"You betcha," she said with a laugh. Grace had never had a man carry her before. She was always too tall, but Mason carried her easily, without staggering, making her feel dainty and oh so feminine. Grace didn't think she would like to be treated like a princess. She was supposed to be independent. But damn if she didn't like it. A lot. Of course, she'd never dated a country boy before.

Hold on . . . were they dating?

Thoughts swirled around in her head fast and furious, like the wind and the rain coming down. When they reached the foot of her bed, he let her slide slowly against his body until her feet touched the floor. But he didn't let go. Instead, he kissed her softly, lingering, and then pulled back and looked at her. "Gracie, I want this to be the start of something, or I wouldn't be in your bedroom. I don't take this lightly, just so you know."

Grace put her hands on his cheeks and nodded. "I already had that figured out," she said. "And neither do I," she added, and it was true. She'd never understood the appeal of casual sex, but she hadn't stopped thinking about what it would be like to be naked in Mason's arms.

And she was about to find out.

As much as Grace wanted to get out of her wet clothes, she couldn't keep her eyes off Mason as he tugged his T-shirt up over his head. The ripple of muscle made her want to moan, and so she did, getting a grin from him. His body was even more impressive than she'd imagined. Her gaze lingered, taking in his wide shoulders, defined pecs, and a lovely dusting of dark chest hair tapering to an enticing line south. She wanted to take that path with her tongue.

Mason held the wet shirt in his hand. "Where do you want this?"

"Anywhere but on your body. Drop it and carry on with the rest of it."

"You want to watch me undress?"

"Well, yeah."

"Are you that easily entertained?" He reached for his zipper, and then looked at her.

"No, I get easily bored, but I could watch you do this all day long," she said, loving the rich sound of his laughter.

"Then I'm flattered."

"You should be."

He laughed again, and then went for his zipper, going slowly just to torment her. But the lines of stress she'd seen on his face softened, and it hit her that he must be under so much pressure these days. Grace had learned from her mother that laughter was the best medicine, especially during the worst of times. This was a man who put his own dream on hold to save his family's business, and he deserved to be happy. She wanted to kiss away his worry, make sweet love to him, and then hold him close.

When he tugged off his boots and then shimmied out of his jeans, Grace's breath caught. He was, in a word, magnificent. No wonder he carried her with ease. She shivered with anticipation.

"Baby, are you cold?"

"I should be, but looking at you makes me warm all over. But say that again."

"Say what?" he asked while he started tugging at her tank top.

"'Baby.' I like it when you call me that," Grace admitted, and then felt a bit of a blush heat her cheeks. In her quest for independence, she'd shied away from endearments. Allowing herself to become attached meant having to settle down, and so when it got to the calling-her-"baby" stage, she was always ready to run.

But not this time.

Mason paused to look at her standing there in nothing but her cream-colored satin bra and bikini panties. "You're beautiful," he said in a simple, straightforward manner. While Grace knew on an intellectual level that she possessed physical beauty, she hadn't ever really felt that way. But she felt that way now.

Mason slipped the straps over her shoulders, nearly but not quite exposing her breasts. Cupping her, he rubbed his thumbs oh so lightly over her cleavage, causing a hot shiver to slide down her spine. Brushing her damp hair to the side, he kissed her neck, teasing with the tip of his tongue, and began a sensual trail of light nibbles. With a flick of his hand, he unhooked her bra, and her breasts happily tumbled free, eager for his touch. When he sucked a beaded nipple into his mouth, Grace groaned. "God, here I thought that whole weak-in-the-knees thing was a bunch of rubbish," she said in a breathless voice, and then sank backward onto the bed.

"So you're saying that I make you weak in the knees?"

"Apparently so." She gazed up at him, drinking in the sight of his gloriously naked body. "I don't think there's a body part on me that isn't reacting to you." She gave him a slow smile. "One area in particular."

"Then let's concentrate on that particular area."

"Oh, please do."

Mason joined her on the bed and kissed her shoulder. "There?"

"Nice . . . but, no, not quite," she said, and sucked in a breath when he grazed his hand over her breasts.

"Then I guess I'll go on a treasure hunt until I find the right spot," he said, and began kissing every inch of her body, slowly, seductively, except for where she wanted him most. Her body quivered when he kissed a hot trail down her torso. "Am I getting warm?"

"Yes!"

"Good." But when he got to her mound, he veered to the left and nibbled on the tender skin of her upper thigh.

Grace could feel the warmth of his breath so very close to where she needed him. She arched her back, wild with wanting his mouth on her core. She felt rather dazed, almost out of breath. "Mason . . ." Grace was going to ask if he enjoyed torturing her when he grabbed her ankles and slid her to the edge of the bed. He tugged her panties off and tossed them aside.

"Here?" The touch of his tongue to her core sent a jolt of hot desire through her.

"Yes, oh God, yes." She felt a deep ache, an intense

longing that only he could fulfill. She fisted her hands in the comforter and her heart hammered in her chest. His mouth was gentle at first, but then he explored her folds, licked, sucked, as if he couldn't get enough of her. She came up on her elbows, thinking that the sight of his dark head between her thighs was the sexiest thing ever. When he took her to the brink, she fell back against the covers. But then he slowed down, making Grace attempt to sit up and pound his back in protest, but her limbs felt as if they were made of liquid. "Mason," she said breathlessly, pleading. "Don't stop."

He paused for a second, making her moan, but then he slid his big hands beneath her bum to get better access and began licking until his silky tongue sent her flying over the edge. Waves of exquisite pleasure washed over her, and she sure hoped that her cry of sheer joy wasn't echoing across the river, alerting all of Cricket Creek and the creatures in the woods that she had just experienced the most delicious, mind-blowing climax of her life. "That was . . . mmm, uh . . ."

Mason scooted up next to her and looked up at the ceiling. "Wait—did I just render Grace Gordon speechless?"

"I . . . do believe . . . so."

He chuckled and then ran his fingertips down her body, making her shiver and gasp. "And we've only just begun."

Grace groaned. "I'll be more than happy to carry on as soon as my body floats back down to earth. I . . . I just need a moment to regroup."

"Maybe I can help rekindle the fire," he said in her ear.

"Oh please, do go on, then."

11

Must Be Doin' Something Right

MASON RAN HIS HANDS OVER GRACE'S WARM, SOFT SKIN, thinking that touching her, tasting her, was something he could never get enough of. He loved hearing her sighs, her moans of pleasure, her low, sexy rumble of laughter. Most of all he loved having her body wrapped around him like kudzu.

When she left the brewery earlier, he'd felt a sense of panic, afraid to go after her but even more afraid not to. Danny had found him sitting on his couch staring off into space and had talked some sense into him. His little brother, of all people, had been dead-ass right. If Grace chose to leave, Mason couldn't do anything about it, but he sure as hell was going to do his best to make her want to stay. He knew he was putting his heart on the line and taking a risk, but not taking it wasn't something he could live with. He was falling for her hard, so hard that there wasn't any use fighting his feelings.

Mason came up on one elbow, leaned over, and kissed her. She responded by turning toward him and pressing her body to his. She entwined those long legs with his and moved against him, letting him know that she wanted him too. He hadn't come over here with the goal of making love to her, but once he kissed her, all bets were suddenly off. "Gracie, God, you're driving me wild," he said, but he paused to give her time to be sure that she wanted to go this far. He didn't want her to have regrets.

She cupped his cheek. "Make love to me." She looked into his eyes and then smiled. "Please."

And that was all the encouragement he needed.

Mason paused for protection and then came back to the bed. She opened her arms and beckoned him. Mason somehow knew that the gesture was meant to convey to him that she was taking a chance too but she was willing and ready. And wasn't that what love was all about? Putting your heart out there and taking a chance? Giving Lauren the power to hold him back from finding happiness was giving her something she didn't deserve. Mason had learned by watching his parents that real love wasn't just about the good times but about standing by the one you loved through thick and thin.

Letting go of his fear of getting hurt felt so damned good!

"Ah, Gracie." He kissed her with the pent-up passion that had been driving him nuts for days. She responded by threading her fingers through his hair, kissing him back with wild abandon. When he moved his mouth to her neck, she sighed and slid her hands down his back. He could tell by her touch that she wanted this every bit as much as he did. When she reached his ass, she squeezed.

"You have the best bum on the planet."

"Why, thank you."

"You're welcome," she said, but then gasped when Mason caressed her breasts. Taking a nipple in his mouth, he licked, nibbled, and sucked, teasing until he heard her moan. "Dear God . . ."

Mason wanted to learn every inch of her beautiful body and find out what drove her wild. When he trailed

his fingers lightly over her skin, he could feel her shiver.
She arched her back, moving sensually against him, letting him know that he was doing something right.

When Mason lightly touched her mound, she gasped.
Knowing what she wanted, he slid a finger into her silky
heat, exploring, caressing, dipping into her folds until he
knew she was close to climaxing. But when she reached
between them and wrapped her delicate hand around his
cock and stroked, he couldn't wait another second to be
sheathed inside her body.

While kissing her deeply Mason entered her with one
sure stroke. She gasped and wrapped her arms and legs
around him, tilting her hips. "My God, you feel good."

"I was thinking the same thing."

Mason moved slowly, holding back, wanting to savor
the feeling of being inside her sweet, tight body. But she
bucked beneath him, grabbing on to his shoulders. Her
teeth found his earlobe, sending a hot shiver down his
spine; holding back flew out the window and never
looked back.

Gracie made love in a wild and free way that he'd
somehow known she would. He loved her taste on his
lips, her scent filling his head, and her soft cries of pleasure. When she pressed her head against the pillows and
arched her back, Mason thrust deeply, taking her over
the edge. A ripple of pure pleasure gripped him, suspended as if in midair, and then rushed through him with
an intensity he didn't know existed. In that moment he
knew with certainty that this went beyond sex, beyond
physical attraction. Mason knew that she felt it too, because she didn't say anything. She didn't need to.

Sometimes words got in the way.

Rolling to his side, Mason held her close, and she
clung to him. Breathing deeply, she shuddered once, and
Mason understood how she felt. He was blown away too.

Wanting to know her thoughts but unwilling to break
the spell, he remained entwined with her for a few more
minutes. Mason knew that everything between them had

shifted, and he wasn't quite sure how to handle it. Finally, she kissed his shoulder and caressed his skin, drawing patterns over his chest. Damn, he couldn't believe it, but he was getting aroused all over again, and he thought he could do this all night long. Or at least give it a try.

Gracie's fingers circled his half-hard cock and she chuckled low in her throat. "I'm impressed."

"As you should be."

She chuckled again, and he smiled, glad that there was an easy flow between them and not something awkward, another clue that this was perhaps meant to be. But he fell silent, wondering what would come next.

"You're wondering what to tell people, aren't you?" Grace lifted her head and looked at him.

Mason nodded. "What do you suggest? You have to know, however we put it, us being together is going to cause quite a stir." He wasn't going to bring up the business end of their relationship right now.

"Should we keep it under our hat until we figure it out?"

A stab of disappointment shot through him. "Is that what you want, Gracie?"

Lowering her eyes, Grace ran her fingertip back and forth over his bottom lip. "No."

"But?"

"We have to figure out what this is first, though, don't you think?"

Mason nodded, and he could feel her pull away a little bit. He understood, though. This was his territory, his home. He was the one who had the most risk of getting hurt. When she glanced away, he put his hand on her cheek. "I know there are complications."

"I don't want to be the bad guy. I make a really awful bad guy. I have this need to have everybody like me."

"You're way too pretty to be a bad guy," he tried to joke, but her eyes turned serious. "Or even a bad girl."

Mason cupped her chin and rubbed his thumb over her cheek. "Hey, you were up front and honest with me.

I'm going into this with my eyes wide-open. You didn't pull any punches, but I'll throw some punches if anyone talks trash about you."

"Ah, my bighearted but tough country boy."

"And don't you forget it," he said with a grin. While he knew she referred to him as being hers as a joke, he liked the sound of it way too much. He was already in over his head, but his damned heart just wouldn't listen to his need to slow down. "And just so you know, I still hate the whole Broomstick Brewery thing."

"You won't when you start making piles of money," she said with some heat behind her words. Good. He wanted to keep the challenge in place for her, because the longer she stayed in town, the better the chance he had to convince her to stay.

"You ready to get something to eat?" he asked lightly. "The storm has let up."

"I'm suddenly starving. I've worked up quite an appetite."

When she grinned at him, Mason almost sighed with relief. "You wanna head up to Sully's and grab a bite?" he asked casually, but he really wanted to get her out in public with him. "Maybe do some two-steppin' with your country boy?"

She winced. "I don't know how."

"I'm a good teacher."

"I'm a slow learner when it comes to dancing."

"Ah, a challenge. I like it."

"I'll do some steppin' all over your feet. Just fair warning."

"I won't mind." In fact, there wasn't much he wouldn't mind her doing to him.

Except leaving. That, he could do without.

But Mason decided not to think about the future at the moment. He was going out on the town with Gracie Gordon on his arm. For now, that was enough.

12

Honky-Tonk Heaven

"OUCH, YOU WEREN'T KIDDIN'," MASON SAID AFTER Grace stomped on his foot again.

Grace pulled up short on the dance floor. "Hey, don't go there. I warned you that I was a terrible dancer."

"Yeah, but there are degrees of terrible."

Grace smacked his shoulder.

"Okay, one more time. It's quick, quick, slow . . . slow. And no bobbing up and down. Keep your chin up and look past my shoulder."

"Too many rules!" Grace shook her head, knowing it was a lost cause. "It's a weird way to dance."

"It's classic," Mason responded, clearly affronted. "Want to give it another shot?"

"Did you just say something about doing a shot? Now you're talking. I'll have a pineapple upside-down cake."

Mason glanced up at the ceiling and then sighed. "Okay, I'll get you the shot if you promise to slow dance with me."

Grace winced. "I suck at that too. Slow, fast, or anything in between. The dance floor and I never did get along. Can we just sit down? Where's the corn hole?"

"That's an outdoor game."

"Oh."

"Darts, then?"

"I have a feeling you'd maim somebody."

"True. So let's just go with the shot."

Mason nodded. "Only if you promise to slow dance."

She rolled her eyes. "You'll be sorry. What are you? A glutton for punishment?"

"Maybe." But then he leaned in close and said, "Slow dancing with you in my arms will be worth a little bit of pain."

"Oh, you say that now," Grace said, but in truth she felt a flash of pleasure slide down her spine. She knew that there was a charmer behind that broody exterior, but what she didn't know was how it would affect her. All it took was his smile, saying something flirty or sexy, and she was putty in his hands.

When Grace walked over to their high-top table, he put his hand lightly at the small of her back. She liked the feeling of being with him, being his girl. And when he headed over to the bar to order her shot, she noticed other women giving him the once-over. Grace sat up a little bit straighter and felt territorial. She couldn't remember when she'd felt this kind of jealous reaction.

Oh boy, I'm getting in deep, she thought, and swallowed hard. Moving back to the U.S. wouldn't be a big deal, though, would it? She, Sophia, and Garret all had dual citizenship in the States and England. When living in London, Grace used one of her mother's furnished flats, so except for clothes, she had nothing much to ship over here. Although Sophia lived in New York, Grace would be able to visit with her sister much easier from Kentucky than from all the way across the pond.

Grace toyed with her napkin, twisting and rolling it between her fingers while she thought about the crazy turn her life had suddenly taken. She never would have thought that her brief visit to Cricket Creek would turn into a life-altering event, and yet here she was, sitting in a honky-tonk tavern with the cutest country boy in the world. The same country boy who had made it clear that he wanted to give their relationship a go.

Grace had noticed curious looks directed their way when they'd first walked in. When she'd asked Mason about it, he'd explained that it had been a long time since he'd been out with a girl. Something in his eyes had suggested more to the story, but tonight wasn't about anything serious, just kicking back and having a good time.

Still deep in thought, Grace was surprised by someone coming up behind her and putting her hands over her eyes.

"Guess who?" Sophia asked, while trying to disguise her voice with a low pitch, but it was a complete fail.

"Sophia!"

"How did you know?"

"Because you're the only one dorky enough to do that."

"I'm not a dork. I'm super cool." Sophia pointed to her outfit and did a little spin.

Grace slid from the stool and turned around to hug her sister. "When did you get here?"

"A few minutes ago," Sophia said, and she did look cute in a pink floral shirt, faded denim skirt, and cowboy boots. Her long toffee-colored hair was braided in one of those fishtail things that only a hairdresser could do.

"Look at you, all cowgirled up."

Sophia laughed. "When in Rome?"

Grace tilted her head and gave her pretty sister a once-over. "Well, you totally pull it off. Where did you get it?"

"At Violet's Vintage Clothing up on Main Street. I need to take you there."

"Definitely." Grace gestured toward a stool. "Join us."

"Okay, whoa, wait a minute." Sophia arched an eyebrow. "Us?"

"I'm with Mason. He went to get me a pineapple upside-down shot but got sidetracked with talking to people he knows," she said casually, trying to ignore Sophia's gasp of surprise followed by a little jig in her boots.

"So are you two seeing each other?"

Grace opened her mouth and then shut it, not sure how she wanted to respond. "It's complicated."

"Oh, I hate when people say that. It's not complicated. Are you seeing him or not?"

"Yes, sort of, I guess, but — "

"I knew it would happen."

Grace lifted her palms upward. "Oh, come on, how?"

"The way you look at him like you want to eat him up with a spoon."

Grace felt heat in her cheeks.

"Oh my God," Sophia whispered in her ear. "Are you sleeping with him?"

"That's an incredibly rude question."

"No, it's not. You're my sister. I have the right to know these things."

"Don't you dare tell anyone — not even Mum."

"You know me better than that. But why are you so uptight about it?"

"I know you'll keep it under your hat." Grace gave Sophia a quick hug. "I'm uptight because Mason is Mattie's brother, for one thing. I don't want to do anything to stir up any family trouble."

"The Mayfields are cool people. They won't hold a failed relationship with Mason against you. But it won't fail."

"We're not in a relationship," Grace said, and looked around to make sure nobody was listening. "So there's nothing to fail."

"Um, you are or you wouldn't be getting so riled up."

"I'm not getting riled up!" Grace said in a very riled-up voice.

"Right," Sophia said. "And you keep glancing over to where that chick is trying to flirt with Mason."

"Not fair. But who is that girl, anyway? Should I go over there and bump her out of the way?"

"Yes, I dare you."

"Oh, stop it," Grace said, but kind of wanted to.

Sophia laughed. "Oh, Grace, I'm so glad you're here. We need to find time to hang out more."

Grace smiled at her sister. "Yeah, we do. So do you want to join us?"

Sophia bit her bottom lip.

"What? Oh, are *you* with someone?"

"Not ... *with* ... with."

"Ha, meaning, you are." Grace gave Sophia's shoulder a little shove. "You little minx, you're holding out on me. Who is he?"

Sophia nodded in the direction of the pool tables. "Avery Dean. He comes into the bistro pretty often."

"Oh, let me think. I wonder why?"

"The food! It is a restaurant, in case you've forgotten. Oh, don't give me that look."

"What, you mean the look you gave me earlier?"

"He's just a friend, Grace."

"And super cute," Grace said. Indeed, Avery Dean was another sexy country boy.

"Stop looking at him or he will know I'm talking about him," Sophia said in an urgent whisper. "He's a friend of Danny's."

"Then most likely a good guy, right?"

Sophia flicked a sideways glance in Avery's direction. "Yes, but he's coming off a broken engagement. I don't want to be a rebound girl, so I'm keeping my distance. We're just hanging out now and then."

Grace looked at Sophia and nodded. "Smart. And you're going back to New York after Mattie can come back to the bistro full-time, right?"

Sophia nodded, but Grace noticed enough of a hesitation before the nod to wonder if staying in Cricket Creek had crossed her mind as well. "I mean, I've built a big clientele by specializing in weddings and big events. What would I do here in Cricket Creek? There's just one local salon and the regular chains on the outskirts of town."

"So you've thought about it?"

"Well, Lily sort of changed everything, you know?"

"Oh, I know. I need to get over to see her and pry her out of Mum's arms." Grace nodded, but then put a hand on Sophia's shoulder. "Wait — do you think Mum will actually move here?"

Sophia shrugged. "I really don't think she can stay away from Lily for any length of time. I asked her about it yesterday when she helped me out at the bistro, and she said that she is thinking about going back and forth with Mattie and Garret when Garret films *Sing for Me* in London."

"Wow," Grace said. "But I guess it makes perfect sense. She'd been cutting way back at BGC, unless you count the new baby line. She's all over that one. But seriously, after all she's been through, maybe it's about time that she sat back and did whatever the hell she wanted to do, or nothing at all, instead of working insane hours."

"Hey, I agree one hundred percent. And I really wish she could find somebody . . . a good guy, you know?"

"Oh, me too. Somebody down to earth and not some wanker who wants to be with her for material reasons. Do you think a bloke like that even exists?"

"In a small town like this? Yeah, I think so. I tried to get Mom out with me tonight, but she's watching Lily while Mattie and Garret have dinner at Wine and Diner. Mattie was getting a little bit of cabin fever and needed to get out."

"Or did Mum convince Mattie she had cabin fever so she could babysit?"

Sophia laughed. "Maybe a little bit of both. Have you been to Wine and Diner yet?"

"No, but I heard that the food is fabulous. We should go soon, maybe after a day of shopping?"

Sophia nodded. "For sure. Oh hey, Avery is motioning for me. I think he wants me to play some pool with him."

"Do you play?"

"Not all that well, but yeah, I get a lucky shot in now and then. Do you and Mason want to take us on?"

"No." Grace shook her head. "I embarrassed myself enough trying to two-step. The only step I did was on Mason's feet, and it was more than twice. I did, like, the ten-step."

Sophia tossed her head back and laughed. "God, I've missed you so much."

"Me too! You'd be good at line dancing, though, and you're dressed for the part."

"Oh, I've seen couples doing it here before. It does look like fun."

"We're still talking about dancing, right?"

"Grace! Do you even have a filter?"

"Chill, I was only kidding."

"And it does look fun. So does line dancing."

"Ha, easy for you to say. You possess something called rhythm, and all I got was the blues."

"Hey." Sophia tilted her head. "You doing okay?" she asked gently.

"It was a joke," Grace said. "I'm fine."

"Good," Sophia said, and the love and concern in her sister's eyes went straight to her heart. While Sophia always had a pretty even-keeled disposition, Grace knew now that she suffered from bouts of depression from time to time, and that's when she became restless and needed a change. Her humor and upbeat demeanor masked her moods, and a new project always chased away the clouds and brought her sunny disposition back. "I think I'll sit this one out, but do come over when you're finished and introduce me to cutie-pie Avery with the dark curly hair."

"Will do. And don't forget I want to shop. Maybe tomorrow? Shane and Laura Lee are going to work the bistro for me, so I get a day off, and Mattie is coming in for a little while. But yeah, we need to catch up."

"We do." Grace pressed her cheek to Sophia's and then watched her sister sashay over there in her cowgirl getup, looking like she fit right in here at Sully's. Although Sophia spent time in London, she'd never lived there for any length of time so never picked up much of an English accent like Grace and Garret. As soon as Grace opened her mouth and spoke anywhere in the States, everyone seemed to want to listen and more often than not try to speak back to her with an accent. It used to drive her bonkers, but she no longer cared about such trivial things. Sweating the small stuff was something her father did, and it was a challenge to purge letting little things get to her, but she'd succeeded.

A moment later, Mason walked her way with her drink. "Sorry it took me so long. I haven't been out lately, and everyone wanted to know how the brewery was coming along. Pete Sully wants to have a couple of varieties on tap here, so we need to keep that in mind."

"Excellent."

Mason handed her the shot, which was more the size of a cocktail. When he saw her eyes widen, he laughed. "That's how we do it round here."

"Are you having one too?"

"Not one of those girly cake things, but yeah." He held up his glass. "Good Kentucky bourbon. Straight, no chaser."

"Can we get a taxi?"

Mason laughed. "Well, if you're lucky, Bubba will answer, if he's in the mood."

"Bubba?"

"The only taxi service in Cricket Creek. Once he falls asleep, you're out of luck."

"Wow." Grace found it hard to believe that there were places where you couldn't hail a taxi when you needed one.

"Pete's son, Clint, runs a free shuttle most weekends. It's a little bit of a walk, but we can hoof it to the marina from here."

"Seriously? On the main road out there?"

"I know a shortcut."

"Are you suggesting through the woods?"

"Are you afraid, my little city slicker?"

"Yeah, but probably not after I toss back this giant shot of pineapple-flavored deliciousness."

Mason laughed and tapped his glass to hers again. "Let's do it."

Grace tried but could only get through half of the pineapple-upside-down-cake shot before making a face and coughing. "Holy moly," she said, but when Mason showed her his empty glass, she polished hers off.

"How do you feel?"

"Like maybe I can two-step," she said, and of course he immediately held his hands out in invitation. Laughing, Grace gave the quick-quick, slow-slow her best effort and actually got the hang of it by the end of the song.

"Want to try for a spin?" Mason asked close her ear.

"Let's not tempt fate," she said and, holding his hand, followed him off the dance floor.

Friends of Mason's stopped by their table, friendly, but Grace could feel their curiosity, and she was rather amused by it. Her accent seemed to fascinate them, and she found herself nudging Mason beneath the table while trying to keep a straight face. At one point he reached over and held her hand, and although she didn't skip a beat, the gesture went straight to her heart. How could such a simple gesture feel so wonderful?

"Did you know my sister is over there playing pool with Avery Dean?" Grace asked in a casual tone, but when Mason rubbed his thumb over the top of her hand, she thought she might slither right off the barstool.

"No, I didn't realize Sophia was here."

Grace leaned closer to him. "Yeah, they're going to join us when they're finished. Sophia says she's just friends with him, but I think she might be sweet on him. Do you know Avery?"

"Not real well. He's Danny's age, but from what I

know of him, he seems like a pretty nice guy." Mason nibbled on the inside of his cheek. "Does Sophia know that Avery was engaged not too long ago?"

"Yes." When Grace nodded, he squeezed her hand.

"Good, as long as she is aware of that fact. I wouldn't want her to get hurt."

"Me neither," Grace said, but she was touched by the fact that Mason was looking out for her sister. She remembered that Garret had said that Mattie's brothers were super protective of her, and it only reiterated what she already knew. The Mayfields were good people. Grace smiled, but fear sneaked back inside her brain.

"Don't," Mason said.

"What?" Grace asked innocently, but she knew he was seeing right though her.

"Don't think. Don't worry. Just feel, Gracie. The rest will take care of itself."

Grace nodded, but felt emotion well up in her throat. What was up with the whole tearing-up thing anyway? She cleared her throat and took the last tiny sip of her giant shot.

"Want another one?"

"Yeah, but you will have to give me a piggyback ride home. And I don't think I will manage to walk the dock without incident. I have a hard enough time sober."

"I don't mind," Mason said, and the lovely thing was that Grace knew he meant it. "Or I could get Danny to come and give us a lift. He owes me quite a few."

"Okay, let's throw caution to the wind and do one more." She held up her index finger. "One. I am quite annoying when I get pissed."

"Angry?"

"Oh, British slang for *drunk*. My voice gets an octave higher. Sophia calls it my drunken voice and it's really super annoying. I can't control it either. You might toss me into the river."

Mason laughed. "Never."

"You say that now . . ."

He laughed again, and Grace loved the sound of it. "You keep thinking that I'm going to change my mind about a lot of things, but I'm not."

"We'll see about that."

"Yeah, we'll see," he said confidently. When she'd first met Mason, he seemed to be carrying the weight of the world on his shoulders. And right now he seemed so at ease. She liked to think she was partly responsible for his good mood. Of course, his good humor might change just a bit when he saw the witch-themed decorations she'd ordered for the taproom. Cauldrons used as beer pitchers were going to be so brilliant, but she somehow didn't think Mason would agree. But maybe he'd finally concentrate on the brewing end and leave the rest up to her. "Another one, then?"

"Oh, why the hell not?" She'd worry about business tomorrow. Tonight was all about cutting loose and having fun.

"I'll be right back with your drink. Look at the menu and pick out something to eat. The wings are good here, just so you know."

"Oh, I love buffalo wings," she said. "The hotter the better."

"Ah, a girl after my own heart," he said, and then turned away.

Grace watched him weave his way through the crowd, thinking that she wasn't after his heart. She hadn't come here to find love at all, but wasn't that the way life worked? Love when you least expected it?

With a sigh, she opened the menu and was trying to decide between wings sauces when her phone pinged. Grace swiped her finger across the screen and looked down to see a selfie of her mum holding Lily. Her mother looked radiant and happy. While Grace knew that the big smile stemmed from the joy of holding her granddaughter, there was something relaxed in her mother's expression that Grace hadn't seen in a while. Maybe never. Grace laughed at the next picture, with Garret photobombing behind the rocking chair.

Being near her family felt wonderful in ways that Grace had forgotten and had dearly missed. She knew that Sophia had gotten the pictures as well and looked across the room to see her sister tipping her head back with laughter. Leaning on his pool stick, Avery leaned close and gazed down at Sophia's phone. Smiling, Avery looped his arm over Sophia's shoulder and squeezed. The gesture was brief, and Sophia gave him a shy smile, but her sister's gaze lingered on Avery when he bent over and took his shot. Grace felt a flash of worry for Sophia. Falling for someone on the rebound was never a good idea. She was glad that they were getting together to shop so they could talk.

When Mason returned to the table with the drinks, Grace showed him the pictures.

"Oh, that's so awesome. Your mother must be over the moon, just like mine."

"She's having a ball," Grace said. She almost added that she didn't know how her mother was ever going to leave Cricket Creek, but she pointed to the menu instead. "Hot wings and extra ranch and celery sticks. Sound good?"

"Perfect, and I'm not talking about the wings."

"Oh, it's the extra ranch that put you over the top," Grace said calmly, even though her heart kicked it up a notch.

Mason tapped his glass to hers. "How'd you know?"

"Good guess, I suppose."

"Good, I plan on keeping you guessing."

Grace wasn't quite sure what to make of that, but before she could ask, he pulled her up from her seat. "What are you doing?"

"Claiming my slow dance."

"But what about the wings?"

"The wings can wait."

"You're quite the bossy pants tonight," Grace said, but was secretly glad to be back in his arms. They swayed to a country song and Mason sang the love song in her ear. "You have a nice voice," she said.

"Hey, I can sing, I can dance, and I brew kick-ass beer. What more could you ask for?"

"Knitting. I love a man who knits," Grace said in the most serious tone she could muster.

"I'll have to work on that one," Mason said without skipping a beat. "But I will learn how."

Grace had to laugh, but in truth she somehow believed him.

13

Against All Odds

BECCA READ THROUGH THE SHEPHERD'S PIE RECIPE SHE'D pulled up on her tablet again and let out a long sigh. "Oh, there are so many steps and so many ways for it to go all wrong." She shook her head. "Why did I say I'd cook dinner when I haven't prepared a meal in a hundred years?" Of course she knew why. Cooking was the last thing Jimmy Topmiller had expected her to offer to do. She'd experienced instant regret after the invitation, but now she was stuck with the task, and he was due to arrive in less than two hours. Maybe she should do the classic thing and head up to Wine and Diner for takeaway. She'd put the meal in her own dish and he would be none the wiser, right?

With a groan she eyed the red wine she'd purchased to put in the gravy and decided that she needed a glass before tackling the task. There was a time when she enjoyed preparing a meal. Her mum had been a great cook, nothing fancy, but good stick-to-your-ribs classic English recipes like bangers and mash, toad in the hole, and steak-and-ale pies. Oh, and her mum's sponge cakes were to die for but something Becca had never mastered. She'd tried, but always ended up with a sheet cake as dry as cardboard that ended up in the bin.

"Brown the ground beef. Easy enough." When she'd first married Rick, she'd been a decent cook, full of newlywed trial and error. But Jimmy wasn't her husband and she just knew he was banking on her failure. Ha, well, she'd show him, all right. She got out the cutting board and eyed the onion. She hoped so, anyway.

Becca took a healthy sip of the wine and smacked her lips together. "Well, Jimmy, odds are in your favor, but I've beaten the odds quite a few times in my life." With a quick nod, she dusted her hands together. "Let's give this thing a go." After putting Pandora on the British Invasion station, she went to work.

Two hours later the kitchen was a complete disaster and she had a bit of a wine buzz going, but the shepherd's pie was in the oven. "Ha, success, Jimmy Topmiller," she said, humming along with "Hard Day's Night." Well, she hoped so anyway. The true test would be when it came out of the oven all nice and bubbly around the edges. "And I've been workin' like a dog," she sang, and then tilted her head to the side. "Oh, hey, was that a knock at the door?" She tucked a lock of hair that had escaped her bun behind her ear and sang, "I hear you knocking . . . ," but then trailed off. "Wait a minute."

Frowning, Becca looked over at the digital clock on the microwave and put her hand over her mouth. "Oh no!" she squeaked, knowing that it must be Jimmy knocking on her door. She glanced down at her ancient *Abbey Road* T-shirt, slouchy boyfriend jeans, and bare feet and put her hand to her chest. Her hair, which had the nerve to get rather curly after menopause for some defiant reason, was escaping the messy bun piled on top of her head. At least she had on some basic makeup, but only because she'd had to run out to the grocery store earlier for the ingredients for dinner. "Bollocks!" she grumbled, but there wasn't time to rush into the bedroom and change into the much sexier slacks and silk blouse that after intense deliberation she had laid out to wear. "Dammit!"

Another knock, impatient this time, had her trying to smooth her hair, without any luck. Inhaling deeply, she reached into her purse and did manage to find her tube of lipstick and apply a hasty swipe to her lips before heading through the great room to the front door. She swung it open and was rewarded with a look of surprise on Jimmy Topmiller's face, making her embarrassment about her casual attire almost worth it.

"Did . . . did I get the day wrong?" Jimmy asked, and had the nerve to look handsome in pressed navy slacks and a light blue button-down oxford shirt that made his Paul Newman eyes appear even bluer. His salt-and-pepper hair looked freshly trimmed, and he sported just a hint of sexy stubble that had Becca wondering what it would feel like to run her hand over his cheek. He had something in a white bakery box balanced in one hand and a bottle of wine clutched in the other.

"Yes, but I, um, do believe you're early," she fibbed, but with a lift of her chin, she stepped back for him to enter.

"I thought you said six thirty in your text message."

"Sevenish, if I remember correctly." She did remember correctly and she'd said six thirty.

"Do you want me to come back later?"

Becca waved a hand as if being disheveled while he looked so amazing didn't bother her in the least. "Oh, don't be silly," she said, and took the wine from him.

"I'm never silly," he said, and followed her through the great room and into the kitchen. "Dear God, it looks like a bomb went off in here."

"The sign of a good cook," Becca boasted, while searching for the corkscrew.

"If you say so," he said, with a touch of humor in his tone. He moved a mound of potato peelings out of the way and placed the bakery box on the kitchen counter. "So, what's on the menu?"

"Shepherd's pie. Do you like it?"

"I've never had it, but I have to admit that it smells good."

"You sound surprised." Becca gave him an arch of her eyebrow as she uncorked the wine.

"Maybe because I am surprised."

"And why is that?" she asked, even though she already suspected the answer.

"I wouldn't have pegged you for a woman who cooked her own meals."

Becca turned around and leaned against the counter. "To be perfectly honest, I haven't prepared dinner in a long time. I thought about cheating and getting takeaway from Wine and Diner."

"Takeaway? Oh, you mean carryout." He grinned as if he found her choice of words funny. "So why didn't you?"

Becca shrugged. "Cheating isn't in my nature." She nibbled on the inside of her lip, and then added, "And I wanted to throw you off balance. Impress you, maybe? Try to figure out why you dislike me so much."

His face registered surprise. "I don't dislike you."

"But you want to." When Jimmy didn't answer, but looked at her with those baby blues, Becca felt a pull of attraction that she wanted to shake but couldn't. "So how's that working out for you?"

"Not all that well." He gave her a crooked grin, and damn if she wasn't the one feeling off balance. "Let's just say you're full of surprises."

"And do you like surprises?"

"Not usually," Jimmy said, and his gaze seemed to linger on her mouth. "For a former fashion model, you seem to be either overdressed or underdressed. But I have to say that finding you dressed in jeans and a T-shirt is a surprise that I like."

"So you can poke fun? You have to know that this wasn't what I intended to wear."

"No, and I find what you're wearing sexy as hell." He

looked down at her bare feet with painted red toes. "Better than those impossible high heels."

"Are you flirting with me, Jimmy?" Becca asked lightly, but her heart beat a little faster.

"Just speaking the truth. Of course, I'm sure you know that you would look good wearing a paper sack."

"Why does your flattery sound more like an insult?"

"Surely you know how beautiful you are, Becca. You were a model and had a poster that sold millions of copies."

Becca shrugged. "My looks have opened some doors and closed others. The poster was a blessing at the time when I needed the money, but somewhat of a curse too."

"I guess I can understand why."

"Yes, no one takes a pinup model seriously."

"That's not fair," he said hotly, surprising her.

"Really? You have your own assumptions about me, though, don't you?" A look crossed his face that she couldn't quite read, but she knew she was right. "Dumb blonde? Spoiled? Vain? Shall I go on?"

"No."

But she did carry on, like a steamroller out of control. "I came from humble beginnings, I'll have you know. Working-class London. And my success was hard-earned. So whatever you think you know about me, you probably don't," she said tightly. "If you think I'm some rich, spoiled bitch living a pampered life, you are all kinds of wrong." She lifted her chin. "Now, can I offer you a glass of merlot, or would you prefer something else?" God, she was blazing with anger and wanted to give him a hard shove. She wasn't one to lose her cool, but Jimmy seemed to be able to rile her up in no time. Oddly, she kind of liked it. "Well?"

"Something else." Without warning, he pulled her into his arms and kissed her. And it wasn't some tame peck on the mouth. Oh no, Jimmy Topmiller meant business. This was a kiss full of pent-up passion and chock-full of heat. And as much as Becca wished she could push at his chest and give him a good slap, instead she wrapped her arms around his neck, threaded her fingers in his hair, and kissed him right back.

Becca's anger dissolved like sugar in hot tea, and she melted against him. It had been such a long time since she'd been held in a man's arms, kissed so deeply. The pilot light that had been extinguished came back to life, and damn, it felt bloody good . . . so good that she wanted to shove the place settings from the table and make wild and crazy love to him right then and there.

Thankfully, an alarm buzzed in the back of her brain, bringing her to her befuddled senses, and she unwrapped herself from around Jimmy.

Oh wait, the alarm was actually the oven timer. *Saved by the bell* went through her brain, and she laughed.

"So you find my kiss amusing? Am I that out of practice?"

"No, I find your kisses to be quite delicious. I thought the interruption from the buzzer was quite funny, because in another moment I was going to have my way with you on the dining room table." She walked over and turned the timer off and then opened the oven door and checked on the shepherd's pie. "Not quite ready," she said, and gave it a bit more time on the clock.

"So you think I'm that easy, do you?" He tilted his head at her as if trying to decide whether she was serious or not.

Good. Let him wonder, Becca thought. "Would you like that glass of wine now?"

"What, I don't get another choice this time?"

"I'm afraid not," she said with a slight smile.

"Then, yes, I'll have a glass of wine, unless you have some bourbon. After what you just said, I need something strong sliding down my throat."

"I believe I saw a bottle of bourbon in the cabinet." She brushed by him closely, hoping he might pull her against him again, but he didn't. "Knob Creek." She turned around held up the bottle. "Will this do?"

"Perfectly. Two fingers over ice, please."

"Coming right up." She poured the drink and pressed it into his outstretched hand. "Would you like to have our cocktails out on the back deck? It's a lovely evening. We could dine alfresco if you like."

"I'm not sure what that means, but I'm hoping for naked."

Becca tossed her head back and laughed. "No, so sorry." She picked up her wineglass and raised it in salute. "But rather tempting."

Jimmy took a sip of his bourbon and then glanced over at the dining room table. "It's going to be a long time before I get that image out of my brain." He gave her a look that melted her panties. "In fact, it might remain there permanently."

"You're making it really hard to stay mad at you."

"And you're making it really hard to dislike you."

Becca laughed. "Well, I suppose it's a start." She waved her hand toward the sliding glass doors. "Shall we?"

"After you."

Becca felt his eyes upon her and hoped that her butt looked cute in the jeans. She almost laughed at her silliness, but she liked the giddy feeling of being attracted to a man. And even though she wanted to box his ears, she couldn't deny that she found Jimmy incredibly sexy. They sat down in side-by-side cushioned patio chairs facing the view of the lake. "It's gorgeous out tonight."

"I have to agree."

"Another step in the right direction, I'd say."

He turned his attention from the lake to her. "What's that?"

"Agreeing with me. I do believe it's a first."

Jimmy shook his glass, making the ice clink, and then took a sip. "You might find this hard to believe, but I'm actually pretty easygoing, Becca."

"Then why have you given me such a hard time?" She tilted her head and waited for his answer.

Jimmy looked down at his bourbon for a moment,

and then gazed back out over the lake. "I shouldn't have and I'm sorry."

"Apology accepted, but you didn't answer my question." She reached over and touched his hand, just a light touch, but she felt an instant reaction.

"I think that's a story left for another time," he said quietly. "Let's just enjoy the evening."

Becca squeezed his hand. She wanted to know what he meant, but didn't press. "When you're ready, then. Assuming you will want to see me again after you taste my attempt at preparing dinner."

"Oh, trust me—I want to see you again, and it will have nothing to do with your cooking skills."

"You're getting better in the compliments category."

"Again, just being honest." He looked at her for a lingering moment.

"Honesty is a good thing, I'd say."

"I'd say you're right." He smiled. "Here we go agreeing again. How long do you think it will last?"

"As long as you keep looking at me like that."

"Then a pretty long time."

Becca wasn't sure how to respond, and so she looked out over the water. She'd had dates here and there over the last couple of years, but mostly for events, mainly to have someone with her. She hadn't had a casual yet almost intimate evening entertaining a man in her home in a very long time. And she had to admit that she was enjoying herself immensely.

Their fingers were nearly touching where they rested on the arms of the chairs. She wanted him to reach over and hold her hand. The thought caused an ache to settle in her chest. Until that moment she hadn't realized how much she missed having a man in her life.

"You've gone quiet, Becca. Did I say something wrong?"

"No." She shook her head, but didn't risk looking at him. "That's the problem. You're saying all the right

things. Making me long for something I've not experienced in a while." *Maybe never,* she thought with a sigh.

"There's always the dining room table," he said, and
she had to laugh.

"That was the wine talking," she joked, but there was
some truth to the statement.

"Then remind me to always bring wine."

Becca leaned her head against the cushion and chuckled. Something warm and comfortable settled between
them, and just like that he reached over and held her
hand. Neither of them said anything, just sat there and
enjoyed the view, each lost in thought.

Although a feeling of peace washed over her, Becca
knew there were complications to getting involved with
Jimmy. She'd already made up her mind that her stay in
Cricket Creek was going to be an extended visit—maybe
even semipermanent—but she still had obligations in London. She planned to go back there with Garret and Mattie
when he filmed *Sing for Me.* And like Gracie, Becca loved
to travel and explore the world. And there was something
that Jimmy wasn't telling her just yet, the reason that he'd
fought his attraction from day one. Before—or if—they
took this thing between them to the next level, she wanted
to know what haunted him.

As if reading some of her thoughts, he squeezed her
hand. Unlike young love, romance at this age had its own
set of complications; the biggest was dealing with the
past. But for now Becca was going to enjoy her hand
being held on a warm summer evening by a handsome
man who suddenly oozed Southern charm. Everything
else would just have to wait.

14

Afternoon Delight

GRACE CLIMBED UP ON A BARSTOOL ARMED WITH A STICK
of chalk to draw up the beer menu. With the first of
their weekend soft openings happening tomorrow, she
was full of nervous energy. The fully furnished taproom
looked ready for action. Twenty tall stools stood around
the large bar, which jutted out into the room in a big
square, leaving a big area to move around for the bartenders. As in many taprooms, upscale smooth wooden
picnic tables were positioned in the center of the room,
with a few high-tops hugging the walls. The actual brewery was visible through a big window taking up most of
one wall, so patrons could see how the beer was being
brewed. In the far corner, Grace had set up a gift shop
filled with witch-themed glasses, T-shirts, key chains, and
baseball caps. The logo, a silhouette of a witch on a
broom, was painted on one wall with a bright yellow
background. State-of-the-art flat-screen televisions hung
suspended above the bar, and later they would add more
along the walls. Grace thought everything looked clean
and fresh, with the added whimsy of the witchcraft theme.

Luckily, Mason had been so consumed with brewing the beer that he'd finally left the marketing to her.

"Is the Belgian strong ale going to be ready for tomorrow night?" Grace looked over her shoulder for Mason.

"Yes, it's been aging for over two months, so it's ready to tap," Mason answered from where he was hanging a dartboard, and then looked over at her. "Gracie, just what the hell do you think you're doin'?"

"Writing the names of the ales on the chalkboard. We're calling the Belgian strong ale Witches' Brew, right? Holy cow, eleven percent ABV. That will cast some black magic on you in no time."

"You're gonna fall and break something. Like your fool neck."

"I'm fine," Grace said, but then wobbled. "Whoa!"

Mason was at her side in an instant. He reached up and put steadying hands around her waist. "I have a stepstool that's much safer."

"I like to live on the edge."

"Not on my watch."

"But then I wouldn't have your hands around my waist, now, would I?"

"Gracie Gordon, you're gonna be the death of me."

"Just keeping you on your toes." She leaned forward and started writing on the chalkboard. "And the American pale ale is called Under My Spell."

"Whatever." Mason groaned.

Grace gave him a look.

"Okay, if you insist. You've got me under your spell or I'd never agree to this whole witches thing."

"A hint of key lime and a citrus-hop blend," Grace said as she wrote in neat script. She looked down at him again. "Oh, come on, it's fun, and I can tell it's growing on you. You even laughed at the bike rack out front with broomsticks resting in it."

"It was either laugh or cry."

"Hey, the *Cricket Creek Courier* gave us a great article and loved the name."

"It was written by Trish Marino. A woman. A guy would have concentrated on the quality of the ale and not gone on and on about the cute logo and gift shop items."

"That's been my whole point all along. Blokes will come for darts and beer, but you needed a hook for women. With Halloween six weeks away, the grand opening is perfect timing. Don't you think?"

"What? Sorry. I was distracted by having your cute butt perched in front of my face."

Grace laughed as she finished writing. After she turned around, he lifted her down and then pressed her up against the counter. "What do you think you're doing, brewmaster?"

"Ah, well now, if I'm the master, does that mean you're my slave?"

"Yes," she answered without a hint of hesitation.

"Well, then come with me."

Powerless to say no, Grace took Mason's hand, thinking that she was the one under *his* spell, not the other way around. He pulled her into his office and shut the door. "What if someone comes in?"

"We're all alone."

"With deliveries of glasses due."

"I thought you liked living on the edge."

"Good point."

"Okay, then." Mason reached over and turned the lock. "Take off your clothes," he said in a stern tone.

"Yes, beermaster," Grace said meekly, and then tugged her Broomstick Brewery T-shirt over her head. "What now?" She loved the way his eyes lingered on her black demi-bra, which pushed her breasts up over the lace edges. A little white pearl bow was in the center, demure and sexy at the same time. She'd recently taken a trip to a new lingerie boutique that just opened up in Wedding Row and had gone on a fun shopping spree. Grace leaned up against the wall and let him look his fill. "Do you like it?"

"Oh yeah. Do the panties match?"

"You're assuming I'm wearing panties."

"You're killing me."

"You did mention that I'd be the death of you."

"Yeah, with slow torture."

Grace pointed to the zipper on her jeans. "Go ahead and find out."

Mason went to his knees and a moment later he tugged her skinny jeans down to her ankles. "Oh God, a thong."

"I'm not really a fan, but I'm wearing it for you."

"Thank you very much."

"I have several colors and styles."

"I will be trying to guess every time I see you."

When he leaned forward and pressed his mouth to the tiny triangle of black silk, Grace gasped and held on to his head for support. The wall felt cool against her back and this seemed so naughty in the middle of the afternoon. He toyed with the lace sides with his thumbs, sending a parade of shivers dancing down her spine. "Oh!" His warm mouth felt so sensual through the thin silk, but she wanted him against her bare skin. "Mason . . ."

"Put one of those endless legs over my shoulder." Knowing just what she wanted, he pulled the thong to the side and slid his tongue back and forth, bringing her closer and closer until waves of pleasure rippled through her. Dazed, she clung to him. He seemed to know her hot spots and found some she didn't know she had. Grace found herself being open and free with him in a way she'd never been before. She knew that it was because she was falling in love with him, and it scared her a little bit. But before she could dwell on her thoughts, he stood up and tugged his shirt over his head. After shucking his boots, he made quick work of shedding his jeans until he stood before her in black boxer briefs.

"Baby, take them off me."

"Gladly." Grace had the boxers down his legs with one swift tug. When his erection sprang forward, she put her hand around him, loving the steely hardness beneath the warm, smooth skin. "I want you," she said, and looked into his eyes while she stroked him.

"You've got me," Mason said. She could tell that his statement went beyond sex, but she wasn't ready to tell him how she felt. The last thing she wanted to do was hurt Mason, and she suddenly felt as if she was in too deep already. "Gracie, don't look at me like that," he said, but when she opened her mouth to try to ... what, explain? What could she say that he didn't already know? "Just kiss me."

"Mason," she began, but he covered her mouth with his, and she gave in to the passion. When she was in his arms, all of her fear melted away, and she told herself that this would all work out some way, somehow. When she wasn't with Mason, she was thinking about him, a sure sign that this was love and they could make this work. Couldn't they?

Mason stepped back and ran a gentle fingertip down her cheek and across her bottom lip. She smiled, thinking how it was so amazing that such a big, strong man had this tender, gentle side. "Stop thinking, Gracie. Just live in the moment and let yourself go." When she nodded, he slipped on a condom and then pulled her back into his arms. He kissed her worries right out of her brain, until all she could think about was making love to him. "Wrap one leg around my waist," he said in her ear.

"Bossy pants," she said, but immediately complied. Her breath caught when he entered her, and she clung to his shoulders. "Oh, Mason," she said. When he kissed her neck, she tilted her head to the side and thought that this was how love should be made, on impulse in the middle of the afternoon. She inhaled the scent of his aftershave ... spice, musk, and a hint of the outdoors. His silky chest hair teased her breasts, and she loved the ripple of muscle when he moved. When Grace wrapped her other leg around him, he held her up with his strong arms, big hands beneath her bum. When he pressed her back against the wall, Grace urged him on, faster, harder, until she cried out and buried her face in his shoulder. She felt him stiffen and shudder with his release, and then he laughed weakly.

"God . . ."

Grace remained wrapped around him, inhaling shaky breaths. "I know . . . that was . . . God, there are no words. Afternoon delight?"

"Delight is way too tame. Afternoon mind-blowing, amazing. I could keep going."

"Really?" She raised her eyebrows and bit her bottom lip.

Mason laughed. "I mean the description. The rest of me needs to recover. Although being with you has my body doing things I didn't know were possible. You just turn me on something fierce."

Grace laughed and then realized that he was still holding her up against the wall and she must be getting heavy. "Mason, you can put me down now, love."

Mason kissed her and then helped ease her feet back to the floor. He rested his forehead against hers as if trying to gather himself together. "That beats the hell out of a coffee break any old time."

"I'm inclined to agree with you. But now we must get back to work, Sir Brewmaster."

Mason tilted his head. "Oh, so I've been upgraded to Sir Brewmaster?"

"I do believe you deserve the lofty title."

Mason nodded and then started gathering up his clothes. "I think I like it." He gave her a lingering kiss. "I'd better get dressed before we start getting some deliveries."

"I'll pull myself together and then do some work on the Facebook page. Then I'm going to meet with Sophia and Mattie and do some last-minute tweaks with the menu. We're going to keep it simple and focus on the ale."

"Smart thinking."

"I have my moments."

He kissed her again and then brushed her hair from her face. "I like having moments with you, Gracie. And I want to have a lot more of them."

"Me too." Grace smiled, but after Mason walked out of the office, she tried not to let thoughts of her limited future in Cricket Creek get in the way of her happiness. During the launch of the brewery, she felt energized and in her element. But once everything was up and running smoothly, the challenge would end and she would crave something new. What could this lovely but laid-back town offer her that could fill that void?

"Don't think about it," she whispered as she tugged her clothes back on. But not thinking about it wasn't fair to Mason either. Grace sat down on the edge of the desk and thought about how her mother had been unhappy because the men she married lived a much different lifestyle than she wanted. But most important was that neither Rick Ruleman nor her father was ever around. Although her mother always presented a positive attitude, even in the worst of times, Grace could see the loneliness lurking in her eyes. Her mother was an amazing, successful woman and deserved happiness. Grace gripped the desk and swallowed hard. How on earth did one combine the two very different backgrounds and lifestyles without being doomed to failure?

But it can be done, a voice whispered in her head. Just look at Garret and Mattie, right? Who would have ever thought that her rebellious brother could have been tamed by a sweet-natured small-town girl? And who would have guessed that Mattie would have followed him to London on her own, prepared to live in a foreign country just to be with the man she loved?

"It can be done," she repeated firmly, planting a seed of hope in her heart. Now all she had to do was let it grow.

15
Taking Care of Business

$\mathcal{M}$ASON LOOKED AROUND THE TAPROOM FOR THE MIL-lionth time and shoved his fingers through his hair, making the shorter cut stand on end. Or maybe his hair was already standing on end and he didn't know it. Although this was a soft opening, with only close friends and family invited, his stomach decided that it would be fun to do a few flip-flops along with a few dips and turns along the way. With a groan he reached into his pocket and pulled out a roll of Tums. After popping one in his mouth, he grimaced at the chalky taste. He didn't think it was even possible to be this damned nervous. What the hell? He'd fished tournaments with thousands of dollars on the line, racing back to the weigh-in station with only seconds to spare, and hadn't been this torn up.

Mason looked across the room and spotted Grace behind the bar drying glasses. She, on the other hand, seemed to be as cool as a damned cucumber, humming along to the music, completely in her element. Everything, from the upbeat tunes being piped in through state-of-the-art speakers to the variety of appetizers paired to go with the ales, was perfectly organized and ready to go. And she'd slept like a baby last night, while he'd tossed and turned.

So what was he so uptight about? As if on cue, Grace looked up. Flipping her dish towel over her shoulder, she caught his eye and gave him a reassuring thumbs-up along with a bright smile.

Mason retuned the gesture, wishing he felt as at ease as Grace appeared. It occurred to him that he could never have pulled this off without her in a million years. When he'd decided to convert the old boathouse into a brewery, all he really thought about was brewing kick-ass, award-winning ale. All of this other promo stuff was just beyond him. His family never had to promote Mayfield Marina very much, just an ad here and there or sponsoring local events and Little League baseball teams, so this hoopla wasn't something he'd thought about. In truth, he'd been concentrating on the quality of the beer so much that he hadn't given this evening all that much thought, until, well, pretty much *now*. What had seemed so far in the future was suddenly upon him. The dream he'd been working toward for the past two years was unfolding before his eyes, so what the hell was suddenly his problem?

Mason glanced through the window to the brewery, thinking that was where he'd rather be right now instead of in all this party-atmosphere crap. Once the taproom was up and running, he'd leave the bartending to Danny and Colby, content to stay behind the scenes for the most part.

But it occurred to Mason that although he'd never been much of a party animal, unlike Danny, at one time he did enjoy the bonfires and gatherings at the marina. But back then he'd had Lauren on his arm and he'd been in a different place, a different frame of mind. But after he'd had to curtail his fishing career, he'd pulled back from everyone, including Lauren. His sullenness hadn't given her the right to cheat on him, but Mason knew that the end of their relationship was partly his own damned fault.

The difference between Lauren and Grace was that Grace had been drawing him out of his broodiness, as she called it. But the cloud that had all but disappeared suddenly hovered above his head without so much as a damned storm warning. Really bad-ass timing, for damned sure. *Shake it off,* he thought. *Shake it the hell off!*

Gracie reached behind the bar, put on a witch's hat, and struck a pose. Although Mason had to admit that she looked cute, he didn't return the second thumbs-up. Try as he might, the whole Broomstick Brewery still didn't exactly sit well with him, but he'd sort of refused to think about it and stayed in the brewery and out of the taproom. Mason knew that Gracie was right about her creative marketing plan to bring women into the fold. But now that the witch theme was staring him in the face, he felt uncertain.

But when Grace's smile faltered, he felt like an ass. She'd been working her tail off for this night, tirelessly, all the way down to having the flying-witch logo on napkins and T-shirts to give away. And while Mason truly appreciated all that she'd done for the brewery, she still drove him crazy with her need to be in control. He wanted to rein her in, but the problem was that he was so completely in love with her that he found more joy in her smiles and laughter than in squashing her ideas, many of which he found a tad out there. One of his continual worries was that his buddies were going to laugh their asses off at the witchcraft thing.

Mason's down-to-earth dad had raised his eyebrows at the Broomstick Brewery concept, but his mother was too caught up in grandma duties with Lily to care about the name. And Danny was the biggest surprise of all, buying into the whole thing, including calling his amazing chocolate porter Black Magic. Mason glanced at the logo painted on the wall and felt an unexpected flash of anger.

"Want to get out of here for a minute?" Grace called

over to him. "You look like you need a breath of fresh air."

"People will be arriving in a couple of hours," Mason protested with an edge to his tone that he didn't like but couldn't seem to stop. "Fresh air will have to wait."

Grace came from around the bar and walked his way. "Hey, you can relax. Everything is more than ready. Mattie, Sophia, and Mum will be bringing over trays of cheeses, fruit, and finger sandwiches."

"What the hell is a finger sandwich?"

"Sandwiches made of fingers." Grace laughed. "Come on, you know, fun-sized beauties that will fit on party plates. Roast beef and baby Swiss cheese, country ham on Mattie's melt-in-your-mouth biscuits, turkey with a tangy cranberry spread that's really amazing. Mattie loved getting the menu together. She plans to leave the sandwiches on Walking on Sunshine's menu, available for early happy hour as soon as she gets her liquor license and can have your ale on tap at the bistro."

Mason nodded and reminded himself that the success of the brewery was going to be an asset to more than just him. He was going to add employees at the brewery, but he would need bartenders in the taproom as well.

"Garret is going to provide some casual live music outside around the fire pit. I just looked again and the weather is going to dip down into the upper fifties, a perfect night for being outside. I checked everything off on my clipboard." She dusted her hands together and gave him another smile. "We're good to go, so you can stop with the scowls."

"When will Colby and Danny get here? Will they be enough at the bar?"

"Sophia is going to pitch in once the food is delivered, and she said that Avery offered to help out too."

"Are you paying all of them?"

"They said they work for beer and food." She gave him a nudge. "Come on, Sir Brewmaster, snap out of your mood." She snapped her fingers in front of his face.

"You've got everything under control," Mason said, but then looked away, trying to keep his odd mood from upsetting Grace. She didn't deserve it.

"Except for you." While her tone was light, Mason could hear a measure of hurt in her voice as well, and he hated to be the cause. He suddenly wished he were out on the lake fishing.

Grace put a hand on his arm. "What's wrong, love?"

"Nothing." *Everything.*

"Talk to me."

"Grace, there's nothing to say. I'm just a little bit on edge. I'm sorry," he said, but it sounded lame to his own ears.

"Hey, it's normal to be nervous for something like this. It's the night you've been working toward. But honestly, I don't see what could possibly go wrong. Tony's wife, Trish Marino, is coming by to cover the event for the *Cricket Creek Courier*. She's such a sweetie that I just know the review will be great. She's going to bring some pizza and desserts from River Row Pizza in exchange for putting some of their menus out on the tables. Nice, since they will be carrying our beer on tap soon, so it's really smart cross-promotion. I've been amazed at how the businesses support each other around here."

"Well, a few years back this town was struggling big-time. Working together was the only way to keep local mom-and-pops afloat, and as you know, the marina was one of them."

"Mason, all of Cricket Creek is proud to have a craft brewery here. It's a perfect addition to the town, when you think about it. You should feel so good about adding this sweet operation that will enhance the lives of locals and attract tourists. Everybody wins. Especially you."

"If not for you, I might not be up and running," Mason said, trying to give her the props that she deserved, but his tone came out stilted and all wrong.

"Oh wow." Grace shook her head and then dropped her hand from his arm. "I get it now," she said quietly. "I forced this Broomstick Brewery theme on you and now you resent me for it. And now that the opening is upon us, the realization is smacking you in the face."

"You know I was dead set against the witches theme from the beginning. I didn't pull any punches."

Grace waved her hand in an arc. "This isn't a whim. You know damned well that I put lots of research into this marketing plan. You have to have a hook. Have to stand out."

"Oh, it stands out."

"Everybody else thinks it's brilliant."

Mason remained silent.

"Except you. If you hated it this much, why on earth didn't you stop me?"

"Are you kidding me?" Mason looked up at the ceiling and then back at her. "You were impossible to stop. And I haven't forgotten that you're the boss of marketing."

Grace gasped. "Oh, so *that's* what this is all about? Listen, when you signed on the dotted line, we became a team. I don't know squat about brewing beer and you don't know a thing about marketing." She patted her chest with the flying-witch logo on the front so hard that her hat slid to the side. "A team! I'm not your boss. I'm in charge of marketing. And you said that you wanted to protect Shane McCray's investment. That meant coming up with something creative and memorable. Drawing in women who already love craft beer and especially those who haven't given it a try. We talked about it! You know all of this. I can't believe you're saying this rubbish to me right now! What's gotten into you, Mason? This isn't like you at all."

He couldn't answer because he didn't know.

"Wow." She tossed her hat at him. "All right, then. I'm out of here." Grace turned and then stomped away. She walked through the door without looking back, and he didn't blame her.

Follow her, a voice shouted in his head. But like a

dumb-ass, he stood there, feet planted, arms folded, and watched the woman he loved go out the door. He looked down at the hat and uttered an expletive that his mother would box his ears for saying.

Mason knew, of course, what had gotten into him. The soft opening was going to be hectic and could quickly turn into a zoo. Although they'd invited a couple of hundred friends and family in an open-house kind of coming-and-going way, he also knew that word spreads like wildfire in a small town and they'd likely have at least a hundred more party crashers. He'd warned Grace that this would likely happen, but she'd shrugged it off, promising that they were prepared for extras and when the beer ran out the party would be over, plain and simple. Leaving people wanting more was part of the supply-and-demand game anyway.

Mason was still standing there in the middle of the room when Danny strolled in. Rusty trotted in with him and came over to have his ears scratched. "Hey there, boy. Sorry I've been so busy lately. What's up, Danny?"

"I just passed Grace heading out, and she didn't look happy. What's up, bro?"

"I was an ass."

Danny looked down at the hat and picked it up off the floor. "What the hell? Why?"

Mason shrugged. "Nerves. I'm a fucking shit show. I took it out on her." He pointed to the witch on the wall. "I told her I couldn't stand the logo. Bad timing."

"Ya think?"

Mason shot him a look.

"Do you really hate it, though?"

"Danny, I hate this crap." He walked over to the bar and sat down heavily on one of the stools. "This place isn't what I expected it would be. Why did I let her call all of the marketing shots?"

"She took over marketing, networking, social media, the parts that you suck at. And she happens to be a genius at it. She landed several articles in the local paper.

Did you know that you have over ten thousand likes on your Facebook page? And lots of them are women."

"I've got more important things to do than jack around on Facebook and Tweeter."

"Twitter."

"Whatever. It's all a bunch of bull."

"Mason, you don't have a clue how important this is nowadays."

"I do, Danny. I just don't like it."

"Well, get with the program. On the grand-opening night, Grace said we'll have the local TV news here. *Southern Way* magazine is interested in doing a huge spread. Mason, the only problem you're gonna have is keeping up with the production."

"How do you know all of this?"

"While you buried yourself in the brewery, I talked to Grace. I'm impressed with her, Mason. She came up with the presale of custom growlers and the special bomber cup that will sell out in no time. Her idea to rotate the beers throughout the night is great. I can't wait to try the coffee stout."

"You mean Morning Magic."

Danny laughed. "I like all of those clever names. When did you lose your sense of humor? Damn. Lighten the hell up."

Mason scowled but silently acknowledged that Danny was right. Somehow Gracie had gotten him laughing again. "This isn't just fun and games. What if I can't keep up? This is the kind of stress that landed Dad in the hospital with a heart attack. I do discuss things with Gracie, but, Danny, she's talking expansion already. It's blowing my mind. I didn't sign for this shit, and I let her do this to me."

"You didn't let her to do anything you didn't want deep down. I know you better than that. Quit being such a girl." Danny went behind the bar. "What beer do you want? Or should I get you something with an umbrella?"

"Ha, funny."

"So what will it be?"

"Belgian strong ale . . . Oh wait." He looked up at the chalkboard. "Under My Spell."

"Comin' right up."

After Danny slid the glass his way, Mason took a swallow and then put it down, since the flavors of this strong ale opened up as the beer sat. "Did you know that Grace is offering scoops of vanilla ice cream to add to the milk stout . . . Oh wait. Witch's Milk."

"I think that a scoop of vanilla ice cream sounds awesome with the full-bodied, roasted flavor. I want to try it, and so will everyone else. Ha-ha! My kind of milk shake. Come on, dude, you know you want to try it too. Did you forget this is handcrafted beer? You're supposed to be creative."

Mason made a face.

"When did you become so damned boring? Do you need to winter in Florida with Mom and Dad?"

"And when did you become so metrosexual?"

"Yeah, right." Danny pointed to his camo hat, faded jeans, and scuffed work boots. "That's me, all right." Danny took a swallow of his ale and then leaned his elbows on the bar. Rusty chimed in with a bark as if agreeing with Danny. "You know what?"

"No, but I think you're about to tell me. When did everybody decide to stick their nose into my business?"

Danny pointed a finger at him and jabbed. "This really isn't about the witch theme. It's about Grace leaving. Now that this is all running smoothly, you're worried that she will move on. Admit it."

"It's not . . . Wait—did she say she was leaving?" Mason felt his heart plunge to his toes. "When?"

"I meant from the beginning, Mason."

Relief flooded his brain. For a minute he thought he'd chased her away. "And you're the jackass who told me to take a chance and give her a reason to stay."

"Being a dick to her isn't part of the plan. But I get it."

"Really? What do you get?"

"Getting her pissed at you solves all of your problems. Push her away and you don't have to put your stupid-ass heart on the line anymore. You're a big chickenshit."

"It was my initial plan, but that went out the window a while ago. So you don't know everything."

"Then what's your deal? Have you lost your mind?"

"Hey, you'd better watch out, baby brother. I can still take you."

"In your dreams."

Mason looked down at his beer, knowing full well that Danny had hit the damned nail right on its stupid head.

"So are you going after her?"

"I have things to do!"

"Yeah, and first on the list is to go after the girl you're crazy about and tell her you were being a total shithead."

"Look, I know you're right." Mason sighed. "But you know what, Danny?"

"What?"

"Sometimes I see her staring off into space like she's daydreaming of where she'll go next. As soon as this is up and running full speed, what is there to keep her here? I'm guessing that Becca will head back to London and that Sophia will return to her job in New York."

"*You*, bro. Why the hell can't you get that through your thick skull?"

Mason shook his head. "Right. Even if I have the ability to keep her here, it would suffocate her to stay in one place. She said that she needs constant change and challenge. Where is she going to find that in Cricket Creek? I shoved all of that worry under the rug, but it's still there."

Danny raised his arms akimbo. "Expand. Make this brewery into something way bigger than what you even intended." He held up his glass. "Mason, you have a knack for brewing beer. It's like Spidey sense when it comes to combining just the right ingredients. Grace is right. You could go way beyond the restaurants in Cricket Creek and even the baseball park." Danny pointed to the window, where the brewery could be seen. "Your production brew house can produce close to a thousand gallons of beer a day. That's a hundred and eighty kegs or, like, ten thousand twelve-ounce cans of beer. And you situated the equipment so you could double the production if you want to expand. Mason, you had big dreams in the beginning. Why change now?"

"It changed when I found myself in way over my head. That's not a cool feeling. Danny, the stress I was feeling was keeping me up at night. It sucks to feel that way. I don't want to live each day wondering how the hell I'm going to pull it off or go under. You know how it felt when we were just scraping by with the marina. It was driving Dad to an early grave. I don't want to live like that. I won't live like that."

"Yeah, but we saved Mayfield Marina. We all put our lives on hold, including Mattie and especially you. I know you don't talk about it, but it cost you your fishing career." He held his thumb and index finger apart. "You were this close to making it to the top, and the hiatus you took cost you big-time."

"You did the same thing, Danny."

"I quit school, but I wasn't on the brink of achieving my dream," he said, but shifted his gaze.

Mason pointed to the handcrafted bar. "Danny, you also have a talent for woodworking that needs to be pursued as more than just a hobby. Just look at this bar. And the addition to the bistro is amazing."

Danny shrugged. "Not enough hours in the day. We all wanted to save the marina. I have to ask, though; if you could go back in time, would you have had it any other way?"

"No. And if I'm honest, being on the road was becoming such a grind. I like it here," Mason said. "I'm not a traveler, a wanderer, like Gracie. I mean, sure, sometimes I do wonder how much I could have achieved in pro fishing. But whatever. Maybe it's a thank-God-for-unanswered-prayers kind of thing. I have given it some thought, though."

"I hate to ask, but does that wondering-what-if include Lauren?"

Mason inhaled deeply. At one time thinking about her caused a hot rush of emotion. "What she did to me hurt like hell and kept me from wanting another relationship."

"And now?"

"Now I realize we weren't right for each other."

"Because being with Grace feels different?"

"She drives me crazy," Mason said, but chuckled. "But yeah." He looked around the brewery and shook his head. "Is this really happening? I can't really believe it."

Danny pushed back from the bar and pointed at Mason. "This is your time to shine. Don't let fear hold you back. This can be something special. I can feel it."

"You're talking about the brewery, right?"

"Not entirely. Look, if Grace is the woman for you, go after her, no-holds-barred, just like I said. Let her decide whether she wants to stay or hit the road after she's done here. You're already past the getting-hurt stage, so what do you have to lose?"

"Yeah, but I just hurt the hell out of her already. And I feel sick about it. Danny, I might have done more damage than I can repair." The thought made his stomach churn. "God . . ."

"Just get her back down here and enjoy the night together. You both deserve it. Sometimes you gotta risk it for the biscuit. Go for it, Mason. Tell Grace you're on board with all of this and more."

"I can't go that far. Right now I'm perfectly happy to use the pilot system to perfect the hops and additives and use the small-batch brew house. I'm telling you, I don't want to grow too quickly. Let me get used to the witches thing first."

"Okay, I get that, and trust me—I don't want you to feel the stress that Dad did."

Mason felt a lump of emotion form in his throat. "But I didn't need to take my frustration out on Gracie that way."

"Dude, she's been working nonstop."

"I know."

"Go get the girl before it's too late." Danny pointed to where Rusty slept on the cool floor. "Even Rusty knew when to make the big move and go after Abigail." Rusty lifted his head at the mention of his name. The Irish setter looked over at Mason with eyes that seemed to agree with Danny.

"Are you both trying to make me feel worse?"

"Yes. Is it working? Mason, everyone has been looking forward to tonight. Don't mess it up. Just look around at how sweet this place is. If you didn't own it, I'd still come here. You'd be here too."

Mason sighed, knowing his brother was right.

"And Mom's been watching Lily so Mattie could work on the menu for tonight. Becca has pitched in big-time too. A hell of a lot of thought has gone into all of this."

"Uppity stuff like finger sandwiches."

"Are you kidding me? I had, like, ten while they were making them, and they are awesome. I tried some Vermont cheddar dip that's kick-ass. Shane McCray smoked some fall-off-the-bone ribs that are ready to roll. They've got crisp shoestring fries and onion rings. It's going to be awesome. You should be having the time of your life today, and celebrating the moment with Grace. You're fucking up something that's pretty hard to wreck. I don't even think I could do a better job, and you know my track record at being a screwup."

"Shit." Mason closed his eyes, remembering what he'd said to Grace about sharing moments with her. "I'm such an idiot."

"Uh, yeah."

"You didn't have to agree with me."

"Mason, you've always been the king of moodiness. Getting you to smile is a major feat."

Gracie makes me smile, he thought. Made him laugh. "What's up with that?"

"Because I'm the oldest." Mason tapped his chest. "I worry. It's in the job description." After taking another swig of his ale, he nodded. "This is some damn good ale." He thought that the Vermont cheddar dip was going to go perfectly with the flavors. Pairing food with craft beer was becoming as popular as pairing wine with food. Grace was right and so was Danny. What he was fighting, he should be embracing.

"This goes beyond Grace leaving, doesn't it?"

"Danny, you know I've kept my guard up after Lauren. Like I said, I know now that she was all wrong for me, but having her cheat put me in a dark place that had me losing friends and worried my family. And yet I'm stupid enough to fall for a woman who never planned on staying here . . . Oh yeah, and she lives on the other side of the damned ocean. I don't want to visit that dark-ass place again."

"Last time I looked, she lived in a cabin out in the middle of the river right here at Mayfield Marina." He angled his head toward the door. "Now, get your ass over there and say you're sorry and make her not want to cross that ocean."

"I hate it when you're right."

"I'm right a lot more than I get credit for." Danny grinned, but being the youngest and always a daredevil, his little brother probably wasn't taken as seriously as he sometimes should have been. "Now, would you just go!"

Rusty barked and trotted over to the door.

Mason raised his hands in surrender. "Yes!"

16

About a Boy

"MUM, QUIT GIVING ME YOUR WORRIED-MOTHER LOOK. I told you I'm perfectly fine." Grace picked up an artfully displayed tray of cheese, fruit, and crackers. She put it in Mattie's new delivery van before turning to give her mother a bright smile.

Becca fisted her hands on her hips. "Right, that's the biggest fake smile I've ever seen."

Grace kept the smile in place and pointed to her lips. "Totally real."

"You can't fool me, Gracie. I've had to put enough fake smiles on my own face to know what's genuine or forced. And yours is forced. So what's bothering you? Everyone seems to be ready for the tasting party. And super excited, I might add."

"Ha, except for one important person."

"You? Whyever not?"

Grace turned away from the van. She needed to go inside for more food, but she paused to answer her mother. "No, I was referring to the broody brewmaster himself, Mason Mayfield."

"Oh, so we have boy trouble." Becca pressed her lips together and nodded.

"Mum, I'm twenty-eight years old. I no longer have 'boy trouble,'" she said, using air quotes.

"Okay, but I can see in your eyes that something is terribly wrong. Please tell me, darling." Her worried-mum look intensified.

"I can't, Mum. I have to get that food down to the brewery." If she started talking about Mason, she feared that she'd start crying and ruin her carefully applied makeup. She'd gone back to her cabin and changed into black palazzo pants and a white tank sporting the Broomstick Brewery logo along with a black silk blouse open but knotted at the waist. Then she'd quickly headed over to Sophia's flat just in case Mason decided to pay her a visit and give her a much deserved *I'm sorry for being a jerk*, because Grace certainly wasn't ready to accept his apology. "I don't want the appetizers to spoil," she said just as Jimmy Topmiller walked out of the bistro with another tray of food. She'd met him one afternoon when he'd stopped by the brewery for a tour.

"Jimmy, would you mind delivering the appetizers to the brewery?" Becca asked.

"Not at all," Jimmy replied, and then smiled at Grace. "You can relax for a few minutes, Grace."

"Oh, thank you so much," Grace said, liking his Southern charm.

"No problem," Jimmy added and leaned forward slightly, as if he was going to kiss Becca on the cheek, but then pulled back.

"Thank you, love. You're a dear," Becca said. Her gaze lingered on him and the soft expression had Grace wondering what was going on between her mother and Jimmy.

Once Jimmy drove away, Grace turned to her mother. "Mum, are you seeing him?"

Becca put a hand to her chest. "No . . . well . . . of

course, I *see* him. He does live directly across the lake, you know."

"Mincing words, are we?" Grace grinned in spite of her crappy mood. "When you mince, that always means yes. Confess."

"I dunno, really." Becca shrugged, and then bit her bottom lip and blushed. "I . . . we . . ."

"Are a thing," Grace provided for her tongue-tied mother. It was rare to witness Becca Gordon flustered, and Grace thought it was cute that her mother was blushing bright pink.

"A thing?" Becca nodded hard. "Yes, I do suppose . . . a *thing* is a good way to put it." She motioned to the brick-paved patio at the side of the bistro. "Come have a chat with me, darling. You can spare your mum a few minutes."

"Do I have a choice?"

"Of course you do," Becca said in her polite way, but she really meant no, you must tell me what's going on.

"Okay." Grace nodded, not only because she really needed to talk to her mother but also because it would buy her more time before she headed down to the brewery. They sat down at a teak bistro table beneath a pretty violet-striped awning. Mattie had an abundance of flowers overflowing from window boxes, and the view of the river was simply gorgeous. "It is really so pretty here," Grace said, and Becca nodded her agreement. "There's just something about a marina and boats, you know?"

"You really aren't very good at attempting to beat around the bush."

"I thought I'd give it a go." Grace leaned forward. "So tell me about your *thing* with the handsome, helpful fishing guide."

"He is a bit handsome, isn't he?" Becca waved a dismissive hand. "But we're just, you know, hanging out," she added quickly. "That kind of . . . *thing*."

"Right. He was totally going to plant a kiss on you and then remembered I was standing right there, and he had a maybe-I-shouldn't moment."

"No, he wasn't."

"Mum . . ."

"Hey, you're just as rotten at changing the subject as you are at beating around the bush. This is about you, darling. We'll talk about me later." She folded her hands, leaned back in the chair, and waited.

Grace closed her eyes and inhaled a deep breath. "I don't know where to begin."

"Are you in love with this boy?"

Grace thought about denying it, but her mother would see right through her. "Yes," she answered softly. "I suppose I am. I mean, I've never felt this way before. I must say, it's a bit overwhelming."

"And does Mason love you?"

"I . . . I think so." Grace rolled her eyes up to the light blue sky and studied the puffy white clouds, thinking one looked just like Winnie-the-Pooh. "I thought he wanted me to stay here in Cricket Creek," she said absently.

"Why would you think otherwise?"

"By the way he treated me this afternoon." Grace frowned up at the sky. "He did everything in his power to push me away. Why would he do that to someone he has feelings for?"

"Open-house jitters? You've been with me at fashion shows when I'm going crazy. Maybe you need to cut him a bit of slack."

"Mum, you're the queen of making excuses for men who don't deserve it."

"I suppose you're right." Becca looked at her for a long moment and then inhaled sharply. "Oh, don't get me wrong. I don't ever—and I do mean *ever*—want you to be talked to or treated in any other way than with the utmost respect. Did he disrespect you?"

Grace shook his head. "No, never, but he just let me know how much he hated the Broomstick Brewery logo and said that I forced the whole thing upon him."

"Did you?"

Grace raised her hands skyward. "I didn't think so . . .

but maybe a little bit. But this is what I'm good at. Drawing in a demographic that's being ignored in the marketplace. And I know I'm spot-on. Women—"

"Gracie, you don't have to explain. But don't you get it? This was his dream, and you swooped in and took over. This all happened very fast, and his head is probably spinning."

Grace gasped and flattened her hands against the table. "Um, I swooped in and saved the day, I'll have you know."

"Something Mason had to swallow his pride for him to allow you to do." Becca reached over and patted Grace's hand. "Put yourself in his shoes, or should I say *boots*?"

"He had an excellent product, but no feasible marketing plan."

"Mason probably didn't know he needed one."

"Mum, the market is saturated. Just like with cosmetics. You have to stand out! Do something clever. Smart."

"Oh, darling, I agree, but that's not the issue here. His beer is named after witches and he doesn't like it. He's probably been too busy to even think about it until today was suddenly here."

"Well, it's too bloody late to go back now." She toyed with the tail of her braid, close to tears that she didn't want to spill. "I wish to hell I'd never gotten involved."

"As you said, it's too late now."

Grace groaned. "I know. Now what am I going to do?"

"Are we talking about the brewery or Mason?" Becca asked gently.

"The brewery!" Grace raised her hands skyward and then shook her head so hard that her braid flipped back and forth. "No, you know what?" she asked, with more than a little heat behind her words, but didn't pause for an answer. "If I hadn't been at the right place at the right time for Mason, he was going to likely go under. And even with my investment, if not marketed well and promoted in the right way, in the end the money wouldn't have mattered. So like the logo or not, it was necessary, so I refuse to feel guilt. Sod that!"

"And you shouldn't. I wasn't suggesting fault on your end, only shedding light on how Mason might be feeling right now."

"And, Mum, I wanted to help. After all, Mason is Mattie's brother. But I'm not going to *not* make the most of my investment either. He's just going to have to get over himself."

"Oh, darling, I think he can do that." She pressed her lips together and gave Grace a level look.

"You have more to say . . . so say it."

"All right, then. I think Mason's worried that he won't be able to get over *you*."

Grace ran her hand over the smooth teak, trying to keep her tears in check. After clearing her throat, she said, "And that's why I shouldn't have gotten involved with Mason in the first place. I knew it was a mistake, and because we're having this discussion, it only proves that I'm right . . . or wrong, depending how you look at it." She took a shaky breath. "I knew it was bloody stupid. What's wrong with my brain these days?"

"Ah, Gracie, we can have control over lots of things in life, but not our feelings. You can fight what's in your heart, but it doesn't change the fact that it's there. You can't stop yourself from loving . . . from caring."

"I understand, but I should have never given in."

"And let love win?"

"No! Now I'm one hot mess, and I don't have a clue what to do about it."

"You could move here, you know. After selling Girl Code, there's nothing to keep you living in London." She pointed to the view. "And Cricket Creek is a lovely town with a lot to offer. Sports, theater, shopping, restaurants; not to mention everyone you care about is here. At least for now."

"No doubt, but you know I could never settle down in one place."

Becca shook her head. "I don't know that at all, and quite frankly, neither do you."

"Mum . . . come on, now," she protested, but her mother merely shrugged.

"Sometimes the things we believe about ourselves are the furthest from the actual truth."

"Did you read that from a fortune cookie?" Grace joked because her mother was hitting way too close for comfort.

Becca smiled. "No, but worth putting in one, I'd say. Actually, it's from experience."

Grace mulled that over while she watched a delicate sailboat glide across the water. Rusty, Mason's Irish setter, ran across the lawn chasing a bird. "Poor thing, he's never going to catch that bird."

"Ah, but it's in his nature to give it all he's got." Becca pointed to Abigail, his little beagle-mix lady companion, who sat in the grass watching Rusty, waiting for his empty-handed return. "I see them frolicking around the marina all over the place, even up by me. I know he belongs to Mason, but he can't seem to leave Abigail's side, and so he stays down here most of the time. Look at them. So very different, and yet inseparable."

"Mum . . ." Grace shot her mother a look. "What are you getting at?"

"Just an observation." She pressed her lips together and then lifted her chin. "Okay, I'll just come right out and say it. Different like you and Mason."

Grace tapped her cheek and then arched an eyebrow. "Hmm, country boy and city girl like you and Jimmy?"

"Changing the subject again, are we?"

"I'm curious about you and your *thing*."

"Oh, Jimmy and I are more alike than what you might imagine. And, darling, don't forget that your mum came from working-class London."

"So do you think there's a chance for you two?"

Becca glanced away, as if not willing to be in the hot seat. But she surprised the hell out of Grace by looking at her and nodding. "You know what? He might not think so, but, yes," she said firmly. "Yes, I do."

"You don't say." Grace leaned back in her chair, a bit stunned.

"I think I just did," Becca said with a slow smile. She splayed a hand across her chest. "Oh wow, Gracie, I do believe I'm . . . in love." Her eyes widened a fraction, and then she laughed with pure delight. "Can that be so?"

Grace's heart pounded with joy. "Of course! So . . . so what are you going to do about it? Tell him?"

"Oh heavens, I dunno. Isn't the man supposed to say those three little words first? And isn't it far too early for such sentiments?" She looked at Grace and shook her head. "And when did this discussion become about me?"

"Just now," Grace said and smiled at her mother. "And it's about time that you thought about yourself and your happiness."

Becca's eyes misted over and she put a hand to her mouth. After a hushed moment, she looked over at Grace. "I do believe you're right."

"Mum, for the record, I don't think any of those rules apply anymore. Didn't you just say that you can fight it but not change what's in your heart?"

"Well, this discussion certainly took a turn I didn't expect." She said it lightly, but there was a punch of emotion behind her mother's admission.

"No, I think you needed to tell me. I want you to be happy, and you should follow your own advice."

Becca brushed at a tear. "You know what? I think that holding Lily just opened up my heart to look at my life from a different angle and to embrace love again."

"Then, go for it."

"Ha, I've never been good at following my own advice."

"But you've never followed rules either."

Becca smiled. "Ah, so true," she said, but then her smile faltered.

"What, Mum?"

"There's something in his past that he's not telling me. Something that caused pain, I'm afraid."

"Ask him. Whatever it is, you need to know before you can go forward."

"I did. I suppose he will tell me when the time is right." She looked at Grace. "Now back to you."

"After that bombshell?" Grace heard her phone ring and knew it was going to be Mason. She was right. She silenced her ringtone.

"Mason?"

"Yes." She almost smiled.

"Are you going to answer him?"

"I'm going to ignore him and give him the cold shoulder at the tasting party."

"And what good can that do for anybody, you included? Some sort of misguided satisfaction? What if he says he's sorry and has been a wanker?"

Grace laughed. "He won't say wanker."

"Jackass."

"Douche bag."

"Oh how horrid." Becca grimaced. "Okay—well?"

"I'd cave in, of course. Why do you think I've been avoiding him for the past couple of hours?"

"You need to be at the event, Gracie."

"Um, yeah, and maybe he should realize the hard way that I need to be there."

"He already knows that, darling. This isn't about him wanting you to stay. That's a given. This is about you thinking that you need to leave."

"I don't think it. I know it. What's that old saying about a zebra not being able to change its stripes, or something like that?"

"Oh, that silly saying doesn't hold water with me. Love changes things, Gracie. I know you're thinking of me and Rick and me and your father. Funny, but I used to view those marriages as failures, but they were part of my journey." She tapped her chest. "Part of what made me who I am right now. I don't have regrets, really. Changing the past would mean I wouldn't have my three lovely children and my adorable Lily."

"Did you love Rick?"

She looked off into the distance for a moment. "Madly."

"So what went wrong?"

"I resented his absence. I guess you could say that I was jealous of his music. Perhaps if I'd gone on the road with him like he asked, he wouldn't have gotten out of control and he would have bonded with Garret early on. I didn't say that I didn't make mistakes. We all do. But I don't have regrets. Does that make sense? Besides, we can't change the past anyway, so what good does it do to dwell upon it?"

"You're right." Grace nodded. "What about Dad? Did you love him?"

"Oh, I thought so. Marcus was so very different from Rick, and I suppose that was the initial attraction. Instead of a wild rocker, I had a buttoned-up businessman. But as you know, your father loved making money more than spending time with his family. Pity, really. He's missed out on a lot. I just don't think he was meant to settle down. Marcus does love you and Sophia in his own way. And Garret too, really. He just doesn't know how to be a father. We grew apart early on and stayed together out of . . . convenience, I suppose."

Grace felt icy fingers of fear slide down her back. "Sometimes I'm afraid I'm like him."

"You've never worshipped money, darling. Far from it."

"But what if I can't settle down?"

"Maybe you need to give yourself the chance to find out."

"And break Mason's heart in the process?"

"It sounds like it's a risk he's willing to take. Now, get

down there and have fun. I'm going to watch Lily so that Miranda can attend her son's big night. Are you okay with that?" she asked, and stood up.

"Of course." Grace pushed her chair back and gave her mother a hug. "I love you so much."

"And I love you, Gracie. And I am also so very proud of you. Not just of your achievements, but of the lovely person you've become. I'll be here for you, whatever you decide."

"I always know that I can count on you." She tilted her head and chuckled.

"What?"

"Wouldn't it just be something if we all ended up living in a small town in Kentucky?"

Becca tossed her head back and laughed. "Yes, indeed, it certainly would. And it's charming here. Now, go meet your prince at the witches' ball."

"Oh, I don't plan on making it easy on him. If he wants me, he's going to have to work really hard."

"That's okay. Makeup sex is the best."

"Mum! I can't believe you just said that."

"Well, you know what? Maybe I'm a bit tired of being so prim and proper. I think I'll buy me some cowboy boots, let my hair down, and live a little."

"You're a grandma now."

"All the more reason. I'm not going to live forever."

"Mum!"

"Will you quit saying that like I'm some kind of loony toon?"

"Then stop talking about sex and dying." Grace stuck her fingers in her ears.

Becca laughed. "It's so fun getting you riled up."

"Why does everyone say that?" she sputtered, but then laughed. "I don't have answers for this crazy life of mine. But you've made me feel much better."

Becca cupped Grace's cheeks. "It was easy when you all were children and I could fix things with a lollipop and a hug."

Grace kissed her mum's cheek. "You're here and that's enough, but I'll never turn down a lollipop or a hug. Okay, I'm off to the party. Wish me luck."

"Somehow, I don't think you'll need it, but good luck anyway."

Grace blew her mother a kiss over her shoulder and gave her one last smile, but her heart skipped a beat as she walked over to her car. After all of her boasting about how tonight's event would be the talk of the town, she'd have egg on her face if Broomstick Brewery flopped.

After starting the engine, she squeezed the steering wheel for a moment, and then put the car in drive. Well, she was about to find out.

17

Shameless

ALL NIGHT LONG AT THE PARTY, GRACE KEPT SLIPPING away from Mason like quicksilver, almost as if she had some sort of superpower. Every damned time he got within arm's length of her, she managed to elude him, and he damned well knew it was on purpose. Mason tried catching her eye, called her phone, and at one desperate point considered following her into the ladies' room. He stopped when he got an odd look from a patron and gazed at the witch's sign on the door as if in surprise. "That was close," he said, and walked across the hallway to the warlocks.

And of course Grace looked gorgeous . . . no, stunning, a fact that didn't go unnoticed by every male in the room. Mason wanted to drape his arm around her shoulders and stake his claim, but that was damned difficult when he couldn't get close to her.

Laughter and music filled the taproom. Mattie's food complemented the ales, which flowed from the taps as fast as Danny, Colby, and Avery could pour. The tasting by any standard was a huge success, and Mason and Grace should have been sharing this success together.

Why he had the meltdown earlier had him so pissed off at himself that he could hardly see straight, and it had nothing to do with the ale he'd consumed.

After only a couple of hours into the night, the gift shop shelves were sold out and just about every woman in the room wore one of the witches' hats. About one million selfies were taken of witches riding the broomsticks parked outside. There was no doubt that the theme captured the festive feel that Grace was aiming for—and there was no doubt that without it, not nearly as many women would be in attendance.

Grace knew her stuff.

Mason almost pinned Grace down while she chatted with Trish Marino for the newspaper article, but just as he approached, Grace excused herself and headed outside. Trish grabbed him and asked a slew of questions. He hoped he sounded somewhat intelligent, because his mind sure was elsewhere. He was eager to get outside and resume his search for his elusive girlfriend, and when he found her, he planned to pull her into his arms and tell her what a fool he'd been.

Mason weaved his way through the crowd. Once again, Grace seemed to disappear, and of course the whole witch's hat thing made it difficult for him to locate her. Every couple of steps someone stopped him and raved over the ales, the food, and the fun atmosphere. Nice, thank you very much, but he was on a mission.

Ah, Mason finally spotted Grace by the bonfire listening to Shane McCray play an acoustic set, much to the delight of the crowd. Laura Lee, his wife of just a few months, watched with adoring eyes, and Mason had to smile in spite of himself. He stood there for a moment, trying to gather his thoughts, knowing Gracie would stay put at least until the end of the song.

"What's that frown all about, Mason? Tonight is your big night."

Mason turned from looking across the lawn at Gracie and spotted Jimmy Topmiller at his side. Mason lifted one shoulder, but when he heard Gracie's laughter, he turned his head in her direction.

"You need some help with the right bait?" Jimmy asked with a little nudge of his elbow into Mason's ribs.

"I'm not fishin' at the moment, Jimmy."

"Oh, son, you're fishin', just not catchin'."

"I'm not sure I follow."

"I haven't seen you and Grace together all night long." Jimmy rocked back on his boots and grinned. "It's been my experience that when you want a woman to take notice, all you gotta do is make her jealous," Jimmy said, capturing Mason's full attention. "So toss some bait into the water and reel Grace Gordon in."

"Are you kiddin'? I'm already in the damned doghouse. Somehow, I don't think that angle will fly," Mason said. "But I'm listening, because at this point I'm desperate. So shoot."

Jimmy jammed his thumb over his shoulder. "Just march over to those witch wannabes close to where Grace is standing and let the flirting begin."

"Ah, flirting with other women doesn't seem like a good tactic," Mason said, but at this point he really was willing to try anything. Anything at all. "Shameless" started playing in his head. One thing he knew for sure. He didn't want to lose Grace before getting the chance to have her in his life. The emptiness he felt after she walked out of the brewery wasn't something he thought he could stand, and it scared the shit out of him.

"They will flirt their cute asses off with you. When women drink, they flirt. It just happens like magic. And let me tell you, that craft beer of yours will do the trick. About this time of night, the beer goggles go on. Hell, they'd even flirt with Bubba Brown. A pretty boy like you is a shoo-in."

Mason had to chuckle. "You tell it like it is, Jimmy."

"Yep, I've always been a straight shooter. Now, head over there and let them do the work for you. And you can be completely innocent. Oh, and flash that smile you like to keep in reserve."

"Seriously?" Mason looked at Jimmy, who seemed pretty confident. "So you think this will work?"

"Like a charm."

"If it doesn't, I'm gonna hunt you down like a dog."

Jimmy laughed. "Well, let me know how it turns out for you. I'm gonna go help Becca babysit little Lily."

Mason was taken off guard. "Really, Jimmy? You and Becca seein' each other seriously?"

Jimmy scuffed the toe of his boot across the grass. "Casual. We get a kick out of getting on each other's nerves," Jimmy answered, but Mason got the distinct impression his feelings went deeper than he was willing to admit. Jimmy clamped his hand on Mason's shoulder and gave him a little shove. "Come on, a supermodel and an old fisherman like me?"

"Old fisherman? You mean world-class pro angler? You were my idol and Danny says you still have the golden touch."

"Would ya quit makin' me feel so damned old?"

"You're seeing a supermodel. 'Nuf said."

"Naw." Jimmy shrugged. "As I said, we like to bust each other's chops. Besides, won't Grace, Sophia, and Becca be leaving Cricket Creek at some point anyway?" While Jimmy's tone remained casual, his gaze sharpened, making Mason wonder if Jimmy had the same fear that he did.

"Well, unless we give 'em a reason to stay, like Danny keeps preaching to me."

"Smart guy, your brother."

"That's what he keeps telling me. But maybe easier said than done."

Jimmy shrugged again. "Best get on over there before Shane is done singing and the group of witches heads back inside for more Black Magic. And they've already had quite a few, judging by how loud they're getting."

Mason swallowed hard. "Okay, here goes nothin'." He walked over to the group of women and gave them what he hoped was a winning smile. "Evenin', ladies. I'm Mason Mayfield, brewmaster. Hope you're enjoying Broomstick Brewery."

"Such a clever idea!" said a wavy-haired redhead as she pulled him to the side. "And I just love the names of the ales. I'm Mary, and you could be my master anytime you like," she said in what sounded like maybe a New York accent.

Mason decided to ignore the suggestive part of her comment. "Why, thank you. Looks like you're having a sample of Black Magic, the chocolate porter. What do you think?"

Mary took another step closer and tilted her head up. "Oh, it's to die for. Chocolate and beer together? I daresay that I'm in heaven." She batted her eyes at him.

"You don't sound like you're from Cricket Creek, Mary," he said, trying to be polite. Was Gracie watching? How did he look without being obvious?

"I'm originally from New York." She waved a hand. "Up from Florida for a visit with friends."

"Ah, well, welcome to Broomstick Brewery, Mary. And who are your friends?" he asked, and noticed that they didn't seem too happy about not being part of the conversation.

"My friends?"

"Over there."

"Oh, them." Mary seemed reluctant to share him, but waved a hand in their general direction and they immediately came over. "Patsy, Deb, Cathy, Jen, Patricia, and Teresa. There, now you know. Who needs them when you have me?" Mary grabbed Mason's arm and steered him away, but Jen stepped forward and nudged Mary out of the way. Mary shot her a glare, and Mason suddenly felt as if he were on *The Bachelor* and a catfight was about to begin.

"I'm Jen," she said, leaning forward to show off her low-cut blouse. Mason blinked, trying to keep his eyes on her face. He suddenly had a feeling this was going way wrong. Another witch stepped forward. Dear God . . .

"I'm Patricia," she said with a flip of her hair, but she was immediately shoved away by a blonde with attitude.

"I'm Deb. What do you say we go for a little walk?" She shot Patricia a look and got a don't-try-it arch of an eyebrow in return. Mary looked ready to start something, but when she made a move toward him, another woman asserted herself.

"Cathy," said another blonde, and stuck out her hand. "Don't mind them. They're a bit out of control tonight." She pointed to the sky. "Full moon gets the witches a little bit riled up, right, Teresa?"

Teresa nodded. "I'm afraid so. But thank you for naming the brewery for us."

"I . . . uh . . ." Mason blinked at them. Were they trying to say that they really were witches or just joking? He decided to go with joking.

"Hey," the one named Mary said, and raised her glass. "I'm empty. Mason, my handsome master, will you buy me another?"

"Brewmaster," he corrected.

Cathy laughed at her friends, but Teresa appeared a bit disgusted and stomped away, mumbling something under her breath. Jen stepped closer, and when it looked as if Mary was going to give her a good shove, Mason decided it was time to take his leave. So much for Jimmy's grand plan. These women were crazy.

"Well, ladies, thanks again for coming to the party. Our ales will be on tap at several restaurants around town and at Walking on Sunshine Bistro soon."

"Oh, I know," Jen said. "I already liked your Facebook page. I'll be back on a regular basis for sure," she said with a suggestive smile.

Mason nodded and took a step backward, but he suddenly noticed that they had circled around him and he was trapped. "I, uh, think I hear my mother callin'," he said, and jabbed his thumb over his shoulder.

"Mason!"

Escape! Thank God. "Mom!" Mason smiled at his mother, never so glad to see someone in his life.

"I've been trying to track you down all night long!"

"Well, now is a good time. I was . . . trapped."

"I could see that. And Grace was shooting daggers their way."

Mason's mood lightened. "Really?" He grinned.

Miranda frowned. "Wait—was that your intention?"

Mason took his mother's hand. "Come take a walk with me."

A couple of minutes later, they were down by the riverside, where it was quiet enough to talk without anyone hearing what he had to say to his mother.

"So, what's up, Mason? You and Grace having problems?" She squeezed his hand and then turned to look at him.

Mason picked up a rock and tossed into the water. "I gave her a rough time earlier about the whole witches theme."

"Well, judging from tonight's crowd, the brewery is going to be a huge success. I mean, I know it's just a party, but of course I listened to what people were saying, and they loved the different ales, Mason. Who knew when you started home brewing that it would turn into this?" She waved a hand in the direction of the brewery. She gave him a smile that trembled at the corners. "I know that you went through a tough time when you left the tour and came back home to help out at the marina."

"I was glad that I did."

"You gave up your dream."

Mason wrapped his arm around his mother's shoulders and gave her a hug. "I'll admit that when I failed at a comeback, I was feeling pretty low for a while. And as much as Lauren was wrong for what she did, I was damned hard to live with after that."

"I'm so sorry."

"Mom, I like living back here in Cricket Creek at the

marina. The tour is a grind. I missed everyone, and if I hadn't come back when I was needed here, I would never have forgiven myself. And I love the art of brewing beer."

"And you would never have met Grace."

"Mom, Gracie will eventually go back to London ... or somewhere. She said that she can't stay tied down and needs challenges. She made that clear from the beginning."

"And that didn't stop you from falling in love with her."

"You can tell?"

"Absolutely. Ah, Mason, you were always so quiet and serious, but I can read your emotions in your eyes, and I do believe you adore her. Am I right?"

"I sure as hell fought it, but you're right on the money. I've fallen for her. But that doesn't mean it can work out. I just have to soak up the time I have with her before she goes on her way. No matter what happens between us, I'm still glad that I met her. Grace opened my eyes to the fact that I do want someone in my life."

Miranda shook her head. "See, your eyes just went all stormy. I can tell even in the moonlight. Not *someone*. You want Grace."

Mason reached down and picked up another rock. "I know that, Mom." He skipped the rock across the water, and then turned back to his mother again. "You're gonna think this is kinda odd, but remember when Aunt Martha died and we had to take care of her pet parakeet?"

"Yes."

"I always felt sorry for that danged bird being stuck in a cage."

"Oh, Mason, I know where you're going with this."

"Mama, the last thing I want to do is hold Gracie back."

She smiled. "You always call me Mama when you're emotional."

"We all do. I miss you so much when you're in Florida."

"Oh, Mason. I love the change of seasons, but your daddy can't handle the cold weather any longer. He thrives in the warm climate, and—" When she put a hand to her mouth, Mason hugged her. "I do it for him. Y'all are all grown up and thriving. I want to be in Cricket Creek all year long, but I want your daddy on this green earth as long as I can have him. Ah, and Lily makes it even harder. But I won't ever tell your daddy that. He thinks I wouldn't come back for a winter for all the tea in China."

"Because you love him."

"Of course. But in the end, it's my choice. And it's Grace's choice whether to stay here or not. Give her the choice, Mason, and don't chase her away because you think you're doing the noble thing."

"Yeah, but that worries me more than if she goes." He felt emotion hit him like a tidal wave. "What if she stays and she's miserable? Just because you love somebody doesn't mean that you're the right match for them. I couldn't wander all over the planet with her, no matter how much I love her. I'd be a basket case."

"Mason, God love you, you're such a worrywart." She chuckled. "You used to follow Mattie around after she learned to walk, worried to death that she'd fall and hurt herself."

"Um, that's because she did. Over and over. It's a wonder she ever grew skin back on her knees."

"And if anybody dared pick on Danny, there would be hell to pay."

"He's my baby brother and always found himself looking for a fight. Blowing his danged mouth off. And a daredevil! If I told you half the stuff that boy did . . ."

Miranda put her hand on his arm. "You always carried the weight of the world on those shoulders. Now, mind you, they are wide and strong, but you got that doggone worry gene from your daddy. I love the marina, but if we'd lost it, life would have gone on for me. Losing him?" Her smile trembled. "Now, that's a different story." She gave him a gentle smile. "Stop your worrying. It only gives you indigestion and doesn't change a thing."

Mason groaned. "Yeah, I should have stock in Tums. But how do I keep from worrying?" He looked up at the sky dotted with stars and sighed. "Now I'm worrying that I worry too much."

Miranda laughed. "Oh, we all have our stuff. But don't feel guilty about the past, and don't fret about the future. You can't undo what's already over, and you can't predict what's going to happen, Mason. Just live the best life you can each day. The rest will take care of itself."

Mason gave her a hug. "How did you get so smart?"

"Living and learning. Now, you'd best get back up there and find Grace."

"She's not made it easy," Mason grumbled.

"But she's expecting you to come after her."

Mason raised his hands to the sky. "Women! Why are y'all so hard to understand?"

"Makes life interesting. Now, go!"

"Why does everybody keep saying that to me? You're the third person tonight."

"Because you're lollygagging around, Mason. Somebody else might be making a move as we speak."

Now, that motivated him. "Thanks for your help, Mom."

"Hey, I want more grandbabies. What can I say? And you and Grace would make some pretty ones," she joked, but then she gave Mason a kiss on the cheek. "And more than anything else in the world, I want my children to be happy." She patted her chest and then pointed up to the brewery.

"I know ... go!" Mason took long strides up the slight hill and looked around. Shane had finished singing, and the crowd was starting to thin down. If he had to guess, the kegs were most likely dry. Still, Grace must be inside, he thought, and entered the back door. When he didn't see her, he walked over to the bar. "Danny, have you seen Grace?"

"She was cleaning up, but she was dead on her feet, so I sent her home."

"I thought the point was for me to find her. Why did you send her home?"

Danny paused from wiping down the bar. "Are you seriously that stupid?"

"We've got this, Mason," Sophia said. She made shooing motions with her hands.

"I can't let you—"

"Just go!" Danny said.

"Wait!" Sophia shouted and held up her finger. "I'll be right back," she said, and a moment later she brought out a bottle of Black Magic and a plastic bag. "I noticed that Grace didn't get much to eat, and I know from experience that Grace and low blood sugar isn't something to play around with, if you value your life. And as you know, this is her favorite ale. She pretty much stuck to water tonight, wanting to have her wits about her as she mingled. She will be ever so grateful for this care package."

"Sophia, you're an angel." Mason leaned over and kissed her cheek. He looked over at Danny, Colby, and Avery. "And I can't thank you enough for all of the help tonight."

Avery held up a cauldron of ale. "We held some back for an after party. Payment enough, and we're glad as hell to have a craft brewery in our hometown."

They all lifted a glass in salute. "To Broomstick Brewery!"

18

Hope Floats

SOMETIMES A PLAN CAN WORK TOO WELL, GRACE thought as she carefully walked down the long dock to her cabin. With each step she took, the cabin somehow seemed farther away. An eerie mist hovered over the river, making her imagine the Loch Ness monster making an appearance. Perhaps he'd be a friendly sort and hang out near her back deck. Grace chuckled at the silly notion, but her laughter faded into the fog, leaving her feeling empty and rather forlorn. Mason's earlier comments no longer seemed to matter quite so much, but there was no turning back the clock, so she might as well just . . . just what? She wasn't sure.

Grace shivered when a damp, cool breeze made her palazzo pants flap around her legs. A glance over to the covered slips showed no signs of light at Mason's houseboat, so he must still be up at the brewery. Grace felt a little guilty about leaving without helping to clean up, but Sophia and Danny said that they were going to hang out with Colby and Avery and maybe a few others for an after party, cleaning up little by little. A crew had been hired to pick up trash on the lawn, so they insisted that she was good to go home if she wanted to leave.

Another gust of wind lifted her witch's hat from her head, sending it flying into the river. "Bollocks!" Grace grumbled, and then felt tears spring to her eyes. "No! You will not cry," she said firmly, and then sniffed. Looking back, she realized her plan to avoid Mason was bloody stupid to begin with. She should have swallowed her pride and mingled with him. But no, she had to go and prove some misguided point. Why did people do that to each other, especially to the ones they loved the most?

Grace should be ecstatic over the overwhelming success of the soft opening, but sadness weighed on her like a wet wool sweater. When the dock bobbed just a bit, she hefted her purse tighter to her shoulder and clung to the bottle of Black Magic that she'd taken home with her. A little later she would be crying in her beer, like the lyrics in one of Shane McCray's country songs.

If that wasn't enough, Grace's stomach growled in protest; she hadn't eaten more than a few bites of this and that while she chatted with the guests. In truth, she'd not had much of an appetite after walking out on Mason, but low blood sugar made her a crazy person, so she knew she needed to eat something.

Only a few more steps. "Thank God I'm finally home," Grace said when she finally reached the front door of the cabin. She fumbled for her keys, praying that she had something in the fridge without mold on it to stuff in her mouth.

After flipping on the lights to scare away anything that might emerge from the mist, Grace put the porter in the fridge. And just as she'd thought, there wasn't anything remotely worthy of consumption on the nearly bare shelves. She looked at the shelves again, as if staring would somehow conjure up some River Row pizza. "Maybe if I still had the hat on, I could make some magic happen," she said with a sad little laugh. "Poof!" she said, waited, and then closed the door.

Grumbling under her breath, Grace headed into the small bedroom and tossed her purse onto the bed so hard that it bounced. Grace thought about phoning Sophia to bring her some leftovers and listen to her many woes, but she knew that her sister wanted to hang out after the party. Sophia might pretend that she thought of Avery only as a friend, but Grace suspected that Sophia was already sweet on the cute country boy. "Whatever is it about cowboy boots and a sexy Southern drawl that makes a girl's good sense fly right out the window?" But then Grace conjured up a vision of Mason in a tuxedo and decided that his appeal had nothing to do with what he wore.

Naked would be even better.

"Oh, stop it!" she whispered fiercely, then decided to change into sweatpants and a hoodie. After she tugged the pants on, spotting the Mayfield Marina logo reminded her of the stormy night she'd first met Mason. But Grace pushed that thought aside, wondering if she'd truly been that difficult to find all night long or if Mason didn't really give locating her much of a try.

Grace pondered whether Mason despised the witch logo as much as he let on or if it was a way to put distance between them. Maybe he was finally beginning to understand that it was pointless to pursue someone who was going to leave.

After retrieving the porter from the fridge, Grace poured the dark frothy ale into a glass and took a sip. Of course the rich chocolate flavor also brought back memories of sitting in the bathroom while keeping safe from the raging storm. There had been something about Mason Mayfield from the moment she met the man.

Grace sighed, thinking that she'd gotten herself into quite a pickle. She'd keep her hand in the marketing end of the brewery, but all too soon she wouldn't be needed at the location on a daily basis. In fact, expansion could mean extensive travel, at least in the tristate area. And Mason did need to seriously consider growing his distribution quickly while the excitement for the new brewery was going strong, getting lots of reviews and press. Grace knew that the beer was excellent and they had that on their side, but momentum was also so very important. Striking while the iron was hot could be the difference between having mild success and having huge success. In the end the decision would be his, but as marketing director she felt she needed to point out what she knew to be true not only through research but from personal experience as well.

Grace picked up her iPad, thinking it was another night for music to soothe her soul. She might even brave sitting outside on the deck while drinking her ale and singing along to sad songs. Surely she had some crisps in the pantry to munch on while she and Billy Joel did another night of duets. If not, she might just have to head up to the bistro and steal some food the way Rusty the Irish setter was fond of doing. Grace remembered a story that Garret still loved to tell about Rusty pinching a ham from the breakfast supplies the day Garret and Mattie met. Of course, thinking of ham made her stomach rumble again. Oh, wait, she didn't have a bloody key! Grace groaned, but then brightened just slightly when she located a can of barbecue-flavored Pringles. She shook the can and the tinkling sound indicated that it was nearly empty. Popping the lid, she peeked in and had to sigh. Ah well, she had a few crumbs to sustain her anyway. After the bottle of porter, she'd be singing with Billy and wouldn't care about being famished any longer. Caring about Mason, though, was another story.

Armed with her drink, her crisps, and her songs, Grace slid open the door and headed outside. The damp, chill air reminded her of evenings in London. She sat down, thinking that she missed the city sometimes, but would she miss this view so much more? She looked up at the stars glittering in the inky black sky and felt the gentle breeze carrying the beginning of autumn with it.

Grace sipped her ale slowly, savoring the taste; since

she had only one, she needed to make it last. The Pringles, however, were consumed in an instant. With a moan she put the can up to her mouth and tipped her head back, determined to get the last crunchy bits.

"There you are! Holy crap, you scared the daylights out of me!"

At the sound of Mason's voice, Grace dropped the can and scooted around in her lounge chair. "I think that's my line," she said, trying not to be so damned pleased that he'd come over. But looking at the stormy expression on his face, perhaps she shouldn't be glad at all.

Mason held up a soggy witch's hat and noticed that Mason was dripping wet.

"You jumped into the river for a hat?"

"Waded in, actually, since the hat was at the dock close to the bank. Now my boots are caked with mud."

Grace looked down and noticed he was in his bare feet. "Why on earth did you feel the need to retrieve the hat? Especially a witch's hat you hate so very much?"

"Gracie, I thought you had fallen in! Imagine my holy terror when I saw the hat floating by the dock."

"Witches do sink," Grace said with a slight smile, but he glowered at her and her good humor faded. "Why are you so mad at me?"

"I thought you could have drowned!"

"So if I had fallen in and drowned, you'd feel better right now?" Grace stood up, angry now too. "Do you want me to jump in and make you feel better?" She walked over to the railing, knowing full well she'd never jump in, but she felt like pissing him off. The wind taking her hat wasn't her fault, for pity's sake!

Mason was upon her in two long strides. He grabbed her around the waist and pulled her up against him. "Don't even think about it."

"Since when are you the boss?" she asked, and then realized that was the very last thing she should have said.

"Oh, really? I thought we were partners," he said hotly in her ear. "In this together?"

"You're getting me all wet!" she sputtered, wiggling.

"Am I, now?"

"Yes!" she said, but then the double entendre made her feel warm in spite of his cold clothes. "You can let go; I wasn't really going to jump in."

"Do you think I don't know that?"

"So it's an excuse to manhandle me?" she asked.

"It's an excuse to hold you, but you obviously don't want me to." When he dropped his arms, she spun around, ready to fight, but she saw the relief in his eyes, and some of the heat faded. "Why did you toss the hat into the water?"

"I didn't." She raised her hands, palms upward. "It blew off!"

"Well . . . ," he said, and then without warning he pulled her back into his arms and hugged her tight. "God, Gracie, I was so scared. It wasn't until I thought to look in the direction of your cabin and saw the lights on that I realized that you weren't in the damned river!"

"I wasn't pissed enough at you to jump to my demise!"

"I know you wouldn't jump in. I thought you probably fell off the dock," he said, and she felt a shiver run through his body.

"Oh. Well, here I am, safe and sound," she said softly. "Ew, you smell like a swamp."

"I fell all the way in when I reached for the damned hat." Mason pulled back and winced. "I'll go home and shower."

"Meaning you're planning on coming back here?" She couldn't keep the hope out of her tone.

"Yes. Of course."

"So, why were you coming here in the first place?" Grace asked. "To tell me how much you hated the event tonight?"

"No, Gracie. To tell you how sorry I was for being such a jerk today. I'm sorry." He shoved his fingers through his wet hair. "I don't know what got into me." He swallowed hard. "I tried to track you down all night long, but you kept slipping away from me. It was really annoying, by the way."

"Really?" Grace arched an eyebrow. "You had plenty of other female attention."

Mason looked up at the sky and shook his head. "That little escapade was Jimmy Topmiller's idea."

"Come again?"

"Jimmy said that in order to get your attention, I should make you jealous. Stupid . . ." He gave her a short laugh and appeared embarrassed.

"Brilliant, actually."

Mason looked at her. "You mean it worked?"

"I wanted to march over there to that circle of women and stake my claim. Tell those ladies that I was the head witch and they'd best back off."

"Really?" Mason grinned. "Why didn't you?"

"It would have ruined my whole cold-shoulder, disappearing routine that I thought was somehow necessary."

Mason laughed, but then pulled her close. She didn't even care about his wet clothes or smelly river scent. She was in his arms, where she wanted to be. "You are a piece of work, my cute little witch."

"I had to stay in character."

Mason kissed her forehead. "I'm really sorry I acted the fool."

"Well, maybe I've been just a tad too controlling."

"Ya think?"

"Yeah . . ."

"No, Gracie, you are amazing at what you do. And I'm grateful, not angry. Yeah, I wouldn't have come up with Broomstick Brewery in a million years, and I still don't totally love it, but tonight the quality of the beer wasn't overshadowed at all. The atmosphere was festive and fun, and you're right—women ate it up."

"Oh, please don't talk about eating. I'm starving."

"I brought food. Lucky for you, I tossed the bag and my cell phone onto the dock before taking the plunge. Yes, I brought you food."

"You did?" Grace pulled back and did a little jig. "Have I told you lately how much I love you?" she asked, but then suddenly stopped dancing. Her heart pounded. She swallowed hard and looked at him.

Mason stared right back. "No, as a matter of fact." He waited, as if daring her to go on. "You haven't."

"I do, you know." She stepped closer, reached over, and took his hand. "I love you, Mason," she said in a serious, husky voice. Grace smiled, suddenly feeling a little bit shy, vulnerable. Humor and sass were her weapons against getting hurt, and now she felt stripped down and naked. "I . . . I told my mum."

"That I was a jackass?"

She tilted her head. "I said wanker, but, yes."

"Not sure what wanker is, but I'm thinking it's not something I want to be called."

Grace put a palm on his chest. "But then I told her that I loved you and didn't want to break your heart."

"And what did she say?"

"That it sounds like you're willing to take that risk."

"Gracie, I'm in love with you too, and there's not a damned thing I can do about it."

"Do you want to do something about it?"

"No." He ran his fingertip over her bottom lip. "If I lose you, if you leave, it will be because that's who you are and what you need to do. I'll never ask you to stay in Cricket Creek unless it's where you want to live. Unless you will be happy living here. Baby, I'll love you forever, and nothing can change that fact. But I'm not going to tie you down or hold you back. I won't like it if you feel the need to leave, and neither will the people who have to deal with me after you go, because my moodiness will be off the charts."

"Oh, Mason . . ."

"But, baby, I'd rather let you go than keep you trapped in a cage. So I want you to promise me, right here and now, that if you have the urge to go . . . if you *need to go* to do new and challenging things, that you'll do it. And don't look back."

She swallowed hard, wishing she could give him reassurance.

"I won't lie. It will be super shitty. But I'll survive."

Grace closed her eyes and felt tears leak out of the corners. When Mason wiped them away with the pads of his thumbs, she grabbed his arms and looked at him. "You know that what you just said is the most oddly romantic thing I've ever heard, much less been told?" And she wasn't joking. Mason was telling her that he'd put his own happiness on the line rather than hold her back. How could she ever leave a man who loved her that much? The thought made her heart constrict, but at the same time she knew she would have to go or shrivel up like leaves in the fall. "I don't know if I can leave you, Mason."

"I want you to promise me, Gracie." When she turned her head to the side, he cupped his hand on her chin and gently guided her back so she had to face him. "Promise."

"This is the oddest thing ever. You want me to promise to leave you. I think we are both weird enough to somehow make this work."

"You are avoiding my request."

"I know. Okay . . . okay." Grace finally gave him a jerky nod. "I promise," she said, barely above a whisper. "Are you happy now?"

"Now? Yes. And that means that if you do end up staying that it's what you really want to do . . . not *have* to do. Does that make sense?"

"Unfortunately, it makes perfect sense. You haven't known me all that long, and I feel as if you understand me more than I understand myself. And that's not an easy task."

"Well, we aren't going to think about you leaving tonight. Deal?"

She nodded.

Mason leaned in and kissed her, softly but thoroughly. "I need a shower so I can make love to you."

"Take one here," she said, clinging to his wet shirt.

Mason nodded. "Get something to eat, and then join me in bed."

"Okay," she said, and watched him walk into the cabin. Warm and tingling happiness washed over her. She hugged her arms to her chest and smiled. The little seed of hope that she'd planted in her heart just sprouted and grew stronger.

Grace looked at the stack of takeaway boxes and smiled. She opened one and ate a few finger sandwiches and then munched on slices of Brie on crackers. A biscuit with a thin slice of country ham melted in her mouth.

The sound of the shower running brought an image of Mason naked with soapsuds slithering down his amazing body into her brain. With a groan she closed the lid and popped the leftovers into the fridge. Eating could wait until later . . . much, much later.

19
We've Got Tonight

MASON LET THE HOT WATER PELT HIS SHOULDERS AND sluice down his body. While soaping up, he hoped that Grace might decide to join him, but that was probably wishful thinking. Having her hands, slick with soap, sliding over his body would be pure heaven. Mason made a mental note that when he built his dream house he'd have a walk-in shower with double heads.

Mason squirted some coconut-scented shampoo into the palm of his hand and then scrubbed his head, thinking he was going to smell like a girl. Damn, she had lotions and potions and strange-shaped scrubbing things dangling from shelves hooked over the shower nozzle. Mason had a sudden image of Gracie in her naked glory scrubbing her body with that big white puffy thing on a rope and he became instantly hard. He glanced through the sheer shower curtain, hoping again that she might feel the need to wash his back . . . and his front and everything in between. He just wanted her touching him anywhere, everywhere. He wanted her slick, soapy body sliding against him while he . . .

"Damn!" Mason turned his face up to the spray and

chuckled, thinking that he should turn the water to cold. Oh, but, God, when he'd spotted that goofy pointed hat floating in the water, his blood had run icy-cold, and fingers of fear had gripped his heart and squeezed hard. Out of instinct he'd waded into the murky water, crazy with heart-thumping worry. When he'd thought to look out toward her cabin and saw lights, he'd nearly sunk to his knees with relief. Once he'd settled his heart rate down, it was in that moment that Mason knew he'd fallen completely ass-over-teacup in love with Gracie Gordon.

Not only had Gracie saved the brewery, but she'd awakened the need for him to have a woman in his life. He wanted a soft place to land, a hand to hold, lips to kiss, but he wanted a family too. He longed for the kind of love that his mother and father shared . . . not perfect, but strong enough to make it through the tough times. And the one thing his parents could always do was make each other laugh, sometimes at silly things that Mason didn't even get.

While Mason couldn't picture Gracie living the white-picket-fence, two-kids-and-a-dog kind of life, he couldn't imagine not having her in his life either. In truth, just like his mother moving to Florida, Mason would have traipsed all around Europe or to the ends of the earth to be with Gracie. But owning the brewery tied him down, so leaving Cricket Creek wasn't an option for him, at least not for now. And he didn't want to leave. This was his home. But he'd live in a damned igloo, a tree house, a shoe, *anywhere*, just to be with her.

And now that she'd said that she loved him, hope was like a living, breathing *thing* dancing around in his chest.

Mason was going to take his mother's advice, chase worry from his brain, and live each day until the days ran together and became his future.

And tonight?

Tonight he planned to make slow, easy love to Gracie until the sun came up. Or at least until they fell into an exhausted sleep, and then they'd start all over again in the morning. With that thought in mind, Mason shut off the shower, stepped onto the cold tile floor, and quickly toweled dry. After wrapping another big fluffy towel around his waist, he looked in the cabinet and found some mouthwash. Finally, satisfied that he was once again presentable, even though he smelled a bit feminine, he decided he was, *yep*, still up for the task.

After breathing in the coconut-scented, steamy air, he opened the bathroom door that led to Gracie's bedroom. The chilly air hit his warm skin, but nothing could even begin to cool his ardor. With a smile, he looked over toward the bed and spotted Gracie snuggled beneath the covers. Her hair fanned out over the dark blue pillowcase and her bare shoulders peeked above the matching sheet. Anticipation, hot and potent, ran through his veins.

This had been one helluva crazy roller-coaster day.

The small lamp next to the bed cast a soft glow in the room. He noticed that she'd added some feminine touches to the basic bedroom . . . a candle here, a bouquet of flowers there, making Mason hope she planned on staying for longer than she'd first expected. *No,* he warned his worry gene. *Don't even go there.*

Instead, Mason concentrated on what it was going to feel like to have Grace in his arms, to make love to her and to sleep next to her. He'd make coffee in the morning and cook breakfast before they headed off for a day at the brewery. Or perhaps they'd walk up to the bistro and have breakfast there, so Grace could chat with Sophia. When Mattie had renamed the bistro from Breakfast, Books, and Bait to Walking on Sunshine because she said falling in love with Garret made her feel that way, Mason had an eye-roll moment thinking that she'd gone a little over the top.

Now he understood.

Mason walked over to join Grace, hoping she was naked, warm, and ready for him, but when he reached the edge of the mattress, he looked down at her beautiful face and realized that she was fast asleep. Disappointment slid like a rock all the way to his toes, but he knew that after the past few days, she must be so exhausted, and that although it was killing him, Mason wasn't about to wake her.

Mason stood there for a few moments and drank in the beauty of her sweet face. Tenderness washed over him, almost like a physical ache, and he longed to reach down and run his fingertip down her cheek and over her shoulders. He even reached out, but then pulled back, remembering that she suffered from insomnia and that sleep was precious to her.

And she was precious to him.

Mason eased his way over to the other side of the bed, telling himself that he was content just to sleep next to her, which was kind of a lie, but he told himself that anyway so he wouldn't be tempted to give her a gentle nudge. But if she did wake up, he would be at the ready. As quietly and gently as he could, he dropped his towel and slid between the sheets. The intoxicating scent of her perfume was almost his undoing, and he had to clench his fists not to reach over and pull her against his body. He silently lifted the sheet and peeked . . . Dear God, she was naked.

Maybe she'd be disappointed if he didn't wake her, the devil on his shoulder argued. *I sure would be*, Mason thought. He stared at the ceiling in indecision and then finally decided that he should just reach over and turn off the light. She was a light sleeper. Maybe his slight, oh-so-innocent movement would be enough to wake her up. Maybe he should just leave the light on. And maybe his worry gene should just shut the hell up!

Mason chuckled silently at the thought and then realized that he was making the mattress shake.

"Mmm . . . ," Gracie mumbled, then moved.

Mason smiled, thinking, *Yes!* She was awake. His disappointed dick responded with immediate glee, and he waited for her to reach over and put her hand on his chest or maybe dip downward to cup his ... Oh damn, she was still asleep. Perhaps he should just say her name super softly so that she wouldn't know that he actually woke her up. "Gracie," he said in a voice not even loud enough to be considered a whisper, and held his breath, waiting. Hoping.

Gracie inhaled a sharp breath, but then started snoring. Not a loud snore, just a cute-as-hell little snore that made him smile. But then he frowned. Dammit! He resigned himself to just go to sleep and to hope that morning came really, really fast. With that decision made, he leaned over to turn out the light.

"W-what are you doing, love?" Gracie asked in a husky, sleepy British voice that was just about the sexiest thing he'd ever heard in his entire life. No, not just about; it *was* the sexiest sound ever made.

"Turning out the light."

"You fancy making love in the dark?"

"No."

"Then you don't want to make love to me?" She sounded perplexed, still half-asleep.

"Is this a trick question?"

Gracie leaned toward him and put a hand on his chest. Ah, now they were getting somewhere. "No, love, truly, what's going on? Do you plan on rolling over and going to sleep?" she asked in the same husky voice.

Mason laughed. "Baby, you were sound asleep."

"I was *not*. I was resting my eyes while you showered."

"You were snoring, sugar."

"No possible way. I don't snore," she said firmly, but then paused and asked in a small voice, "Do I?"

"A cute little rumble that I find totally adorable." Mason tried to give an example, but his snore sounded way worse than she did, and her eyes widened.

"Oh no!" she cried, as if snoring was the worst thing in the world. "That's ... horrible!"

Mason laughed harder.

"Stop it." She shoved his shoulder. "It's not one bit funny. I need to get some of those strip things to put on my stupid nose. Or maybe one of those machines. Would you quit laughing?"

Mason tried to control his laughter, but it was as if the tension of the day and his guilt over hurting her feelings came pouring out of him. He couldn't remember the last time he'd laughed this hard, and he simply could not stop.

"I think you've gone stark-raving mad."

Mason swiped at tears. "Oh God . . . ," he said in a voice weak with laughter. "First I wade into the river after your runaway hat and now this." He shook his head against the pillow and then raised his index finger. "No, *first* I tried to flirt with that crazy bunch of ladies to get you to notice me."

"Well, that was pretty funny." Gracie started laughing with him. In fact, she laughed so hard that she snorted and was mortified again. "No, I did *not* just snort."

"You snort and snore. I'm telling everyone."

"No!" she wailed. "Don't you dare."

"I'm going to Tweeter it."

"Tweet," Grace corrected, and laughed harder. The mattress started shaking as if in the middle of an earthquake. "Oh, dear God," Gracie said, wiping at her own eyes.

"Thank you," Mason said, and then reached down and took her hand.

"For making you laugh?" she asked softly.

"For coming into my life."

Gracie squeezed his hand. "I can't really take credit for that, now, can I? It all started with Rick coming here to undo the mess that Garret found himself involved in. Rick found lovely Maggie. Garret fell in love with Mattie. And I've fallen in love with you. Funny how life works, you know?"

Mason came up to his elbow and smiled down at her.

"Yes, it is." He leaned down and kissed her gently, tasting her lips, exploring her mouth, while he trailed his fingers lightly over her soft skin. She shivered, arched her back, telling him with her body how much she wanted him. He cupped her breast and moved the pad of his thumb over her nipple, knowing by now what drove her wild with need. Mason moved his mouth to her neck, kissing, nuzzling, while letting his fingers trail lower until he found her sex. When she gasped and parted her legs, Mason dipped his finger inside her silky folds, finding her wet and ready for him. He tossed the sheet aside, pausing for protection.

Grace reached up for him and he entwined his hands with hers. He kissed her while he entered her body, and her fingers squeezed him hard. Mason moved slowly, pulling nearly all the way out and then inching back in until she wrapped those long legs around him and urged him to go faster, harder. When she cried out his name, he kissed her and thrust deeply, finding his own heart-pounding release.

Mason rolled sideways, bringing her with him.

"Well, I can tell you one thing. I'm wide awake now," Grace said with a low chuckle.

"Good, because, baby, we've only just begun."

20

Thank God I'm a Country Boy

JIMMY KNEW HE WAS A GONER WHEN THINKING ABOUT Becca made him unable to concentrate on fishing. Usually, when he was out on the lake, he stayed relaxed yet sharply focused, but that sure wasn't the case today. Watching Becca holding and cooing to baby Lily last night was his complete and utter undoing. When Becca looked up and caught him staring, she'd given him a smile that melted his damned heart on the spot.

He loved the woman. There wasn't a shred of doubt in his mind. But that didn't change the fact that Becca was completely wrong for him. And while he got the impression that she intended to spend a great deal of time in Cricket Creek, Jimmy was damned well positive she wouldn't want to live in a plain and simple cabin and ride around in a beat-up pickup truck. He knew that just wasn't her style, but it was how he preferred to live, and he was too old to change his stubborn ways.

In truth, Jimmy had piles of money; more money than he wanted or knew what to do with. Even though he'd retired from competitive fishing, cash kept pouring in from endorsements and his extensive line of fishing products. Funny, but Jimmy knew that part of his success stemmed from the fact that he never cared about the money end of it, and so when he fished tournaments, winning didn't make him nervous. He just liked to fish, and he was really good at knowing where the big bass were hiding and what kind of bait would catch them.

But because of how hard Jimmy's father had worked to put food on the table and the tragic way his dad died, spending money on anything more than necessities always somehow felt wrong. So, out of guilt, Jimmy wore old boots, drove an ancient truck, and fixed his fishing poles rather than purchase new ones. And he sure as hell didn't see any of that changing. So while he'd fallen hard for Becca, he knew that she liked the finer things in life and enjoyed extensive traveling. When he'd seen pictures of the fancy home she owned in Hyde Park, along with the flat she owned in Notting Hill, which she kept just for her kids to have somewhere to stay while visiting London, he was a little blown away. Becca casually mentioned that she was thinking of putting the house on the market or renting it out for a monthly amount that made his head spin.

Jimmy's own pockets were deeper than most people even suspected. He wasn't impressed by money, nor did he even care about it. Some people thought he was just a cheapskate or that maybe he'd gambled away his fortune. People talked—he knew it—but he didn't give a rat's ass what people thought of him. In fact, Jimmy thought it rather amusing when people suspected that he'd pissed away his fortune. The only real joy he felt in spending money had been when he spent it on his mother, and now that she was gone, his money simply sat in the bank and wherever his financial adviser put it. When statements came, he looked at the numbers with mild interest and then filed them away.

With a sigh, Jimmy used his trolling motor to weave his way to some shallow water in a hidden cove. One of the reasons he'd won so many fishing tournaments

stemmed from his uncanny ability to troll into shallow
water most anglers would end up getting stuck in. He
cast his plastic frog over to hop along the lily pads where
smallmouth bass liked to feed. But it didn't land where
he thought he'd aimed; instead Jimmy ended up snag-
ging his line in a tree branch for the second time that
morning. "Well, hell's bells," he grumbled when he had
to cut his line, and decided he might as well call it a day.
"And that was my favorite damned frog."

After easing his way back out of the narrow passage,
Jimmy opened the motor up and whizzed down the middle of the lake, hoping the wind in his face would help to
clear his head. When he got near the cabins, he slowed
down, intending to head over to his dock and button the
boat up and maybe go back out and catch the evening
bite.

After a cool morning, warm sunshine glinted off the
lake, making the water look as if diamonds were dancing
around playing tag. The trees were changing colors, turning the shoreline into a gorgeous display of orange, red,
and gold leaves.

Jimmy felt the weight of sadness grip him, because he
knew that he needed to have a talk with Becca. They'd
come close to making love, and he didn't want to cross
that bridge and then tell her that they needed to break
things off. He inhaled a deep breath and blew it out. No,
he needed to be honest and tell her now. Taking their
relationship to the next level would only end up in disaster, and he cared way too much about her to inflict any
kind of emotional pain. While they enjoyed each other's
company and chemistry, they weren't a good fit as a couple, and so they'd be much better off in the end if they
broke things off now and could remain friends. He
wanted her to know that she could count on him, come
to him for anything she ever needed.

Jimmy turned his face up the light blue sky and shook
his head, thinking that he had to be out of his ever-lovin'
mind to break off a romantic relationship with the beau-

tiful Becca Gordon. But he needed to give her the let's-be-friends speech before it was too late.

Jimmy looked over to her cabin, and as if on cue, Becca walked out onto her back deck and waved to him. He waved back and a moment later his phone pinged. He looked down at the text message from Becca inviting him over for lunch. Jimmy almost declined. The thought of telling the woman who had managed to capture his heart that he wanted to be just friends wasn't something he wanted to do, but he decided that rather than brood about his decision, he might as well face the music. He sent a message back that he'd be right over and drove his boat across the lake.

While Jimmy tied his boat to the cleats on Becca's dock, he rehearsed the let's-be-friends-and-nothing-more speech in his head. But when he saw her beautiful smiling face, he dug deep for courage.

"I brought chicken salad sandwiches and fresh fruit home from the bistro. Sophia makes superb chicken salad. She uses yogurt rather than mayonnaise and you'd never know the difference," Becca said, but when she saw his face, her smile faded. "What's wrong, love?" She gestured toward the wrought-iron chairs beneath an umbrella table. "Bad day on the water?"

Jimmy nodded and then sat down. The chicken salad sandwiches on marble rye and the dish of fruit should have looked appetizing, but his stomach churned at what he was about to tell her. "I couldn't concentrate. Snagged my line, lost my favorite frog in the process."

"Oh, I'm so sorry," Becca said as she poured sweet tea from a pitcher into a tall glass. "So do you have something on your mind? You looked a bit stressed." She reached over and gave his arm a squeeze. "Want to talk about it?"

Jimmy looked at the pretty cloth napkin and nibbled on the inside of his lip.

"Jimmy?" Becca asked softly. "What is it?"

Jimmy looked at her lovely face. She'd pulled her hair

straight back into a ponytail and wore jeans and a button-down light blue sweater with pearl buttons. She looked soft and sweet, and with her eyes so filled with concern, it hit him hard that she really cared about him. Jimmy had been a loner for such a long time that he'd forgotten how good it felt to have someone give a damn about him. Instead of the speech he needed to give Becca, he longed to tell her that he'd fallen love with her. But where would that get him?

Becca took a sip of her tea and then said, "Let me make this easy for you."

"Okay." Jimmy's heart thudded. Was she about to give him the let's-be-friends-speech and beat him to the punch? He sure hoped so.

"I'm in love with you." Becca tilted her head, waiting for his response, but Jimmy didn't know what the hell to say to her. "This is the part when you say it back," she prompted with a smile.

"I . . ." Jimmy cleared his throat while thoughts buzzed around in his head like angry bees. "I'm completely wrong for you, Becca."

"And why is that, precisely?"

"I'm just a plain ole country boy."

"Evidently, I like country boys." She lifted one delicate shoulder and continued to smile. "Who knew?" she asked as she unfolded her napkin and placed it on her lap. She picked up her fork and stabbed a strawberry.

"Won't you be going back to London soon?"

"I've succeeded in renting out my house." She snapped her fingers. "It happened that quickly, as I knew it would. I'll have to go back now and again for business purposes, and I promised Garret that I'd help out with Lily when they head back to London to film *Sing for Me*."

"So you'll live in this cabin?" he asked, while his brain tried to process what was going to be a much different conversation than he expected.

"For now." She chewed the strawberry, but when he remained silent, she put her fork down.

"Becca . . ."

She pressed her lips together and her smile finally faltered. "So you don't feel the same way about me, then?"

"It would never work."

"You're avoiding the question." She toyed with her straw, waiting.

"So would you live in a plain little cabin and ride around in my old truck?"

"Why are you so afraid to spend money?"

"Because I hate it."

"Money?"

"Being wealthy."

"How odd."

He shrugged.

"Why?"

Jimmy felt a muscle jump in his jaw. "Because I grew up dirt-poor." He paused to swallow hard. "My father was a landscaper in Florida. He worked for rich folks and was treated like a dog most of the time."

"I came from humble beginnings, Jimmy. I'm not and never will be like that. I'm so sorry that your father wasn't treated with respect. There's nothing more despicable."

"I know you better than that, Becca. You're one of the kindest people I've ever known."

"Then what's the problem?"

"The problem is, that spoiled, rich—I'm sorry—*bitch* insisted that my father get her yard ready for a damned party. Rather than risk being fired, he worked during a storm and was struck dead by lightning while trimming dead leaves from a palm tree."

Becca sucked in a breath. "I'm so very sorry."

"Yeah, I was just a kid." He ran a hand down his face. "And my poor mother . . ."

"And you've held it against wealthy people for all these years?"

Jimmy nodded. "It's not fair. I know that now. In large part because of getting to know you, Becca. I was wrong to be so judgmental and narrow-minded. Ironic if you sit back and think about it, you know?"

Becca reached for his hand again. "None of us are perfect."

"You're pretty damned close," Jimmy said with a small smile. "Ah, but, Becca, I wouldn't be able to make you happy."

"Don't you think I should be the judge of that?" She rubbed her thumb over his knuckles, and he felt such a strong pull of attraction that he almost picked up her hand and kissed it.

"Look, you've worked hard for what you've got, and you should live the kind of life that you're accustomed to. Baby, I just can't do it."

"Spend money?"

He nodded. "I don't expect you to understand."

"You're wrong. I do understand. I was married to a man who lived for making money and not much else, so I developed my own issues with it. To me, it's just a commodity. I don't even think about it all that much. I've lost lots of money and made it back, and I actually found the challenge of rebuilding more enticing. Other than caring for my children, I didn't think about it all that often. When I stumbled, I picked myself back up and started all over again."

"A healthy attitude."

"You still have a lot to learn about me, Jimmy."

"I could never live the kind of lifestyle that you enjoy. You travel in very different circles. Damn, you're so far out of my league it isn't even funny."

"That's utter nonsense."

"Becca . . ."

"Do you love me, Jimmy?"

He looked away so she couldn't see the answer in his eyes. "It wouldn't work."

"So what were you going to tell me?"

"That we should just be friends."

"It's too late for that, and we both know it," she said with stormy eyes.

Jimmy shook his head. "I just can't stomach riding around in fancy cars and traveling all over the world. We're just too different to fit well together. I've given this some serious thought."

"Oh, I've thought about how well we'd fit together . . . ," she said, and slanted him a look that made his toes curl.

"Believe me—I have too, but you deserve a man who is willing to share your life, not just your bed."

"Then do both!" She gave him a level look and her eyes widened. "I just had a lightbulb moment." She smiled and then laughed. "The answer is so bloody simple!" She raised her hands so her palms faced upward.

"Are you going to enlighten me?"

Becca raised her chin a notch. "Admit that you love me first, country boy. I deserve that much, don't you think?"

21

Joy to the World

BECCA'S HEART POUNDED WHILE SHE WAITED FOR JIMMY to answer. She'd never told a man she loved him before he'd said it first, and it felt empowering to take her love life into her own hands. Jimmy's story about his father broke her heart, and she could understand why he detested the arrogance of wealth. "Well?"

"Becca, there's no use denying it. I love you," Jimmy finally said, but with enough regret in his voice to make it hurt rather than feel good.

"Well, I guess since I forced that out of you, I shouldn't be disappointed about how you sounded when you professed . . . or rather, woefully admitted your feelings for me."

"Because admitting how I feel about you won't change the sad fact that our lives will never mesh." He leaned back in his chair and sighed. "Why can't you see that?"

"Are you forgetting that I have the solution to your so-called problem?"

"Okay, then, lay it on me, sugar."

"Jimmy." Becca leaned forward and tapped her fingertip on the table. "Use your money for the greater good. Find some way to give back. Money can do wonderful things too, you know."

Jimmy lifted one shoulder, clearly not impressed with her lightbulb moment. "I give a lot to charities, Becca."

"No," Becca said, really warming up to the idea. "I mean do something that you can get involved with on a personal level, so you can see your money working. Make it part of your everyday life. A nonprofit of some sort," she said, and felt a sense of excitement when his eyes lit up with interest. "Shall I go on?"

"Is there any stopping you?"

"Absolutely not."

Jimmy cupped his chin, rubbing his thumb back and forth, while seemingly taking her suggestions seriously. "But I don't know what that might be. Becca, I'm good at fishing. It's really been my whole life. I don't know anything else that I could get involved with."

Becca mulled his answer over for a moment. "Who taught you to fish?"

"My daddy." Jimmy's eyes misted over and he swallowed hard. "We had fun fishin' together, but it was to put food on the table, not just for sport. But it bonded us." He threaded his fingers together. "And fishing is something that, once learned, you can do for life." He shook his head. "I don't see where I could do anything . . . ," he said, but then trailed off and nibbled on his bottom lip.

"What? You just thought of something. I can see it in your baby blues." Becca felt a flash of excitement. "Come on and tell me."

"Well . . ." Jimmy pointed across the lake to where his cabin sat with other similar small dwellings. "Those cabins are used by the Mayfields for fishing tournaments and summer rentals. But now that Mason has the brewery and Mattie has the bistro, they aren't doing many tournaments and the cabins have mostly been sitting empty. I'm supposed to help Danny out, but we haven't gotten as much interest as in the past."

"Carry on."

"Well, if the Mayfields would be willing to sell the cabins to me, I could envision having fishing camps for underprivileged children."

"Oh, I love it!" Becca nodded firmly. "Fishing requires concentration and patience. I could see how learning to fish would help kids in more ways than just having an affordable hobby." Becca felt her breath catch. "Oh, Jimmy, your idea is simply brilliant!"

Jimmy grinned, making Becca's heart fill with absolute joy. "I have my moments. They are few and far between, but still," he said, and looked down as if seeing his lunch for the first time. He popped a chunk of pineapple in his mouth. He seemed lost in thought while he ate more fruit, and then ideas started spilling out of his mouth as if floodgates were opened.

Becca picked up her iPad and started taking notes, adding suggestions here and there when she could manage to get a word in edgewise.

"There are plenty of men over in the Whisper's Edge retirement community who would be great helping out. Instant grandpas for these kids, and they would have plenty of patience."

"And feeling good about having the ability to help out. Seniors and kids are the perfect combination."

Jimmy nodded and then took a healthy bite of his sandwich. "Oh wow, this is really good."

"Mattie's recipe, but Sophia has mastered it, I daresay." She held her finger and thumb an inch apart. "She's this close to getting the biscuits down pat."

"You must be so proud of your kids."

"They are the joy of my life. And now I have little Lily . . . ," she said, and then felt her eyes tear up. She gave him a watery laugh. "I just adore her. I can't wait until she can call me Nan."

"I could see the love in your eyes while you held her, Becca. It's when I knew that I'd fallen deeply in love with you."

"Oh, Jimmy." She had to use her napkin to dry her eyes, but then she had to laugh. "I remember being so pissed at you at Sully's when you snubbed me. And I was sitting there thinking you were so sexy."

His eyebrows shot up. "Are you serious?"

"Oh, I sure didn't want you to know it."

"And now?"

Her heart thudded. "Now I want you to kiss me."

Jimmy stood up and offered his hand. Once she was on her feet, he pulled her into his arms. Becca melted against him. When he dipped his head and captured her mouth, she felt a thrill of excitement that slid all the way to her toes. It was as if his kiss healed all of the hurt she'd felt in her life, and the broken pieces of her past fell into place.

Jimmy pulled back and cupped her chin in his big, callused hand. "Thank you."

Becca leaned her cheek into his palm. "For what?"

"For knocking some sense into my fool-hard head."

"Anytime." Becca laughed. "You're quite welcome."

Jimmy rubbed his thumb back and forth over her chin. "We're gonna do good things together, aren't we?"

Becca nodded. "There's absolutely no doubt in my mind."

"I'll give Danny Mayfield a call later and see if they're interested in selling the cabins and the surrounding land. If not, I'm sure we can set up a rental from them. To be honest, I think that Danny needs to spend more of his time with his carpentry work anyway."

"Oh, I agree. The coffee table is gorgeous, and the rocking chair he made for Mattie is so pretty too." Becca nodded. "And I'll get Gracie involved with the marketing end of this. Hopefully this will be another project to keep her in Cricket Creek. It's hard to keep her in one place for very long before she feels the need to roam." Becca sighed.

"I thought maybe Mason Mayfield might solve that problem for you."

"Oh, she's in love with the boy. I have no doubt. She even told me so."

"Maybe that love will be strong enough to keep her grounded. Keep her here."

Becca nodded but wasn't so sure. "Let's hope so."

Jimmy kissed her on the forehead. "You might be able to talk some sense into her. If you can get through my thick head, you can get through to anybody."

Becca tilted her face up and nodded. "You make a good point, darling, but as much as I would adore having all my children living in the same place, Gracie will have to figure it out on her own. It's my fondest wish that my children find happiness and hold it close to their hearts." She smiled. "And give me more grandbabies."

"You are the most gorgeous grandmother on the planet."

"Thank you." She put her palms on his cheeks. "I love you so much, Jimmy."

"And I love you too, Becca. With all my heart."

"And I didn't have to wrangle it out of you this time."

"And you never will again."

22

Sooner or Later

$\mathcal{A}$FTER HAVING DINNER WITH SOPHIA AT RIVER ROW Pizza, Grace had decided they should walk around and do some window-shopping to work off some of the calories. A brisk evening breeze had failed to deter two city girls from strolling past the various shops and artful window displays. "I'm so glad you talked me into coming out tonight, Sophia. I needed a break from the brewery. The last couple of weeks have been nonstop planning."

"Yeah, I've missed hanging out with you. I have to say that having all of us together has been so wonderful," she said with an unmistakable note of wistfulness.

Grace nodded slowly. "This past month has just flown by."

"Oh, would you look!" Sophia said as she stopped in front of a jewelry store. "Why have I not been in here?"

"Oh, quite lovely," Grace said as she paused to admire the jewelry glittering in the display window of Designs by Diamante. "Too bad it's closed," Grace said. "I love that silver necklace with the moon and the stars." She cupped her hand to her ear. "I do believe it's calling my name."

"It's exquisite." Sophia nodded. "Look, there're matching earrings. We'll have to come back here and bring Mom with us."

"If we can pry her away from Jimmy," Grace said. "It's so wonderful to see her so happy, don't you think? It's like she's glowing. I've never seen her quite like this, have you?"

"No," Sophia replied. "And do you know that Jimmy's teaching her to fish? Can you picture Mom . . . *fishing*?"

Grace laughed. "I think it's awesome. And the idea for the fishing camp for kids that they came up with yesterday is just so cool. Mum can't stop talking about it."

"I think so too. Oh, look at the beaded peace-sign pendant." Sophia pointed to the display at the back of the window. "So Bohemian. We definitely have to come back here and have a look."

"No doubt." Grace glanced around. "This is such a lovely strip of shops. It has a very throwback feel to it that I really like. The gas streetlamps are a nice touch. A lot of planning went into this development. And I agree with you that the fishing camp is perfect for them both, actually. Mum has always been big on giving back, and she said that this is a way for Jimmy to feel good about spending his money. Leave it to Mum to come up with a solution that makes everyone happy, including herself. Mason said that his family is on board with the project and is willing to sell the property and pitch in with help, as well."

"The Mayfields are such good people." Sophia nodded. "Yes, Danny Mayfield is getting involved with the fishing camp. And so is Avery. They've had a meeting this morning at the bistro."

Grace arched an eyebrow at her sister. "You seem to talk about Avery a lot. Is something developing between you two?" Grace turned from the window and looked at Sophia. "More than friendship?"

"No . . . it's still too soon after his breakup. I won't be *that* girl. And besides, my time here will be up soon. Mattie is getting stronger every day and eager to come to the bistro."

"Have you thought about moving here, Sophia?"

"To be honest, it's crossed my mind. Cricket Creek is just such an idyllic little town. I just don't know what I'd do. Working at the bistro is a fun change of pace, and I do love to cook, but it's not my true calling."

"But there are hair salons here," Grace pointed out.

"I know." Sophia played with the fringe on her purse. "I've sort of looked into it. Well, I should say that Mom did. There's only one small salon on Main Street, and you know that what I love best is doing weddings and events. I don't see having enough of that here to keep me busy."

"But you could see yourself living here?"

Pressing her lips together, Sophia nodded. "I do like it here, and I have to say that I don't miss the drama of a high-end salon and dealing with bridezillas."

"Something to think about."

"I guess I've never considered living in a small town because we didn't ever have this experience, only city life. What about you, Grace? I thought you'd settled in, but I've seen that look in your eye lately."

Grace shrugged. "The brewery is doing fine. The soft openings have been a total success and we're sold out for the grand opening. I won't be needed here much longer either."

Sophia slanted Grace a level look that pinned her to the spot. "Oh, you're needed here, and I'm not just talking about the brewery."

Grace sighed. "But you know me, Sophia. Like you said, would there be enough to keep me busy?"

"What about expansion? Distribution in other counties or even states?"

"Mason has the capacity to double his production, but he's hesitant to move too quickly. He seems content to keep things local, and he could make a living doing so, but his beer is so amazing that it would be a shame not to go bigger."

"And keep you occupied?"

"Yeah," Grace said with an edge of sadness. "Mum wants me to help with the marketing of the fishing camp, and of course I will, but that wouldn't keep me busy enough."

"You're leaving something out."

Grace slowed her pace. "Marco Cosmetics has been coming at me hard to develop a line of nail polish for Girl Code."

"And that would mean going back to London."

Grace nodded. "I'm afraid so," she said, and started walking.

"But what about Mason? Grace, you're totally in love with him. And I know he adores you."

Grace stopped in her tracks and took in a deep breath. "But it's not enough. Look at Mum and Rick Ruleman. And she was so miserable with Dad. I don't want to live like that."

"You wouldn't have to."

"Lifestyles have to blend together, Sophia. If not, no matter how much you love someone, it will eventually tear you apart."

"Um, there's a thing called compromise," Sophia said, and then put her hand on Grace's arm. "Oh, would you look at that?" She pointed to a bridal shop called From This Moment. "That wedding gown is stunning."

Grace looked at the dress and felt an odd longing wash over her. "Yes . . ." Her breath caught and she couldn't look away.

"Do you dream of your wedding day? Fantasize? Wonder what it will feel like to see your groom standing at the altar?" Sophia asked in a dreamy voice.

"No," Grace insisted, but a vision of Mason dressed in a tuxedo waiting for her with a smile on his face slid into her brain. "You're such a romantic. I'm a realist. Marriage and settling down just aren't for me." And yet she still couldn't take her eyes from the dress.

"Would you look at this? We're on a street called Wedding Row."

"Maybe there's more for you to do in this town than what you know," Grace said. "Look at the lovely florist called Flower Power." She walked over and peeked in the window, eager to get away from the dress. "Charming!"

"Oh right, Gabby Marino owns it. She's married to Reese Marino from the pizza parlor. They come into the bistro for breakfast from time to time. Really cute couple. Evidently, Reese was a bit of a bad boy who came back to Cricket Creek to open the restaurant with his uncle Tony."

"Oh right, Trish is Tony's wife. She did a couple of articles in the newspaper about the brewery. I liked her a lot."

Sophia chuckled.

"What?"

"Reese and Gabby told a funny story about how Trish gave River Row Pizza and Pasta a rather bad review in the paper when they first opened. Apparently Trish was Tony's landlord at the time and she didn't realize that the restaurant belonged to him. Talk about a rocky start to a relationship. Wow . . ."

"And now they're married?"

"Yes."

"Oh, that's brilliant."

"Seems to be the way of things here in this little town."

"How do you know all of this?" Grace asked.

Sophia waved a hand through the air. "From the bistro. Working there provides a wealth of information. I love listening to all of the stories. Everyone here is just so . . . real, you know?"

"You just sounded rather forlorn."

"Well, Mattie is back on a limited basis. Meaning my time here is limited as well, in spite of Mom's efforts."

Sophia stopped and looked out over the river. "I'll be sad when I have to leave. It's been so fun having all of us together in one place rather than scattered all over. Grace, I'm going to miss you so much."

Grace felt a lump form in her throat. She reached over and hugged her sister. "Me too."

"Oh, Grace, I can tell by the tone of your voice that you're leaving soon. When?"

"After the grand opening. Like I said, after that I won't be needed much. I'll become the silent partner that Mason wanted from the beginning."

"I somehow think he's changed his mind on that one."

"I'm best at launching a business, Sophia. If he doesn't want to expand, my work here is just about done."

"And if Mason asks you to stay?"

"He won't. He made me promise that I would leave when I felt the need to move on."

"And are you feeling the need?"

"Yes," Grace said, but what she was really feeling was the odd need to cry. "The longer I stay, the harder it will be to go."

"Perhaps that's the point."

"You're being awfully cheeky tonight," Grace said, trying to change the subject, but her voice wobbled.

Sophia stopped and grabbed Grace's arm. "You just decided to leave, didn't you? Like, right now. I know that faraway tone."

Grace nodded. "I'm afraid so."

"And miss the grand opening? How could you?"

"Everything is in place. It would just be too hard for me."

"So what brought about this sudden decision?"

"It's not sudden, Sophia. I only meant to come here for a couple weeks at the most, and I've gone way beyond that. We're halfway though October."

"Well, that was before you invested in the brewery and fell in love with Mason Mayfield. Both unexpected, but game changers, Grace. So what the hell just happened in the span of seconds? Oh my God . . . this!"

"What?" Grace asked innocently, but her sister knew her all too well.

"Wedding Row. The bridal shop. You had an attack of . . . something. Anxiety?" She looked at Grace. "No." She shook her head hard. "Hope. Longing." She pointed her finger at Grace and then back at From This Moment, before turning to face Grace again. "You were feeling it while you looked at the dress. The possibility of getting married to Mason slipped into your mind."

"I don't want to get married or settle down!"

"Are you trying to convince me or yourself?"

"Oh, Sophia, you were sort of right. The idea did slip into my brain. Quickly followed by anxiety. The whole ball-and-chain thing scared the daylights out of me. Looking at that wedding gown made me want to run for the hills."

"You are horrible at lying."

"I'm not lying to you."

"No, you're lying to yourself. Let me ask you something. What would you do if Mason proposed?"

Grace's heart thudded at the thought. "First of all, he isn't going to. It would be too soon for something that big."

"That's not what I asked."

"It's a moot point! This whole conversation is a moot point. You know me, Sophia." She sliced her hand through the air. "I have to move on."

"The only thing you have to do is be happy." Sophia hugged Grace again, and then said, "I'm dropping the subject."

"Thank you!"

"After one more question."

Grace blew out a long sigh. "I don't suppose I can bloody well stop you."

"When are you going to tell Mason you're leaving? You're not just going to up and go, are you?"

"Of course not!" Although that idea held some appeal. Grace's heart thudded with dread. "I'll tell him tonight."

Sophia groaned and raised her hands skyward. "Well, here we went out for a simple dinner, and this had to go and happen. I feel responsible for suggesting eating up here."

"I was going to bolt sooner or later."

"Oh, Grace." Sophia swiped at a tear. "No! At least wait for the grand opening that you've worked so hard on."

"I think being here for that will make it even more difficult."

"But Mason is going to be so disappointed. How can you do that to him? And won't you miss him terribly?"

"Of course! I will miss everyone. But my life will get back to normal as soon as I'm in London working on the nail polish line. And then I think I'll take a holiday to Paris or something."

"There's nothing normal about you or your life."

"Part of my charm, right?"

"No, it's not. I hope you go back there and then come to your senses. If I had a guy like Mason in love with me, I'd be over the moon. You should be thanking your lucky stars instead of running away."

"Sophia, I would make us both unhappy if I tried to be someone I'm not. I'm doing us both a favor. Think about it."

"You wouldn't be this damned afraid if you didn't really love him. Think about *that*."

Grace looked out over the water, knowing that Sophia was right. "Why is love so frightening?"

"Because it's the most powerful emotion we possess. And in the end it's what we care about the most. Love is what we live for, Grace. Think about that when you're deciding upon nail colors."

"Since when does sweet Sophia not pull any punches?" Grace tried to joke.

"Having us all together has tugged at my heartstrings. And holding Lily has me thinking about my future too, I guess." Sophia glanced back at the display window and sighed.

"That tiny little girl has had quite an impact on us all. She's the reason we're all in Cricket Creek, if you stop and think about it." Grace cleared her throat. "Well, I'd better get going."

"Okay . . ." Sophia nodded slowly. "I love you, sis. If you need to talk, be sure to call me, okay?"

"I will. And I love you too." She squared her shoulders. "All right, then, here goes nothing," she said, but she thought . . . *here goes* everything.

23

Whatever Gets You Through the Night

A S SOON AS GRACE WALKED INTO THE TAPROOM, MASON took one look at her face and knew that something was terribly wrong. He tossed the dish towel down onto the bar and walked her way. "How did dinner with Sophia go?"

"Good. I'm proud of myself for refraining from ordering the turtle cheesecake," she said lightly, but her smile seemed to be forced.

Mason had a flashback of feeding cheesecake to her, and he smiled back. "Good for you."

"Why, thank you. We'll forget all about the three slices of pepperoni pizza."

"I won't mention it. Hey, listen, I'm all done here. Want to head over to my place and share a nightcap? Listen to some music or watch a movie?"

"Actually, I need to have a chat with you about something."

When she swallowed hard, Mason's heart thudded.

"Okay. Should I sit down for this?" he asked, but he was pretty sure what was coming.

"Maybe." She suddenly seemed even more distraught, and on the verge of tears. When there wasn't even a funny comeback, he knew for sure he was in trouble.

"All right." Mason nodded and then took a seat on one of the barstools and waited for her to join him. "So what's on your mind?"

"Marco Cosmetics has been after me for weeks to develop a line of nail polish for Girl Code."

Mason nodded. "You mentioned it," he said, trying to remain calm.

She sucked in her bottom lip. "They sweetened the pot, and so I've decided to accept their offer."

"You can do it from here, though, right?" Mason asked, but he suspected the answer.

"No." She frowned and looked down at her hands rather than at him. "Not really. I have to meet with the design team, and it wouldn't be feasible, especially with the time difference."

"So you're moving back to London?" Mason tried his best to sound casual, but his heart felt as if it was splitting in two.

"Yes, I have to, Mason."

"You don't *have* to."

She finally looked at him. "Okay, I need to."

"No, you don't need to."

"I . . . I want to, then."

"Are you sure?"

"Mason . . ."

"And you can't even wait until after the grand opening?" Hurt slammed him hard in the gut. "Wow . . ."

"You don't need me here. Everything is all set up and ready to roll. I'll revert to the silent partner that you wanted in the first place."

"Nothing I have now is what I wanted in the first place." He paused for her to respond, but she gave him a slight shake of her head. "Everything might be all set up, Gracie. But you're dead wrong. I need you here." He reached over and put his hand on top of hers. "And it has nothing to do with the brewery. But I won't ask you to stay." He looked down at their hands and then into her eyes. "And I expect you to keep your promise."

"That's what I'm doing. Keeping my promise."

Mason dug deep for a smile, but he failed. "That doesn't mean that I like it."

"I'll keep in contact, Mason. If there are any loose ends that need to be tied up or—"

"No, I've got this." He glanced away and then slid his hand from hers.

"I'm sorry, Mason."

"It's okay," he said, but it wasn't even one bit okay. "I've been preparing myself for this day. I've seen that look in your eye recently, and I knew you'd eventually feel the need to move on. I just hoped . . ." He trailed off and shrugged. He wanted to say that he hoped that she loved him enough to stay, but that wouldn't be fair. "So when are you leaving?" He didn't even try to keep his voice light.

"Tomorrow."

Mason couldn't speak, and so he nodded.

"I'm going to head over to Mattie and Garret's after I leave here."

He nodded again. Every fiber in his being wanted to beg her to stay. "I love you, Gracie. And I'll miss you something fierce." He stood up and slapped the dish towel over his shoulder. The urge to hug her had him fisting his hands at his sides. If he hugged her, he wouldn't be able to let go.

"I love you too, Mason." Her eyes swam with tears. "I always will," she said, but when she stepped closer, he backed away.

"Don't," he pleaded softly, and when he saw regret flash in her eyes, he had a moment of hope, but then she nodded and turned around.

"I understand."

Mason stood in the middle of the taproom and watched her walk out the door. He remained motionless for a long time, thinking that the aching emotion he was feeling could only be described as ... despair.

A few minutes later, Danny walked in the front door. "Hey, was that Grace I saw driving down the road?"

"Yeah," Mason said in a voice that sounded like a croak. "She's leaving, Danny."

"Wait." Danny shook his head. "You mean leaving, as in leaving Cricket Creek?"

"'Fraid so."

"Why the hell aren't you stopping her?"

"Because I promised I wouldn't."

"Well that was a dumb-ass promise. Who cares? Do it anyway."

"No." Mason shook his head firmly. "I can't keep her here if she doesn't want to be. What good would that do in the long run?"

"Change her mind. I can't believe it. I have to admit that I'm kinda surprised."

"Hey, she was up front from the beginning, and I did what you suggested and gave her a reason to stay. Apparently, loving her just isn't enough."

"There has to be a way to work things out. Give her space and freedom but still have her in your life."

"Danny, we're small-town people. I want a wife, children, the whole nine yards at some point, and I'm not getting younger. I adore Gracie, but we want way different things out of life. I knew that all along, and now I have to let her go." He shoved his fingers in his hair and sighed. "So I'm trying to decide whether to get shit-faced or throw things ... punch a hole in a wall?"

"Hey, I'm the wild brother who does shit like that. I've got a better idea."

"Shoot."

"How about doing some night fishing?"

Mason managed a small smile. "Now you're talkin'."

"And if you want to get shit-faced, we can do that later while we fry the mess of crappie we catch."

"I'll hold you to that." He wasn't able to smile again, but he was so glad to have his brother with him right now.

Danny reached over and squeezed Mason's shoulder. "I've got my money on Grace coming to her senses and ending up back here."

"I can't even put that hope in my head."

"Well, I just put it there for you. Now, let's get out on the river and head up to the lake. We've had enough rain to make it through the creek to some of the sweet spots."

"Sounds like a plan. I'll button things up here and meet you at the marina."

"Bring some beer."

"I've got that covered. Having a brother who owns a brewery has its perks."

"You can say that again." Danny gave Mason a playful shove, but then pulled him in for a quick hug. "Hey, I'm here for ya—you know that, right?"

"Absolutely. And you know I'll always have your back."

"Good." Danny gave him a nod. "See you in a few."

Mason rolled his head back and forth, trying to get the knots of tension to ease. He remembered that he'd told Gracie that if she left, he'd survive. And he would. But it wasn't going to be easy. He knew that the best thing would be to keep busy. Luckily, he had plenty of work to do.

But first, he had to get through tonight.

24

The Look of Love

*H*OLDING LITTLE LILY WAS ALMOST GRACE'S UNDOING. She looked down at her niece's sweet cherub face and had to blink back tears. Grace started making noises in the silly baby-talk voice that adults were compelled to use. "You're such a pretty girl," Grace said, and melted when Lily smiled. "Yes, you are. Oh, yes, you are. Goo, goo, goo!" She looked over at Garret. "She's smiling at me!"

"She loves her aunt Grace."

"Oh, Garret, she is just the sweetest thing."

"Do you think I can have a turn with my daughter?" Garret asked, but Grace shook her head. "Come on, love, I've been at the studio all day long."

"No way. I'm leaving tomorrow. I want to treasure every last second."

"Then, don't leave," Garret said gravely. "There, that was an easy solution. Anything else I can do for you?"

Grace pretended to ignore him and smiled when Lily put her tiny hand around her pinkie finger. "You are the best baby in the whole wide world. Wait, no, the entire universe. And I will miss you dearly."

Mattie walked in from the kitchen and smiled over at Grace. "Well, you know that our door is always open."

"She means that quite literally," Garret said in a tone that usually would get a laugh from Grace. "People in Cricket Creek think that locks are a decoration meant for show."

"I lock the door now that we have Lily."

Garret rolled his eyes.

"Well, at least I try to remember to lock it. But, Grace, I'm serious."

"Thank you, Mattie. I'll take you up on that." Grace refused to give up Lily until she started fussing and rooting around to be fed. "Oh, can't help you there, sweet pea." As she walked over to hand Lily to her mother, Grace felt emotion well up in her throat. "Here's your mum." After gently lowering Lily to her mother's arms, Grace lifted her sleeve to her nose. "Oh, such a lovely sweet baby smell. They should make a baby-scented candle." She snapped her fingers. "Hey, I think I'll work on that one. When I miss Lily I'll burn the candle."

"And miss her even more," Garret pointed out.

Grace responded by swiping at a tear. "You are a heartless bloke, Garret Ruleman."

"Just telling you the truth, Grace. Why can't you commute back and forth like Mattie and I are going to do? Keep a place here too?"

"It's not that simple, Garret. I just can't come and go as I please. I'll have work to do. I'll have to travel to do market testing with the new line of nail polish. This isn't easy." What she left out was that as much as she could come and go with her family, she didn't see her traveling lifestyle blending with Mason's. It wouldn't be fair to him to have a girlfriend who needed to roam.

"Oh, Grace, we'll be in London in just a few months," Mattie said. "I hate seeing that sad look on your face."

"That seems ages away." Her nearly three-month stay in Cricket Creek had flown by in a flash, though. Time could be so weird that way.

"And we will all be staying at the Notting Hill flat, since Becca is renting out her house. By that time, Lily will be sitting up and rolling over," Mattie said.

"I know," Grace said glumly. "And of course I'll come back to visit family, especially with Mum having what she calls her 'thing' with Jimmy." Grace did air quotes. "I don't see her leaving until you head to London. Especially now that they are doing the fishing camp together."

"Well, it's a serious thing, if you ask me," Garret said, "and the fishing camp is brilliant. But I won't lie. I'm going to miss you. And Sophia when she leaves too."

"Even though Sophia says she's going back to New York, I'm not so sure she'll pull that trigger. She really likes living here."

"Well, I've never seen Mum this happy," Garret said with a crooked smile. "There's just something special about people from Cricket Creek." He gave Mattie a cute wink.

"You're such a flirt," Mattie said, and put a possessive hand on Garret's leg when he sat down on the sofa next to her.

"Only with you," Garret said, and leaned over to give his wife a kiss.

"Well, yeah, or else!" Mattie raised her fist, but laughed. She looked over at Grace and said, "We get to start cereal next week! That means a better chance that Lily will sleep through the night."

"And I get to help feed her," Garret said with such joy that Grace had to laugh in spite of her somber mood. Her bad-boy brother had finally settled down, and it suited him.

Grace smacked her hands on her knees and pushed up. "Well, I'd better get going. I promised Mum that I'd stop by, and I'm not looking forward to her giving me another round of reasons to stay."

"You have one big reason," Mattie said. While there

wasn't any accusation in her voice, Grace still felt a stab of guilt.

"Mattie, I never meant to hurt Mason. He knew I'd leave at some point. I'm so sorry."

Mattie tilted her head to the side. "I'm not placing blame, Grace. But Mason loves you dearly, and you can't do any better than him. He has a heart of gold."

"Oh, believe me—I know that, Mattie. This decision didn't come lightly to me, but I value his happiness too. He needs a woman by his side, and I'm not meant to stay put. It might not seem like it, but I'm doing the right thing by leaving."

"I don't agree with you, but I understand your way of thinking." She smiled softly and gave Garret a look of love. "But, hey, I didn't think this little country girl would have the courage to up and travel across the ocean to be with your brother, but what was in my heart was strong enough to overcome my fear. And now I love London and I enjoy traveling and seeing the world! As my daddy would say, where there's a will, there's a way. Just remember that, okay?"

Grace nodded.

"I love you like a sister, no matter what, so don't you fret. I just think that you and Mason belong together."

"Mattie," Garret said. "You promised not to do this, remember?"

Mattie glanced up at Garret. "I did not promise not to speak my mind. I promised not to cry," she said, and sniffed. She shifted her gaze over to Grace. "You can change your mind, you know."

"Mattie!" Garret said, but leaned over and kissed her. "You need to keep out of this, love."

"Hey, I'm Southern. We meddle. It's a way of life. I'm sorry, Grace. I just can't help myself."

"It's okay," Grace said, and wondered if she'd lost her mind leaving this loving, wonderful family and quaint town. "Well, I'm going to whistle off."

"I'll walk you out," Garret said.

"Okay." Grace paused to kiss Mattie on the cheek and run a fingertip down Lily's cheek. "Make sure you FaceTime me so I can see her smile."

Mattie reached over and squeezed Grace's hand. "I will."

Grace nodded and then stood there for another heartbreaking moment before finally turning and walking out the door.

When they were by her car, Grace gave Garret a hug, clinging a little bit longer than usual.

"Grace, are you okay?"

"No, not at all. Am I doing the right thing by leaving?"

"Only you can answer that. But, Grace, I have to say that there's nothing in this life that can replace the feeling of someone loving you beyond all reason. You know I'm a flawed piece of work. I feel so damned lucky to have Mattie in my life. I wouldn't trade her or having Lily for anything in the world. And you know what a selfish wanker I used to be. But I'd make the same mistakes all over again to end up right here and now. Does that make sense?"

"Yes, but we've always understood each other." Grace put her hands on his cheeks. "You were confused there for a while and gave Mum some gray hair that she hates, but you were always an amazing brother. I love you dearly." She kissed his cheek and then stepped back. "Wait. I can tell you're going to say something more. I can see it in your eyes."

"Just think about what you really, truly want out of life. It took me a while, but when I figured it out, it was crystal clear."

"I will." Grace nodded briskly, knowing she had to leave before she simply could not. "See you in London soon."

Garret hugged her again. "If not before. Now, get over to Mum's. She's been blowing up my phone."

"Sorry, but you're going to have to put up with her grumbling after I leave."

"You're going to owe me big-time. Safe travels, love."

"Thanks." Grace nodded, but as she drove over to her mother's cabin, she knew that announcing her sudden departure wasn't going to go well. Just like Sophia, Garret, and surprisingly Mattie, her mum wasn't going to pull any punches or hold her tongue either. But Grace knew she had to stand firm. With that in mind, she braced herself and then knocked on the door of the cabin.

"Gracie!" Her mother's face lit up with a smile. "Come on in, darling."

"Is Jimmy here?"

"He just left a little while ago," she said, but then took another look at Grace and put one hand to her chest. "Oh, Gracie, please tell me you're not thinking of leaving."

"I'm not thinking of leaving."

"Oh, good."

"I *am* leaving, Mum."

"Now?"

"Tomorrow afternoon. I'm packing my things tonight and driving to Nashville tomorrow and taking the red-eye to London."

"This is sudden. Why now, before the grand opening?"

"Because the longer I stay, the more it isn't fair to Mason."

"You're way past that part."

"I've not been unfair. Honesty isn't unfair," she insisted. So why did it feel that way?

"Really? I don't think you're being honest with yourself." She gestured to the sofa. "How about a lovely glass of wine? And then we need to talk about this decision of yours."

"Yes, and make it a generous pour."

"Will do, coming right up," she said, and hurried into the kitchen.

"Thank you," Grace said as she took the large glass from her mother. After taking a sip she said, "Life sure isn't easy, is it?"

"Not in the least," Becca said, and sat down in an

overstuffed chair facing the sofa. "So tell me why you feel the sudden urge to flee."

"I'm not fleeing. I'm going back to London, where I've lived for the past few years. I'm simply going home. And the offer to do the nail polish line was just too generous to pass up. Plus, you'll be back in a few months when Garret films *Sing for Me*. And this time we'll all be living at the flat. It will be fun."

"Yes, your tone sounds utterly joyful." Becca took a sip of wine. "So what brought this on? It had to be something. Did you and Mason have a row?"

"No." She ran a fingertip over the rim of her glass. "I wish we had a fight, and then this wouldn't feel so horrid."

"Then what happened, Gracie? Didn't you and Sophia go to dinner?"

"Yes." Grace stared down into her red wine, playing with the stem of the delicate glass. "We ended up walking around up on Wedding Row." She took a bracing sip of the wine. "And when Sophia and I stopped in front of a bridal boutique, there was this spectacular wedding gown in the window. A spotlight caught the beaded bodice, making it almost glow. The train was magnificent, and I felt this longing . . . followed by sheer panic."

"Did Mason ask you to marry him?"

"No, but if I stay here, I know that he will at some point. He wants a family life, and I love him, but I don't have that in me," she said, and patted her chest. "If I leave, he can move on and find someone right for him," she continued, but picturing Mason with another woman made her throat constrict.

"And you'd be able to live with that knowledge? Come back here for family functions and see him with someone else?"

"I want him to be happy. He wants me to be happy. We made a promise to each other that he wouldn't ask me to stay, and I promised that when the time felt right, I would leave."

"And does the time feel right, darling?"

"Yes, Mum. That doesn't mean that it isn't tearing me to pieces. Why doesn't anyone get that? This isn't a selfish move on my part. But it's the right one. And I don't want Mason to come running after me like a Hallmark movie. We've been realistic about the whole thing. And it makes me love him even more that he's not asking me to stay."

"Oh, darling, but what if he would ask you?"

Grace closed her eyes, trying desperately to ward off tears. "I don't know if I'd have the willpower to deny him. That's why I have to go now, before it's too late. Don't you see? I'm terrified that in a few years I'll be miserable, and I don't want to put Mason through that." She took a sip of wine. "Everything will be okay after I return to London. My life will go back to normal. My normal, anyway."

"Do you seriously believe that?"

"I don't have a choice."

"It took me a long time to figure it out, but there are always choices, darling. Remember that."

Grace nodded. "I will," she promised, but she thought that she wasn't choosing to leave Cricket Creek. She simply had to get back out there and continue to explore the world.

25
In My Life

"Mason, for the love of God, call Grace and ask her where to order the witches' hats," Danny said. He pointed to the empty shelves in the gift shop. "We're out and we need a slew of them for the grand opening."

Mason looked up from the computer screen. "No, Danny. While I appreciate all of the help you've been giving me, I'm not going to contact Gracie."

"Why not?"

"You know why. I made her promise that it would be her choice to come back," Mason said, and of course the mention of Gracie's name brought her face floating into his mind. It had been only a little over a week since she'd been gone, and it felt like a lifetime. "Who needs those silly-ass hats anyway?" he asked gruffly. But then he thought about fishing Gracie's hat out of the river, his terror, and then his knee-buckling relief when he knew she was okay.

"You do!" Danny walked over and sat down on a barstool. "It's Halloween, bro. By the way, what are you going to dress up as?"

"I'm not getting dressed up," Mason replied.

"But it's part of the grand-opening theme. You have to wear a costume. I think I'm going to be Robin Hood."

"You're wearing tights?"

"Hey, I have great legs. Why not show them off?"

Mason shook his head and went back to entering the new ales into the main menu. He knew that Danny was trying to cheer him up, but he just couldn't muster even a hint of a smile.

"Mason, you need to do what Mattie did and head to London and bring Grace back to Cricket Creek, where she belongs."

"She doesn't belong here. That's the problem. It worked with Mattie and Garret because he has his music at My Way Records. Becca has the fishing camp with Jimmy and needs to be near Lily."

"Have you heard from her?"

"No." Mason glanced away. He left out the part where he'd sent Gracie an invitation to the grand opening. She might not want to live here, but he wanted her to know that she was welcome and that she deserved to celebrate the success of the brewery too. But when he didn't get the RSVP back, he knew she wasn't coming. And as much as it hurt, he respected her decision. "I'm sure she's really busy. And that's the way she likes to live her life. Slow and laid-back like it is here just isn't her style. Hey, I know I've been grumpy since she's been gone, but I'm getting over it," he said, which was completely untrue. "Just don't mention her again, okay? I'm sure she's over me already, and . . ." Mason shrugged, unable to think of Grace out with some other guy. "Is it too early for a beer?"

"You're asking the wrong guy that question," Danny said.

"No, I'm asking the right guy."

Danny chuckled. "Well, I should really get back to the marina and check on a few things. I can come back later and take you up on a beer. Or better yet, why don't we head over to Sully's later and shoot some pool?"

"I'll let you know," Mason said, not sure how social he

could be at Sully's. "I've got to get into the brewery and roll the fermentors into the walk-in cooler in a little while. I hope I've tweaked the pumpkin ale to perfection."

"It's that time of year when everything is flavored with pumpkin."

"It will be subtle. People have been asking for it. Seasonal ales date way back to when beer was first brewed and brewers had to use the ingredients on hand. I think it's a pretty cool tradition."

"Is there anything you don't know about the history of beer?"

"Probably not."

"Need some help?"

"No, I can handle it. Hey, Danny, I can't thank you enough for all you've been doing for me."

"It's called family. No matter what happens, we can always count on each other."

"No doubt," Mason said, and no sooner did Danny leave than Mattie walked through the door. "Well, hey there. Where's Lily?"

"Mom and Dad are watching her. I wanted to show you the menu I've come up with for the grand opening. Do you have a minute?"

"Of course."

"Great," Mattie said, and slid onto a barstool. Mason braced himself for another go-get-Gracie lecture, but Mattie stuck to chatting about the side dishes to go with the pulled-pork barbecue they'd already decided upon weeks ago. "I've ordered the buns from Grammar's Bakery. They're also making a huge sheet cake with the Broomstick logo on it."

"Very nice."

"I'll make the slaw up a day ahead, and Mom and Dad are going to help me scoop it into plastic containers. We'll need room in the cooler, if that's okay."

"Sure."

"And I sure wish you'd quit talking so much . . ."

Mason sighed. "Don't look at me like that. I'll get over her, Mattie. It will just take some time." *Like until the end of time,* he thought darkly. He searched for something to say to change the subject. "What are you and Garret being for Halloween?"

"We're trying to decide whether we want to come as Sonny and Cher or the Captain and Tennille. I think I'd rather be Cher so I can do the hair flip. I already have the wig." She did a fake flip and licked her lips in an imitation of Cher. "What do you think?"

"Perfect."

"I've been practicing." She propped her elbows on the bar and rested her chin in her hand.

"What?" Mason asked.

"Nothing."

"Mattie, I know that look. Just go ahead and get it off your chest. I've been bracing myself."

"You're bored without Grace. Just going through the motions."

"I'm not bored. I have a craft brewery to run. Orders to fill," he said, even though his sister had hit the nail right on the damned head. Without Gracie, it was as if the light had gone out of his life.

Mattie shook her head. "Grace brought excitement into your world. She made you laugh, Mason. Go get her and bring her home."

"Mattie, I told Gracie that I wouldn't try to stop her from leaving. I love her and she knows it. So if she comes back to Cricket Creek, it's because she wants to . . . not because I want her to. What don't you and Danny understand about that?" He patted his chest. "End of story."

"But what if—"

"No, Mattie. Look, I know you and Danny mean well, but I'm having a hard enough time with this without a constant reminder of what I no longer have in my life. Just let it go. Please."

"Okay, you're right. I'm sorry. I won't mention it again."

"Thanks."

"It's just that—"

"Mattie!"

"Okay!" She raised her hands in surrender. "Well, I'd better get back. My breasts are about to burst."

"Too much information."

Mattie laughed. "Come on over here and give your baby sister a hug. But don't squeeze too hard. I might leak on you."

Mason came around from the bar and gave Mattie a hug gingerly. "The next time you come over, bring Lily with you."

"Prying her out of the arms of her grandmas is difficult, but I'll try." She reached up and put her hands on his shoulders. "If you need to bend my ear, just give me a holler, okay?"

"Will do," Mason promised. He watched his sister walk out the door, thinking that he might be hurting from missing Gracie, but he was lucky to have such a close, loving family. He told himself to stop feeling sorry for himself and to count his many blessings.

But later that evening, when Mason sat outside on his back deck, he looked over at Gracie's empty cabin on the water and felt sadness wash over him. He didn't care how much time passed; he knew in his heart that he would never be able to look over at the cabin and not think of her. He took a sip of his bourbon, liking the bite lingering on his tongue. Blowing out a long sigh, he gazed up at the stars glittering in the inky black sky, wishing to find an answer as to why fate had to be so cruel to bring Gracie into his life, only to have her slip away from him.

He looked into his empty glass and decided he needed another splash of bourbon over ice while waiting for Danny to arrive. He'd already decided not to go to Sully's but to stay home instead. If Danny wanted to hang out and listen to music with him, that was fine, but he didn't feel like going out. As the ice was clinking into his glass, Mason heard a knock at the front door. He never kept it locked, and Danny wouldn't knock, making him wonder who would be visiting who wouldn't just come on in. He'd fantasized about Gracie showing up and throwing herself into his arms, and his heart kicked into high gear as he walked across the living room. But when he opened the door, he found Jimmy Topmiller standing on his houseboat.

"Hey, Jimmy, come on in," Mason said.

"Sorry to stop by unannounced. I tried calling your cell, but you didn't pick up."

"Oh, I've been outside, and I had it in here charging. Can I get you something? Beer? Or I'm sippin' on some fine bourbon."

"I'll take a bourbon on ice, if you don't mind."

"Coming right up," Mason said, curious as to why Jimmy had stopped over. "Everything okay with Becca?"

"Yeah, she went up to Wine and Diner. Girls' night out."

"Oh, good." He handed Jimmy the glass. "Wanna go on the back deck? It's a little bit cold, but I don't mind if you don't. And Danny should be over soon."

"Oh, good, I wanted to run some more ideas by him about the fishing camp."

"Hey, it's a great idea, by the way."

"Thanks. I'm really excited." He accepted the glass. "Sure, outside is fine."

Mason nodded and headed to the sliding doors. He zipped up his hooded sweatshirt and sat down. "So, let me guess. You came over to jump on the go-get-Gracie bandwagon?"

"Nope, not me." Jimmy took a sip of his bourbon, but shook his head. "I've never been on a bandwagon in my life. I do things my own way. Always have." He looked down at his drink. "Smooth stuff."

"Knob Creek single barrel."

"Mmm . . ." He took another sip. "It's hitting the spot."

"Why do I feel as if there's something you want to tell me?"

"Well, I'm not one to meddle, but I love Becca. There's something about fallin' in love with a woman that turns a man's brain to mush and makes him do fool things. Like meddle in someone else's business."

Mason sat up straighter. "Go on."

"I'm like Silly Putty in her hands. Lord help me, but there's nothin' I wouldn't do to make her happy. Do you know that I'm going on a European vacation? Yep, just applied for my passport. Stayin' at fancy-ass hotels . . . and I think in a castle somewhere along the line."

"Jimmy, what does this have to do with me?"

"Well, Becca wants Grace to come back to Cricket Creek to live. Spilled a bucket full of tears over it last night."

"Well, there's a long line of people wanting the same thing." And he was first in that long line.

"Yeah, well, there's only one person who can make that happen." He pointed a finger at Mason. "And I happen to be lookin' at him."

Mason gazed up at the stars and shook his head. "I've explained to everyone over and over. I won't go to London to bring Gracie back—not that I don't want to. If she wants to come back to Cricket Creek, it has to be her decision."

"Well, you didn't hear it from me, but I've got that part covered."

"Wait . . . what?"

"Grace is at Wine and Diner with Sophia and Becca."

"She's in town?" His heart knocked around in his chest like a pinball.

"Yeah, apparently she wanted to come back for the grand opening of the brewery after all. But you didn't hear it from me."

Ah, so his invitation had worked? Mason's heart beat so hard, he was sure that Jimmy must hear it. He tried to process the information. "So she's just back for the grand opening."

"Yeah, well, that's where you come in, my friend. It's up to you to make her want to stay."

"I . . . uh . . ."

"If I were you, I'd head on over to her cabin and be there when she arrives."

"I don't know. I . . ."

"Mason, for the love of God, do you really think she came back for a doggone party?"

"Well, she is invested in the brewery."

"Which you are more than capable of running." He drained the rest of his drink. "Is your skull really that thick?"

Mason smiled for the first time since Gracie left. "No."

"Then you'd best hightail it on over there. And don't blow it this time. You only get so many chances, you know. I'll wait here for Danny. Now, get on over there!"

26

The Other Half of the Sky

THREE GLASSES OF MERLOT, A GENTLY BOBBING DOCK, and jet lag had Grace gingerly making her way to her cabin. Well, she thought of it as her cabin, anyway. The wheels of her suitcase made a clunking noise as she tugged it along behind her, and her progress was further hindered by the weight of her laptop case hanging on one shoulder and her purse over the other one. At one point she almost took a sideways dive into the water. She suppressed a little shriek and did a little tap dance back to safety. "Okay." She stopped and hefted her purse higher on her shoulder, trying for balance. After regaining her composure, she forged ahead. Had the dock gotten longer since she'd left? It certainly seemed so.

Grace breathed a sigh of relief when she reached the front door. Luckily, she still had a key. Before sliding it into the lock, she glanced over at Mason's houseboat and noticed that no lights were on, so he must not be home. She wondered if he would come over later when he noticed lights on over here.

Grace had considered calling Mason, but she'd rehearsed what she was going to say to him a million times while driving in from Nashville, and the speech was meant to be given in person. Of course, after the third glass of wine, Sophia and her mum were full of advice on how to handle the situation, most of which she had no intention of using.

Grace lugged her stuff into the bedroom, switched on the small lamp on the nightstand, and decided to change into her Mayfield Marina sweatpants. Then she planned to go out onto the deck and listen to some music to wind down before getting some much-needed sleep. But when she looked at the inviting bed, she immediately decided that she needed sleep more than sitting outside. After a good night's rest, she would call Mason and give her speech.

"Yeah, that's a good plan." Closing her eyes, she tilted her face upward, yawned, and stretched her arms overhead.

"When were you going to let me know that you were back in town?"

Grace yelped, took a step backward, tripped over her suitcase, and stumbled. Luckily, she landed on the bed with a little bounce. "Mason?" She pushed up to her elbows and looked over to where he stood in the doorway. The sight of him sent her pulse racing.

"Why didn't you tell me you were coming home? I mean to Cricket Creek." He casually leaned one shoulder against the doorframe and waited for her answer. "And you didn't RSVP. Very bad form for a proper British lady."

"Because I . . . ," she began, trying to remember the speech, which had flown out of her head. She sat up and cleared her throat. "Because what I have to say needed to be told in person." She licked her bottom lip, suddenly nervous.

"Okay. Well, here I am. In person."

"I love you . . . no wait, that part was supposed to come at the end. Let me start over."

"No, I like that beginning." Mason walked over and sat down on the bed next to her. "So, go on."

"Well . . ." Grace swallowed hard, but when Mason reached over and took her hand, her courage returned. "It all started with the invitation to the grand opening. When it came, I held it in my hand like it was a lifeline to you."

"I didn't mean it as pressure, only that you deserved to be here. And I wanted you here."

"I know, love." When Grace nodded, he brought her hand up to his lips and kissed her knuckles, a gesture so tender that she had to stop and catch her breath. "That same night I was sitting out on the terrace of Mum's flat, working, while listening to music and drinking a lovely cup of tea. I looked up at the sky and wondered if you were watching the same stars as me . . ."

"A romantic notion."

"Well, yes, but of course with the time difference I realized that couldn't be true. But as I tried to concentrate on the color wheel I was studying, my mind kept wandering back up to the sky and to thoughts of you, the grand opening, and that you reached out to me. No pressure, no guilt, but it was like having your hand reach across the ocean."

"Oh, Gracie . . . I had to do something, and the simple invitation seemed like the right thing to do. No one knows I did it. I didn't want you to get pressure from anyone to come."

"In truth, I'd gotten very little work done with the nail polish the entire time I was there."

"Why is that?"

"I guess you could say that my heart wasn't in it."

"Ah . . ."

"This might sound a bit odd, but as I gazed up at the stars, the lyrics of the John Lennon song 'Woman' drifted to me as if carried on the night breeze. I get songs playing in my head a lot."

"I don't think that's odd at all."

Grace smiled. "Do you know it?"

"I do. I happen to be a big Beatles fan."

"In that same moment, I wondered how I had ended up in Cricket Creek, Kentucky, investing in a craft brewery of all things. And I realized that I had no control, really. Does that make sense?"

"Perfectly."

"Good, because the speech I rehearsed was much better."

"You're doing just fine. Go on."

Grace gave him a soft smile. "When I gazed up at the sky again, I thought to myself that our love was somehow 'written in the stars,' just like in the John Lennon song."

"Gracie, oh wow . . . that's beautiful."

"I know! So being on the other side of the ocean from you was just plain silly."

He cupped her cheek. "I've thought so all along."

"Mason, I finally figured out that my need to travel, roam, was an urge, the quest to find happiness." She leaned over and patted his chest. "You are my happiness. My journey's end," she said in a tone laced with emotion.

Mason put his hand over hers. "Hey, no need for a GPS, and you'll never get lost again. I will always be here for you."

Grace laughed. "Good thing, with my track record, right?" Sudden tears blurred her vision, and her smile trembled. "I was lost the day I met you, and now I know that I'm completely lost without you. After I left, it didn't take me long to figure that out. But I needed to have that horrid feeling of missing you so I knew for sure. And when the invitation came, it was my ticket back to you."

"Gracie, Cricket Creek is my home, and I love it here, but I'll go wherever you want me to, live wherever you want to live, or travel around the world with a backpack and nothing else. We can sell the brewery. I don't care."

"Mason, there is no doubt that I belong here in Cricket Creek. You are my other half of the sky."

"Gracie . . . mercy, I love you so much." He pulled her onto his lap, threaded his fingers through her hair and kissed her.

Oh, it felt so good to be in his strong arms. She missed the smell of him, the touch of his body, and the taste of his lips. Her need to wander was over.

She was home.

Don't miss the next charming
Cricket Creek Novel,

WISH UPON A WEDDING

Available in May 2016 from Signet Eclipse.

White Lace and Promises

"SOPHIA GORDON, NOW JUST WHAT IN THE WORLD ARE you doin' reading *Good Housekeeping*, for pity's sake? That's for my older clients, not for a young cutie pie like you."

Sophia looked over at Carrie Ann through her foil-covered bangs. "Well, there's a recipe for—" she began, but Carrie Ann tugged the magazine from her fingers so quickly that the salon chair swiveled sideways.

"This is what you should be reading, sweet pea." Carrie Ann placed the latest issue of *Cosmopolitan* in Sophia's hands.

Sophia gazed down at the scantily clad model on the cover and looked at the hair and makeup with a critical eye. "That eye shadow is way too shimmery."

"Oh forget about that and turn to page thirty."

"Page thirty?" Sophia flipped through the magazine and stared at the hot male model lying in bed, wearing nothing but boxer briefs and a wicked smile. "'Twenty-five surefire ways to drive your man wild'?" When Sophia shook her head and laughed, the foils made a light tinny sound next to her ear. "Unfortunately, I don't have a man to drive wild."

Carrie Ann looked at her in the mirror and fluffed her big auburn hair. "My motto is to always be prepared." She arched an eyebrow. "Know what I'm sayin'?"

Sophia chuckled at the owner of A Cut Above. In her mid-fifties, Carrie Ann Spencer had the hair and curves of a vintage pinup girl and a sassy Southern attitude to match the look. She'd been styling Sophia's hair since Sophia arrived in Cricket Creek, Kentucky, last summer to help out at her pregnant sister-in-law's bistro after Mattie had been put on bed rest. "You crack me up."

Carrie Ann fisted her hands on her hips and tilted her head. Her big hair was so full of product that it barely moved. "I'm serious, girl. Hey, how about me and you head over to Sully's Tavern after your hair is all done up with those highlights? I'll be your wingman."

"Have you forgotten that I'm heading back to New York City soon?"

"No." Carrie Ann took a seat in the chair beside her and swiveled it around. "But now that your mama, sister, and brother all live in Cricket Creek, I was hopin' that you might consider moving to this sweet little town too. I've grown fond of your smiling face both here and at my many breakfasts at the bistro." She leaned in closer. "Don't tell Mattie I said so, but I do think you've mastered her melt-in-your-mouth biscuits," she said in a low voice. "Add some strawberry jam and it's like having a party in my mouth."

"Oh thank you, Carrie Ann. And I'm fond of you too." Sophia shifted in her chair and inhaled deeply. Of course she'd thought about staying in Cricket Creek, especially recently. The peace and quiet of a small town drew her in more than she'd expected, and living in the same town with Garret, Grace, and her mother would be sorely missed once she moved back to the city. She'd sublet her apartment to a friend, and Sophia had no doubt that Janie would be more than happy to take over permanently. "But Lily is nearly six months old and Mattie is back full-time at Walking on Sunshine. While I love cooking and enjoyed filling in as a chef, I'm a hair stylist and makeup artist. I've worked hard to develop my clientele. It's time for me to head back to New York before I lose them. I've stayed through the holidays, but I really need to get back for the June bridal season. I've already stayed way longer than I intended. My salon is running out of patience with me. They will only hold my position open for so long before I'm permanently replaced."

Carrie Ann pressed her deep red lips together and gave her a level look. "And just why did you do that?" she asked but continued without waiting for an answer. "Um, maybe because you want to stay in Cricket Creek?" She raised her eyebrows. "Hmm? And you could have a chair here." She waved her arm in a wide arc. "I could certainly use someone with your reputation and skills. Girl, after you helped with the updos for the Snow Ball Dance, requests for you started pouring in."

"You've mentioned that a time or two."

"Or ten." Carrie Ann gave her a slight grin.

Sophia loved the little salon situated in the heart of Main Street, and while she didn't miss the drama of the high-end bridezillas she'd had to deal with, her expertise was in elaborate updos and makeup for elaborate events and weddings. But how could she tell Carrie Ann that the little salon wouldn't be enough of a challenge without sounding uppity and rude?

"Hey . . ." Carrie Ann raised her palms upward and inclined her head. "I know what you're thinkin'. You're used to the hustle and bustle of that fancy salon in New York City, and this wouldn't be enough for someone with your skills."

"Carrie Ann . . ."

"Hear me out, sweet pea."

"Okay." Sophia gripped the magazine and waited.

Carrie Ann nibbled on the inside of her cheek for a few seconds as if gathering her thoughts. "We've been slow today but A Cut Above still holds its own against the chains popping up outside of town. I have lots of loyal local clients, and I could use a couple more stylists." She put her hands on her knees and leaned forward. "But I've been tinkerin' with the idea of opening a salon up in Wedding Row. You know, in that pretty strip of wedding-related shops overlookin' the river?"

"I've been up there with Grace." Sophia nodded her foiled head and felt a warm flash in interest. "If I remember right, there's a florist, jewelry store, and lovely bridal boutique, among other things."

"From This Moment is owned by Addison Monroe, daughter of Melinda Monroe, the famous financial guru. She married a local boy."

"I know." Sophia nodded slowly. "Um . . . Addison was engaged to my half brother, Garret, before she married Reid Greenfield. It was kind of a messy story in the tabloids for a while until Rick Ruleman, my mom's ex-husband, came to Cricket Creek to straighten out the rumors and crazy lies fueled by the media. Rick was a rock legend with a reputation to match, but he would never have had an affair with Garret's fiancée." Sophia shook her head in disgust.

Carrie Ann slapped her hand to her forehead. "Well, hell's bells, how in the world could I have forgotten about that little detail?" She winced.

Sophia sliced a dismissive hand through the air. "Oh, no worries where that's concerned. Addison and Garret are on great terms now. She even sent a baby gift for Lily." Sophia lifted one shoulder. "My mom and Rick have mended their fences too. Crazy, but I never thought I'd see the day when he'd retire from his hard rock days and settle down in a small town. And his wife, Maggie, is such a sweetie." Sophia chuckled. "Life is so weird."

"Tell me about it. Your fashion model mama married a bass fisherman, and they run a fishin' camp for under-privileged kids right here in Cricket Creek. Your sister, Grace, swooped into town and helped Mason Mayfield save his craft brewery from going under."

"Oh, Mason was none too happy about Grace's marketing plan. They butted heads over calling it Broomstick Brewery."

"I thought it was genius. Sure brought in the local female crowd who might not have tried craft beer. I didn't know how delicious a glass of flavored ale could taste. And names like Spellbound and Witches' Brew are so clever."

"Oh no doubt, but Mason didn't go down without a fight." Sophia groaned. "Oh, I love Mason's chocolate porter."

"Um, yeah! I'd say your family is pretty damned awesome."

"Why, thank you. I totally agree," she said with a firm nod.

"This is why you need to consider staying in Cricket Creek." Carrie Ann stood up and checked one of the foils. "Not done processing yet." She folded it back into place.

"Carrie Ann, why are you so adamant about my staying?" she asked but had an inkling of where this conversation could be heading.

"What would you say to opening up a wedding-themed salon as partners? I'm thinking I'd like to call it White Lace and Promises," she said in a dreamy tone.

Sophia's heart thudded with excitement, but about a dozen questions popped into her head all at once. While her mom and sister were all about taking financial risks, Sophia was much more conservative. "Would there be enough weddings to keep the business brisk?"

"Good question. I spoke with Reid Greenfield's sister, Sara, who said that she's getting big barn weddings booked from Nashville, Tennessee, and Lexington, Kentucky. Sara's wedding-reception venue with the gorgeous river setting is growing by leaps and bounds. She's also booking more intimate receptions at Wine and Diner right here on Main Street. We might be a small town, but we're close to some big cities. And don't forget that there's a convention center down by the baseball stadium now. I'm sure there will be some black-tie events, which could mean even more business. Sophia, sugar, with your expertise and reputation, I truly think the clientele would grow quickly." Her voice picked up speed, and her hands did the talking as she became more and more excited. "The businesses up on Wedding Row support and feed off one another. There's a shop available for lease right next to Flower Power and it's just two doors down from the bridal boutique!" She paused to take a breath. "So what do you think? Not that you have to give me an answer right now. But thoughts . . . Give me some feedback."

"I'm definitely interested."

Carrie Ann smacked her knee. "Sweet! I've been thinkin' about this ever since Wedding Row opened up, but I didn't have anybody like you who could take the reins for me. And I have to keep on top of things here at A Cut Above. My mother opened this shop, and I want to keep the doors open in her honor." She raised her arms skyward. "This is so perfect! We definitely need to head to Sully's or down to the taproom at the brewery and celebrate."

"Carrie Ann . . . I said I'm interested," Sophia said with a note of caution in her tone.

"Okay then . . ." Carrie Ann flipped her palm over and put her index finger to her opposite pinkie. "Let's start a list of reasons why you should do this: You'd be your own boss. I would basically let you run the whole thing. You'd live in the same town as your family. The cost of living is nothing compared to New York City. You already told me that you love your condo overlooking the river." She leaned forward and put her hand next to her mouth and whispered, "And you already know that most of the hot Cricket Creek Cougars baseball players live there. Thought I'd toss in that tidbit."

"I hadn't noticed," Sophia said.

"Oh . . . well maybe that's because someone else in this town has caught your eye."

"Pffft . . . no way." She pointed to her eyes. "Not caught."

"Right, and I'm a natural redhead."

Laughing, Sophia pointed to her own hair. "And I'm *about to become* a natural blonde."

Carrie Ann sat back in her chair. "You're gonna look that way because of my expertise. Actually, those highlights will be just the perfect little boost to your gorgeous caramel color. A very Jennifer Aniston look. You kinda remind me of her . . . so pretty but not in a flashy way."

"Coming from one of the flashiest women I know."

"At my age I have to pile on makeup and bling to camouflage my flaws."

"Oh shut up! You're gorgeous."

"Ah, bless your heart, Sophia. But, sweetheart, you're a natural beauty."

"The girl next door, right?" While Sophia didn't have the stunning long-legged beauty of her mother and sister, Grace, she was content with her looks for the most part. Although it was super irritating that Grace could eat whatever she damn well pleased and not gain an ounce. Having a slow metabolism really sucked. While Sophia also didn't share the big personalities of her mother and sister, she was happy to stay in the background. She'd much rather do hair and makeup than be in front of the camera. But being the quiet one also gave her the ability to get away with some pretty epic practical jokes. Garret and Grace were always blamed for things first, so there was a definite upside to flying under the radar.

"Why so quiet? Did I say something wrong?"

"Oh no." Sophia shook her head. "Not at all. I'm just trying to process what you've just thrown in my lap."

"You mean the twenty-five ways to drive your man wild?" Carrie Ann asked with a chuckle.

"No! I'm just a little blown away by your offer to go into business together," Sophia replied but then glanced down at the article. Because she'd thought she'd be heading back to New York, she'd been careful not to get entangled in a relationship but looking at the hot guy with the wicked smile suddenly had her longing for a little skin on skin. Damn, it'd been a long time since she was in the arms of a man. And there was one man in particular . . . *No, don't go there!*

Carrie Ann stood up and checked the foils again. "About another ten minutes." She patted Sophia's shoulder. "No rush on your answer. It's good enough for me right now that you're considering my offer," she said, and hurried off to answer the phone. Because Sophia had come in rather late, everyone else was gone for the day. She glanced at her reflection in the mirror and winced, thinking that she looked like an alien Medusa, with the silver foils sticking out everywhere. The blond highlights were a bit of a whim, but she was glad she was getting them done, since she was ready for a change. Of course hair stylists were always ready for something different.

With a sigh she started scanning through the article, just for shits and giggles. The suggestions called for sexy games using props like ice cubes and feathers, mostly silly in her opinion. The painting of each other with chocolate syrup and then licking it off seemed a little messy, she thought, but then closed her eyes and groaned. Dear God, was she becoming a . . . *fuddy-duddy*? Yes, because she was pretty sure nobody her age even thought of expressions like *fuddy-duddy*. Determined, she kept her eyes closed and tried to imagine the chocolate-syrup scenario. Perhaps if you used thick chocolate fudge and warmed it up? Oh, now that might just be very nice. Hmmm . . .

"Are you sleeping?" asked a whiskey-smooth male voice that slid over her like the chocolate fudge she'd been daydreaming about. She smiled, thinking that this body-painting thing might be the ticket after all. "Um, maybe I shouldn't interrupt," the voice continued cutting through her chocolate-coated fantasy.

Oh shit.

Sophia opened her eyes and looked at the sexy country boy who had been invading her thoughts and dreams over the past few months. "Avery!" She almost sighed, but then caught herself and cleared her throat instead. Foils sprung from her head and *oh dear God* the magazine in her lap was open to the twenty-five ways to drive your man wild. She gripped the armrest, dearly wishing there was an eject button. "Hi." Her smile probably looked like a wince.

"Hey, Sophia. Haven't seen you in a while." He put his toolbox down and shrugged out of his jacket.

"I've been busy babysitting Lily a lot."

"Oh well, I miss seeing you at breakfast," he said, which created a vision of him sitting across a kitchen table in the morning, all sleep tousled and sexy.

She swallowed hard. "I miss you . . . I mean seeing you at the bistro too." She glanced down at the nearly naked model. Her fingers itched to turn the page.

"Watcha readin'?" Panic set in when he angled his head at the glossy pages in her lap.

"I . . . um . . ." She felt heat creep into her cheeks. "I was just, you know, thumbing through a random magazine while my hair processed." She looked over at Carrie Ann, who was chatting away on the phone. "What, um, brings you here?"

Avery jammed his thumb over his shoulder causing Sophia to notice the bulge of his biceps, which stretched the sleeve of his red T-shirt. The Fisher and Dean logo printed inside of a toolbox rested above a nicely defined pectoral muscle. "I'm here to fix the washing machine that's been giving Carrie Ann fits. I would've been here sooner, but I was slammed with repairs all day." He gave Sophia a grin that caused a dimple in his cheek. His dark hair, which he had usually worn short, had grown out a bit since she'd last seen him, while she'd still worked at the bistro. Dark tendrils curled around his ears and forehead. As though reading her thoughts, he shoved his fingers through his hair.

"I know. I need a haircut. Just been too busy to get it done."

"I like it longer," Sophia heard herself say and then lifted one shoulder.

"Well, then, maybe I should keep it that way." He shot her a grin.

"As a stylist I'm always thinking about hair," she responded quickly.

"Oh, I'd forgotten that was your career. If you ever decide to stay a cook, you'll never be broke either." He flashed another grin that made her melt like the ice cube in "How to Drive Your Man Wild" number five. "I really do miss you at the bistro, Sophia."

"Oh, I was getting pretty good, but Mattie is still the best cook around and is getting even better."

"I was referring to the company," Avery said in a sincere but slightly flirty tone. "Your sweet smile was a great way to start my day."

"Why, thank you." Sophia inclined her head but then was mortified at the tinny sound. "Sorry. I must look a fright." She pointed to her head and caught her bottom lip between her teeth.

"Aw, you still manage to look pretty," he said just as Carrie Ann hurried over.

"Hey there, Avery. You gonna take a look at my washing machine from hell?"

"Sure thing." Avery nodded. "Sorry I'm late. Busy day."

"Oh, that's okay." Carrie Ann peeked beneath one of the foils. "You're just about ready to get rinsed," she said to Sophia but then looked back at Avery. "We're thinkin' about heading up to Sully's Tavern later. Stop on in and I'll buy ya a beer."

"Well, now, that's an offer I can't refuse," Avery said, and then angled his head toward the back of the shop. "I'd better get working." He picked up his toolbox, causing another delicious ripple of muscle. "See y'all tonight."

"Let's get you back to the bowl, sugar."

"Carrie Ann!" Sophia said in an urgent whisper. "Just what do you think you're doing?"

"Gettin' an early start on bein' your wingman," she whispered back. "Avery Dean's got the hots for you, Sophia. And judging by the blush in your cheeks I think you're sweet on him too. Why are you not taking advantage of the situation?"

"Because when we first met at the bistro he was just getting over a broken engagement. I didn't want to be his rebound girl. And I never intended to stay here, so I didn't want to hurt him all over again either."

"Well, now, I'd say enough time has passed since his breakup. And I'm hoping you'll take me up on my offer and move here. In other words, everything has changed, sweet pea."

Sophia stood up and had to grin. "I think you're playing matchmaker to give me another reason to stay."

"Would I do something like that?" Carrie Ann placed a hand over her ample chest. "Little ole me?"

"In a heartbeat."

Carrie Ann laughed. "Ah, child, you already know me too well. That's why we're gonna make great business partners. You just wait and see."

Sophia shook her head as she followed Carrie Ann back to the shampoo bowls to get rinsed. Through the open door to the laundry room she could see Avery bent over the washing machine. She couldn't help but admire his very fine denim-clad butt.

Carrie Ann turned and caught her staring. "What?" Sophia sputtered with a lift of her chin, desperately trying to appear innocent, which of course only made her appear guilty.

Carrie Ann laughed. "Thought so . . ." She rubbed her hands together. "I do love it when a plan comes together."

Sophia rolled her eyes, but when Carrie Ann turned around, Sophia angled her head to get another glimpse of Avery. Of course he picked that very moment to straighten up and look in her direction. She did one of those lightning-quick look-away moves, but she caught the blur of his smile in the corner of her vision. A warm tingle of awareness washed over her as she leaned her neck against the cool porcelain bowl. She and Avery had been tap-dancing around their attraction for months and for very good reasons. She firmly reminded herself that nothing would change if he showed up at Sully's. No matter what matchmaking scheme Carrie Ann was cooking up, Sophia knew she needed to make her decisions with a clear head that wasn't clouded by the desire to know what it felt like to kiss Avery Dean.

Also available from *USA Today* bestselling author

LuAnn McLane

WALKING ON SUNSHINE
A Cricket Creek Novel

Cricket Creek, Kentucky, is a sweet small town. But that doesn't stop Mattie Mayfield, a tomboy breakfast cook, and Garret Ruleman, a tabloid-magnet musician, from getting into a little trouble together....

"No one does Southern love like LuAnn McLane."
—The Romance Dish

Also in the Cricket Creek series
Sweet Harmony
Wildflower Wedding
Moonlight Kiss
Whisper's Edge
Pitch Perfect
Catch of a Lifetime
Playing for Keeps

Available wherever books are sold or at
penguin.com

facebook.com/LoveAlwaysBooks

LOVE
ROMANCE
NOVELS?

For news on all your favorite romance authors,
sneak peeks into the newest releases, book
giveaways, and much more—

"Like" Love Always on Facebook!
f LoveAlwaysBooks